When I Became INVISIBLE

maret johanson

Suite 300 - 990 Fort St
Victoria, BC, V8V 3K2
Canada

www.friesenpress.com

First Edition — 2016

ISBN
978-1-4602-8067-6 (Paperback)
978-1-4602-8068-3 (eBook)

1. FICTION

Distributed to the trade by The Ingram Book Company

Table of Contents

Part One

Fall 1955

Summer 1955

Part Two

Dedicated to the memory of my father, who was imprisoned for thirty years by MS. Despite his severe limitations, his determination, optimism, and appreciation of the simple joys in life has been my inspiration.

Part One

Fall 1955

MOLLY

The Day They Took My Daddy Away

I am five years old. I live on a farm with my mommy and daddy and Rex, who is a dog. The summer is so hot it makes my face and hair all sticky. In the winter, it's so cold my eyelashes freeze. There aren't many people around except for Nell. She helps with farm chores. She was like my pretend big sister all summer long. Then she stopped coming.

The farm is my castle. The animals are my friends. My mommy says I have a big imagination. I think that means that I can make pretend things real. Pretending is fun. Sometimes I talk to the animals and they say things back. They all have names. Rex is my best friend.

I see other people when we drive into town to get groceries. I like hot days, because we stop for ice cream. Daddy lets me pick my favorite flavor. I love nutty chocolate swirl. Summer is over now because the ice cream shop is closed.

I thought today was going to be just like any other day. But it wasn't. Everything changed today. I became invisible.

The wind was blowing really hard. I like windy days. I like the way the wind makes everything dance. The wind today felt cold. I guess summer was really over. I was sitting at the kitchen table. The shutters were banging against our windows.Every time the shutters banged it made me jump in my seat. Daddy just got home. We were gonna have lunch. We were having cheese sandwiches that Mommy had made. She was not hungry and was laying down. I put a jug of milk on the table. It was still warm from Bella. Daddy was getting glasses from the cupboard. They were too high for me to reach.

That's when I heard a noise outside. I peeked out the window and saw a car. It was strange, because we never got visitors. They were in a hurry. The tires made a screeching sound when they stopped. Loud footsteps came stomp stomp up our front steps. Someone banged on the door hard. Daddy just stared at the door. I wondered why he didn't go answer. Suddenly two big men pushed our front door open and came inside. I thought that was rude. They should have waited until we opened the door. They were dressed in the same clothes. They wore black and had hats on. There were words that I didn't understand written on their shirts. I knew my daddy was surprised because he stood still and did not say anything. His eyes got very big. That made me scared. I ran over to him and grabbed his leg. I was afraid that something bad was going to happen. I held onto his leg tight.

"Are you William Mulgrave?" one of the big men asked in a loud voice.

My daddy looked like he had forgotten who he was.

"What's the meaning of this?" he asked. "How dare you just barge into my home?"

"Just answer the question, sir. Are you William Mulgrave?"

"Of course I am, and this is my house! Explain what this is all about!"

The two men walked up to him. One stood on one side of him and the other went to the other side. They pulled his hands behind his back. Then they put big hard rings on his hands. These were the hands that had just cuddled me. Why were they being so mean and rough with his nice hands?

"Leave my daddy alone!" I screamed.

They paid no attention to me.

"You're under arrest!" one of them said.

I didn't know what that meant. They started pushing him toward the door. He was trying to shake them off. I got more and more scared. They began dragging him. His shoes scrapped along the kitchen floor. I could not keep hold of his leg. I was left behind on the floor. I was crying so hard I couldn't see. My tears dribbled down my chest and my shirt got wet all the way through to my skin. I couldn't let these bad men take my daddy away. I reached out my arms and ran after him.

"Daddy, Daddy, come back!" I yelled.

One of the men had a long dark mustache. He reminded me of the villains in the books my mommy and daddy had read to me. He pushed me with the side of his leg. That's how we sometimes pushed our cattle when they wandered off. I wanted to bite his leg like Rex did with the cows. The bad men dragged my daddy down the front steps.

"Don't hurt my daddy!" I screamed.

They pulled him toward the car. I tried to run after him but tripped and fell on the steps. My knee was bleeding but I couldn't feel the hurt. I felt numb all over. I just stayed there. I could tell my daddy was very mad. He was fighting to get free. I'd never seen him fight before. He was shouting at them. "This is all a big mistake!" The two big men were stronger than him. They pushed him into the car and slammed the door hard. The bang that the door made felt like a punch to my stomach. I bent over in pain and cried some more.

"What about the kid?" I heard one of the men ask the other.

"We'll have to send someone to come pick her up. First let's deal with Mulgrave," the other answered.

Did that mean that they were going to take me away too? I hadn't done anything wrong. My daddy hadn't done anything wrong, but they were being mean to him.

The last I saw of my daddy, he was looking at me through the back window of the car. His face was red and wrinkled. He was shouting something, but I couldn't hear the words. I'd never seen my daddy cry before, but his face was wet like mine. The tires threw stones at Rex when it drove off fast. I watched the car get smaller and smaller. Then there was nothing but a big bunch of dust.

Rex came and licked my face. I think he liked the salty taste. Mommy was not around. She always disappeared when things were bad. Today was the worst day ever, so she was probably hiding.

"It's a bad day," my daddy would say when I'd go looking for her. "Leave her be, child."

I learned that when Mommy's bedroom door was shut, I was not to disturb her. Her bedroom door was shut now.

I had not had my lunch, but my stomach wasn't hungry anymore. The milk was still sitting on the table. I thought maybe I should put it away before it turned bad, like I had been taught to do. The milk didn't seem very important. I couldn't stand up. My legs felt like jelly. I sat on the steps of the veranda, staring into the cornfields. The wind felt cold on my face. I thought maybe I should get my sweater, but I couldn't move. It was getting late because the sun made the meadows sparkle like gold. Everything looked like it did every day. But nothing was the same. I had disappeared, just like my daddy.

I sat there shivering when I heard a banging and clattering noise. A car was coming up the bumpy road. Rex started barking. I wondered if more bad people were coming to take me away now. The car stopped and I saw that it was my aunt Edna. I knew it was her because she always wore a hat with a big feather when she came to visit us. It had been a long time since I had seen her and Uncle Jake. I wondered why they were coming today. She swung the door open before Uncle Jake had stopped the car. She had a big scarf wrapped around her shoulders and her skirt was flapping like Mommy's laundry does on a windy day. I watched her big boots stomp up towards me like there was no nonsense.

"Where's your mother?" she demanded.

I looked up at her, wondering if she was real or just a ghost. I felt like I was a ghost. I tried to say something, but no words came out of my mouth.

"Oh dear," she gasped. She ruffled my hair as she passed by and swung open the door to the kitchen. The slam of the swinging door was extra loud. I still couldn't move my legs, so I kept sitting on the veranda. Uncle Jake came up the steps and grunted as he walked past me. I could hear Aunt Edna's screechy voice telling Uncle Jake what to do. She made a phone call, but I couldn't hear what she said. There were banging pots and pans, then the sound of running water. Rex wagged his tail as he watched through the screen door. They were walking back and forth between my mommy's room and the kitchen. I guess they didn't know that when the door was shut, they shouldn't go in.

The next thing I saw was Uncle Jake carrying my mommy. He put her in the car. She was wrapped in a blanket. I wondered if she felt cold like me. I wished someone would wrap me up too. Aunt Edna came out after him and closed the door. She scooped me up in her arms like a rag doll and carried me to the car.

"We have to take your mother to the hospital," she said.

I had never been to a hospital before, but I knew that was where sick people went. My grandpa went to the hospital when his heart didn't work anymore. He died there. Did this mean my mommy was going to die too? I sat in Edna's lap as we drove away. I squirmed in her lumpy lap that did not feel like my mommy's. I looked out the window and saw that Rex was no longer wagging his tail. I reached my arms out the open window towards him. He looked so sad. Mommy lay fast asleep in the back seat. I wondered why the bumpy road didn't wake her up. Maybe she was very very sick. Aunt Edna and Uncle Jake didn't talk. Uncle Jake looked white, like I did sometimes when I was sick. He held the steering wheel so hard that his knuckles stuck out. His eyes stared straight ahead like he was afraid to turn his head. Aunt Edna patted her eyes with a hanky and made sniffling sounds.

I sat sideways watching our farm go by. Everything looked the way it always did. The cows were in the meadow. Daddy would have been bringing them in by now, but he wasn't here. I wondered what would happen to them. The sun was so low in the sky that it hurt my eyes. I started counting lamp posts. I could count up to twenty and then had to start over again. It helped me not to think about bad things. Everything was whizzing by me so fast as I sat there on my auntie's lap. My daddy was gone and now my mommy wasn't talking to me. I didn't know why we were going to a hospital. I wondered if we would be coming back again soon. I missed my daddy so bad that it made my tummy ache.

Where Did My Voice Go?

The curtains fluttered in the breeze when I opened my eyes. They reminded me of butterflies dancing in the sunlight. I looked around the room. I'd never been here before. There was a white dresser with pictures on top. The people in the pictures looked happy, because they were smiling. My clothes were on the chair beside the dresser. I was in a nightie that wasn't mine. I didn't remember putting it on. Drawings were stuck to the walls. They were better than I could draw. They must have been drawn by someone older than me.

Where was I? I pulled the sheet close to my face. It smelled the way my mommy's sheets did after drying in the sun. I pretended I was a baby bird hiding in a nest waiting for my mommy or daddy bird to come and take care of me. Where was my mommy and daddy? I felt achy deep inside of me. I missed them so much.

There was a knock at the door.

"Molly, are you awake?"

It was Aunt Edna's voice. I tried to say something but I couldn't. My mouth made no sound. Aunt Edna peeked in the door, and then swung it wide open when she saw that I was awake. A big smile was on her face and I could see a shiny gold tooth. She must be rich … to own gold.

"How did you sleep, honey?" she asked.

I still couldn't say anything, even though I tried.

"Oh child, you've been through a lot. I hope you got a good sleep, but the day is half over and you must eat something."

I didn't remember eating anything since yesterday, but my tummy wasn't hungry. She tore my nest apart and pulled me to my feet. She went to the closet and came back with a sweater that was too big for me. She pulled it over my head.

"Now come child and sit in the kitchen while I fix you some lunch."

The kitchen smelled of fresh baked bread and sweet things. I liked the smell. It reminded me of my mommy's good days, when she would bake. Sometimes she would hum a tune when she was really happy. I liked to lick the bowls after she was finished.

My eyes and mouth opened wide when I saw Rex lying under the kitchen table. His tail was thumping like a drum against the floor. I ran over to him and wrapped my arms around his neck. He licked my ear like he always did. I was so glad to have Rex back. He was my family

"I have some bread fresh from the oven and soup on the stove," Aunt Edna said.

I didn't want to leave Rex, so I stayed under the table.

"I bet that poor dog is hungry. Maybe you'd like to come out and give him something to eat?"

I felt worried that maybe he hadn't eaten anything since yesterday either. I crawled out from under the table.

"I brought his food bowl along. Why don't you go and give him the leftovers from breakfast. I'm sure that will make him happy."

She led me to the stove and scraped the grub from the pan into Rex's bowl. Rex knew it was for him, because he stood behind me with his tongue dripping wet stuff on the floor. I gave him the bowl and patted his head. He gobbled up his food.

"Now it's your turn to eat, young lady."

She put the soup and bread on the table. I sat down, trying to be polite like my mommy and daddy had taught me.

"Eat now," she said.

I tried a little sip, but it dribbled down my chin. It tasted funny, nothing like what my mommy had ever made. Aunt Edna shook her head. She got up and went into the pantry. She came back with a big cookie with chocolate on top.

"This goes against my better judgment," she said, "but maybe we can do things backwards this one time and have some dessert before lunch."

I liked Aunt Edna a whole bunch more. I took a bite of the cookie. I chewed it for a long time. It felt like my throat was stuck closed. It took me a while to swallow it. It was so good that I ate the whole thing. She put the soup and bread in front of me again, but I just stared at it.

She gave up waiting for me to eat. She pulled me to my feet and took me to the bathroom. She rubbed my face and hands with a wet cloth. I wished she wasn't so rough. I pulled away but she didn't stop. Then she helped me put my clothes back on.

"We'll have to go and get you some new clothes soon, but for now this is all we have," she said.

I wondered why I needed new clothes when I had lots of nice clothes at home. Then she took me out to the backyard.

"Now go play," she said. "Ricky and the others will soon be home from school. Won't it be nice to see your cousins again? Sally was so excited to have you here. That was her room you were sleeping in. She insisted on it last night. She just slipped in with her sister for the night. You were so sad and tired with the day and all. Now go get some sunshine and exercise and all that's good for you."

She waited for me to say something, but I just looked up at her. I didn't know what to say to her. Even if I did, I couldn't say it anyway.

Aunt Edna was much bigger than my mommy. She was even bigger than Uncle Jake. She looked like she had pillows on her chest and her behind. Everything looked extra soft. Except her hands were rough and red. Her arms were hairy like a man's. Her voice sounded like she had something caught in her throat. I sometimes sounded like that after I shouted loud for a long time.

Uncle Jake reminded me of Pinocchio. He had a long pointy nose, big ears, and skinny arms and legs. My daddy called Aunt Edna "Sis" but didn't see her much. If I had a sister, I would be with her all the time. My mommy and daddy didn't have many visitors. It was just the three of us most of the time. When they were busy, I always found something to play with on the farm. I had Rex as my best friend. Then there was Nell. She was like my new big sister for the summer. Then she disappeared. I missed her and wondered what happened to her. Both Mommy and Daddy looked away when I asked if Nell was coming back.

What was I supposed to do out here in Aunt Edna's yard? I didn't know where to play or what to play with. I was feeling sad and didn't feel like playing. The yard was small. My farm had so much room to play. The lawn smelled like it was just cut. There were pretty white flowers along the fence. I walked over to the vegetable garden. It only had some straggly looking beans. Daddy needed to teach Aunt Edna how to grow crops. We always had more than what we could eat. There were no trees to climb or hiding places to crawl into. I stood there looking around. I felt lost. Aunt Edna looked like she was losing her patience with me. The droopy corners of her mouth made her look sad or angry. I wasn't sure which. She made a sighing noise. I thought she was about to say something important, but then she changed her mind. She turned to go inside. She stopped at the door and said, "Now go and play." Then she flapped her hand at me and shut the door behind her.

I wandered from the back yard to the front yard and looked around. The house was on a street with cars driving by. The roaring sound hurt my ears. It was so different from being home in the big fields. There I could hear the crickets chirp and birds sing. The houses here were so close together. I could hear the cackling laughter of the lady next door. She was talking loudly on her telephone. It was strange that I could hear someone I didn't even know.

I stood there looking around. I wanted to cry, but no tears came. I wanted to scream, "Daddy, where are you?" but no words came out. He wouldn't hear me anyway. I started to walk. I walked up the driveway and out to the street. I turned and walked along the sidewalk. A man in a suit passed me by. He wore shiny black shoes and was carrying a big black bag like the doctor who came to see me when I was sick. I thought he was probably important. He looked at me like I was in his way. I felt like I didn't belong. I walked faster along this street that I did not know. Rex stayed by my side. I decided I was going to try to find my daddy.

The Big City

There were strange people everywhere. The noise was loud in my ears. I didn't know where I was going. It felt good to keep walking. I did what other people did. I'd stand at curbs and wait until there was a large crowd. Then we would all walk across the street together. Rex stayed by my side. People looked down at me, but no one talked to me. That was fine with me, 'cause I couldn't talk anyway.

I stopped at a shop window. There were ladies standing there looking at me. They had on fancy clothes. I wondered why they were standing there and didn't move. They looked like real people, but maybe they were big dolls. I tried smiling at them, but they did not smile back. Their eyes looked really bored. I guess I would be bored too, if I had to stand in a window all day long.

I stood for a long time at the window of a toy shop. It was filled with a magical land of toys. There were doll houses, a moving train spinning around a track, teddy bears that were big and small, and soldiers with rosy cheeks. I put my hands on the glass and pressed my nose up against it. I wanted to grab one of them through the window. A mean-looking lady came out and frowned at me.

"I just cleaned those windows," she scolded. "Now move along."

That magical land did not belong to me. I kept walking.

I stopped to listen to a man playing a fiddle on the street corner. No one else would stop to listen. I thought that was rude. He had long gray hair and a beard. I thought he looked like Santa Clause, except his beard wasn't white and he wasn't fat and jolly. Christmas time was not here yet, so it couldn't be Santa. I noticed that his feet were bare. I wanted to give him my shoes, but they would be too small for him. I stood there listening to him sing. Music always made me feel happy. I liked Sunday afternoons at home when Daddy would put on a record and spin me around the room. I felt like I was flying. I would laugh so hard my sides ached. Music was a happy thing, but this man looked sad. Maybe because no one but me was listening to him. When he was finished, I clapped my hands. He gave me a wink and made a funny face. That made me giggle. I thought he was a nice person. Everyone else was too busy to notice me.

I decided to keep on walking. I needed to find my daddy. I was starting to feel tired and hungry. Both Rex and I needed something to drink. I found a fountain across the street at a park. I tried to climb up to get a drink but couldn't reach. I kept trying, until a car pulled up to the curb with lights flashing on top. Out jumped two men in matching clothes. They looked like the bad men who took my daddy away. Maybe they were bringing my daddy back to me. I felt excited. I tried to see into the back seat of the car. No one was there.

"What's your name little girl?" one of them asked.

All I could do was look up at him. No sound came out of my mouth. I started to cry, because they scared me. I was worried that they would take me away too. Rex started to bark at them. People were staring at us.

"Don't be afraid. We're here to help you get back home."

They put me in the back seat of the flashing car and Rex climbed in beside me. Here I was, just like my daddy, with two strange men taking me away. I remembered the look on my daddy's face when they took him away. I cried harder. They made a call on a crackling phone in the car and drove away.

The car pulled up in front of Aunt Edna's house. Aunt Edna was standing at the curb. She had on the same scarf she wore when she had come to get me. It was pulled tight around her shoulders. She was chewing on her knuckle. When I got out of the car, she squeezed me so tight I couldn't breathe.

"Don't you ever wander off like that again, Molly," she said. "I was so worried about you. Thank goodness you're safe."

The men in matching clothes left me there. They lied about taking me home. This was not my home. They took my daddy away and then they lie to me. I knew for sure now that they were bad guys.

Tea at Aunt Edna's

I slept in the same room with my cousin Sally. She was in grade two. She was the one who had drawn those pictures on her wall. I didn't go to school yet, so I stayed home with Aunt Edna all day. After I had wandered off, she wouldn't let me out of her sight. I'd have to sit and watch her cook meals and do housework. I played with Sally's toys while Aunt Edna talked on the phone or had her neighbors over for tea.

"Poor child," her friend Trudy said, shaking her head. I guess she thought that, if I was not speaking, I also couldn't hear her.

"She's been through so much at such a young age, with losing her parents and all."

"What's strange though," says Aunt Edna "is that I can't read her. She doesn't speak and shows no emotion. It's like she's gone into another world of her own."

"Maybe you should take her to the doctor to see what's wrong with her," Trudy said. "I've heard that if children aren't treated right away after something bad happens, there could be permanent damage. Remember Gertrude's daughter? The one who was … you know ... by that strange man? It scared her so bad that she won't be in a room with any man without her mother present. She will probably never have a normal relationship with a man in her life. It's best to get these things looked at early, before they get worse."

"I guess I should," Aunt Edna said with a sigh. "It's just that I don't really know what she was like at home with Billy and his wife. They just kept to themselves, so we lost touch. When I got the call from Billy from the police station, it was the first I'd heard from him in months. He just told me to get over to the farm and check on Dora and Molly. I knew that Dora wasn't too stable and something like this would throw her over the edge. I'm his sister, so I couldn't refuse. I got more than I bargained for when I got there."

I turned my back to them. I rocked baby doll in my arms. I wanted to make her feel better.

"How long do you think she will be here for?" Trudy asked.

"Hard to say. These things with the courts take time you know. I had to find a lawyer for Billy, and with the charges he's facing, it's not going to be over quick. Poor Dora's not well after that overdose. They're watching her pretty carefully right now at the sanatorium. We're all that Molly's got."

I looked over at Rex, who lay by my side as I took care of Dolly. He was all I had. As long as I had Rex, I was okay until my mommy and daddy got back to take me home.

I don't know why I couldn't get words out of my mouth. It was like being locked in a dark closet. I peered out around me through a small crack. I didn't want to be seen or heard. I wasn't able to make myself disappear, but I could pretend I wasn't there. If I was quiet, I was almost invisible. I was like Rex, watching everything but no one noticed him much. After a while, I don't think I could have made a sound if I'd wanted to. It was like I'd swallowed my voice.

When Sally got home from school, she'd play with me like I was her doll. She'd dress me up with ribbons in my hair. She'd make me drink her pretend tea from her tea set. Then she'd be my teacher and make me draw pictures. If she thought it was good, she'd give me a gold star. Sometimes she was a nurse and I would have to pretend I was sick so that she could take care of me. What I hated the most was when she made me pretend to be her pet dog. I'd have to follow her around on my hands and knees. She'd make me lie on the floor and patted my head. She asked me to bark, but no sound came out. Then she'd get mad and make me go under the table. Rex would crawl in beside me. We would cuddle there together. At night, when I tried to sleep, she would sing to herself as if I wasn't there. All I wanted was to close my eyes and pretend I was back home. This was like a bad nightmare that wouldn't go away.

My New Family

Uncle Jake was a ghost like me. He didn't say much. When Aunt Edna asked him questions, he grunted. She talked all the time. I didn't know how he could get a chance to say anything anyway. He left for work early in the morning. Everyone else was still in bed. I listened to his footsteps while he did his morning chores. The back door slammed outside my bedroom when he left. I listened to the roar of his car as he started it. Then it was quiet again. I liked this time, because it reminded me of home. All I'd hear was birdies outside my window. Then Aunt Edna made everyone get out of bed and get ready for school. That's when the noise started.

My cousin Ricky was the oldest. He was twelve years old. He was big and round like Humpty Dumpty. He wanted to play football all the time. He wore a shirt with large letters on it. Sally told me that it spelled the name of his football team. He carried a football under his arm when he came to eat. He slammed it back and forth from one hand to the other hand. I was afraid he would drop it on the table and break Aunt Edna's nice dishes. Aunt Edna yelled at him to put it away. He hid it under the table until he was finished eating. He'd peek at his football cards. He always carried them in his back pocket. He stayed for practice every day after school. He was always late for dinner. He gobbled down his food so he could go back outside to throw his ball again. I could see his friends making funny faces through the screen door. They were waiting for him to come and play.

"What about your homework?" Aunt Edna yelled after him, as he headed out the door.

"I don't have any."

He always said that.

"Well then you need to study. You've been failing everything at school this year. If you want to continue on that football team, you better pull up your socks young man. Wait until your father gets home. He'll deal with you if you don't listen to me."

Before she finished, the door slammed shut. Ricky probably knew that his father wouldn't get home until he was in bed. Uncle Jake would be too tired to punish anyone.

Lenny was ten. He was very different from Ricky. He was skinny. He had freckles all over his face and arms. He looked a lot like Uncle Jake. Ricky looked more like Aunt Edna. He wore glasses like the thick glass my mother used to put thread through a needle. He put things close to his face to see it. In the mornings, when he didn't have his glasses on, he slid his hands along the wall to find the bathroom. I stayed out of his way so he wouldn't trip over me. I was invisible to all of them, but especially to him. After school he went to a library. Sally told me that was a big room full of books. Sometimes he came home with his arms full of big books. He was panting like Rex from carrying so many. At home he always had a book in front of his face. He'd even have a book at the dinner table. He'd take a mouthful of food and chew it and chew it forever and read at the same time. When Aunt Edna asked him a questions, he shrugged his shoulders. He was like me and Uncle Jake. He didn't speak.

"You're becoming more and more like your father every day," Aunt Edna said when he ignored her. She'd scoop his plate away. He wouldn't even notice.

Ricky would tease him and call him "four eyes". He'd sometimes throw a football at his head. I thought that would hurt, but Lenny just ignored him.

"Pansy," Ricky would say, and walk away shaking his head.

I thought pansies were flowers that my mother grew in her garden. Lenny didn't look anything like them.

One day his sister hid his glasses. He sat at the table staring at the wall. He wouldn't eat or talk. Everyone went to bed but he just sat there.

"Go to bed. We'll look for your glasses in the morning," Aunt Edna told him. The next morning, he was still there. He'd fallen asleep with his forehead on the table. His sister saw that this wasn't much fun anymore, so she threw the glasses at him.

"Here put your eyes back on," she sneered.

He felt around the floor for them. They were all bent and wobbly. He put them back on anyway. He picked up his book and started to read again like nothing had happened.

Elizabeth was the one who hid Lenny's glasses. She was nine years old. She thought she was more special than everyone else in the family. Sometimes Aunt Edna or her brothers would call her Lizzie or Beth, but she didn't like it.

She'd say, "My name is Elizabeth, understand?" and then she would spell it for them. Everyone would make a groaning sound or their eyes would roll around.

She did this funny thing before she answered questions. She turned her head slowly towards the person who asked her something. Then she would raise her chin high in the air and look down her nose. She would just stare at them. She would say things like "You have to be kidding," or "I can't believe you really said that," or "Eat my shorts." That one made me giggle. I tried to picture someone eating shorts. She walked like she was dancing all the time. She'd go high on her tipsy toes, raise her hands up high, and make a circle. She did this even when she was getting ready for school or cleaning the table. She had long hair that I liked to touch. It felt like the blanket I had when I was a baby. She brushed it for a long time in front of the mirror. She told me it was a hundred strokes. I didn't know how much a hundred was, but it was more than I could count. Sometimes she would let me brush it. I liked to play with it and she said it felt nice. She put on a pretty new dress every day, and it was always clean and had no wrinkles. Her shoes were so shiny that she could see herself in them like a mirror. She carried a purse over her arm like my mommy did when she went to town. She showed me the lipstick and powder in it. Aunt Edna told her that she was too young to wear such nonsense. When Aunt Edna wasn't watching, she would put it on in front of the mirror and smile at herself. Then she would wash it off. She went to ballet lessons every week. I had a music box at home with a ballerina that danced when I opened it. When Elizabeth got home, she circled around the house just like that ballerina. She flapped her arms and raised her chin up high. Her ballet teacher probably taught her to talk with her chin in the air too.

"Help me get these dishes done," Aunt Edna said after dinner.

"But Mom, I don't want to ruin my nails. See? I just painted them." She held her bright pink nails out for Aunt Edna to see.

"I've told you before that you are too young to be painting your nails," Aunt Edna scolded.

They argued back and forth for a while. Elizabeth started to cry. Aunt Edna then agreed to let her dry the dishes instead. Aunt Edna was up to her elbows in dish soap at the sink. Elizabeth fluttered like a bird around the kitchen, waving her dish towel. She would spin around before she placed dishes up on shelves. A song that no one else could hear must have been playing in her head. She danced from one end of the kitchen to the other.

Then there was Sally. She was seven. She was Elizabeth's chubby younger sister. She was my tormentor. She always said what she thought. She made a big fuss if she didn't get what she wanted. When she was upset, she screamed so loud that it would hurt my ears. I'd have to cover them with my hands. Everyone would do anything to try to make her stop. When she was happy, she had a big laugh that made her belly jiggle. When she was mad, she hit things. Sometimes she hit people too. I tried to hide to stay out of her way when she was mad. When she liked me, she gave me big bear hugs and wet kisses. I don't think she knew just how strong she was. I was scared that she would squeeze me so hard that I would break in half. I learned to keep her happy (so I wouldn't get hit), but not too happy (so that she wouldn't hug me either). She treated me like her favorite doll. I wasn't real. That was fine with me. This was not my real world and being a doll that didn't feel anything was just what I wanted to be.

This was a very different family. My daddy was always gentle with me. He rocked me in his arms when I was sleepy. He had long answers when I asked questions. He taught me new things when I was being like Curious George. He made me laugh when I was sad. He listened to my stories as if I was the most interesting person in the world.

My mommy was sad a lot. I didn't understand why. She needed lots of sleep even in the daytime. I knew she loved me though. Some nights, when I couldn't fall asleep, I'd crawl into her bed. She would cuddle me. She felt warm and soft and smelled like flowers. She would hum into my ear until I drifted back to sleep. She called me her precious little angel. Sometimes she said that she was sorry, but I didn't know why.

Now I was in a very strange new place with people I wasn't used to. I felt like none of this was real. There was no one to hold onto who made me feel safe like my mommy and daddy did. I was floating in a never

never land. Like Alice in Wonderland, I was falling down a rabbit hole. I didn't know where I was going to land next.

The Mean Doctor

"Say 'Aaah'," the doctor demanded.

He was making me open my mouth so wide it hurt and was looking down my throat. Nothing but a hissing sound came out.

"Now young lady," he scolded, "you aren't trying hard enough. I want you to say 'Aaah'."

I tried again, but this time not even a hiss came out. His wood stick was so far down my throat that I started to cough. He pulled the stick out but kept staring at me. He had bulgy eyes and he looked mean. I looked at Aunt Edna for help. She sat in the corner. She was holding her purse in her lap. She would hold things tightly like that when she was worried. She wore her favorite hat. It had a yellow flower. She called it her happy hat. She didn't look happy and neither was I. She had fussed over what to wear, like we were going someplace special. The dress that she wore made her look lumpy. The tight sleeves made her arms look like mashed potatoes. She was not like my mommy. Mommy always looked so pretty in a dress. I don't know why Aunt Edna made so much fuss getting dressed up for this mean doctor.

"She hasn't spoken a word since she arrived," she said to the doctor. "I haven't had a chance to talk to my brother ... since the incident that is." She paused. "I imagine he would have mentioned to me if she wasn't speaking at all before. She is five years old and should know how to speak."

"There is absolutely nothing wrong with her throat and no reason for her to be silent. This is nothing but bad behavior," he said. He crossed his arms like he was hugging himself. Probably because no one else would ever hug him. "What does she do when she wants something?"

Aunt Edna held her purse even tighter.

"Well, she usually points."

The doctor put on his glasses. He scribbled something on a piece of paper and spoke without looking at us.

"I would suggest that you need to force her to talk by not rewarding her when she doesn't speak. If she wants something bad enough, she'll ask for it. So don't give in to her."

Aunt Edna looked down at her lap. She looked like she was going to say something but wasn't sure whether to say it or not.

"The child has been through a very difficult thing, losing her parents so suddenly. It must have been very frightening for her. Could that have scared the voice out of her, doctor?"

"Rubbish," he said. He had a big frown on his face. "You can't go making excuses for her behavior. Children of Molly's age adapt quickly. If she's not talking, she is being disobedient and needs to be punished. As I suggested, make her ask for what she wants. That includes her meals, her toys, and anything else that she may want. She'll talk soon enough."

Aunt Edna looked like she didn't believe what the doctor was saying. I think she was afraid of him too. I wanted to make myself disappear. I looked around, but there was nowhere in the room to hide.

"Yes, doctor. We'll do what you say," she said.

"Bring her back in two weeks for a checkup. I'm sure that everything will be fine by then."

He picked up a lollipop from a glass jar on his desk. It had red and yellow paper wrapped around it. He held it in front of my face.

"Would you like this, Molly?"

I nodded.

"Well then, ask for it."

My face scrunched up. I tried not to cry.

He put the sucker back into the jar and left the room.

Aunt Edna had promised to take me to Woolworth's after the doctor's appointment. We were going to sit on the high swervy chairs for a soda.

"Would you like to go for a soda, Molly?"

I was wondering why she was asking. She had already promised to take me. I nodded.

"Tell me that you want a soda," she demanded, "or we're going straight home."

I moved my lips. I tried pushing out air from my throat. No sound came out.

"Well you obviously don't want it badly enough."

She grabbed my arm and dragged me home. I cried all the way.

I sat at the dinner table with everyone. I'd had no lunch. I was very hungry. Aunt Edna put a big chicken on the table. There was also mashed potatoes and a bowl full of peas and carrots. The plates passed around the table. Ricky took the biggest meat pieces. Then he passed it to his brother. Lenny took what was left of the cut pieces. Elizabeth took a chicken wing. Aunt Edna glared at her.

"You need to eat more than that," she scolded.

"I'm on a diet," she said.

"Diet? Look at you! You're just skin and bones already."

"I'm a ballerina and I have to look like a ballerina. I don't want any more."

Aunt Edna shook her head.

Sally scooped up a big pile of mashed potatoes. She poured gravy all over it.

"Take some chicken," Aunt Edna scolded.

She took a small piece. She didn't eat it though.

The plates kept passing me.

"Would you like some dinner, Molly?" Aunt Edna asked.

I nodded hard.

She sighed. "What would you like to eat, Molly?"

I sat there and blinked up at her. I could feel the corners of my mouth feeling shaky. I knew that I wasn't going to get any dinner, because of what the mean doctor said. Sally tried to slide her piece of chicken to me. Aunt Edna caught her and made her take it back.

I sat and watched everyone finish eating.

"Ah let the child eat." Uncle Jake wiped his mouth with his hanky.

"The doctor made it very clear that she has to ask for things," she said.

"Well we can't starve the poor child, now can we?" Uncle Jake asked.

"Eventually she will speak if we do this. It's for her own good."

Uncle Jake shook his head but didn't argue with Aunt Edna. If he argued, Aunt Edna always won. I liked Uncle Jake for trying. I went to bed with a grumbly tummy. I had dreams about the delicious smell of chicken all night long.

The next day was worse. I sat in a corner all day without my dolly.

"If you want your doll, you have to say her name," Aunt Edna said.

"Missy," I tried to say. No sound came out.

"That's not good enough. When you want your dolly, let me know."

I had to sit at the table for breakfast and watch everyone eat. I only got a small glass of juice to drink. I was so hungry that my head was spinning around and my tummy hurt. Aunt Edna didn't make me any lunch like she always did. I was so tired that I couldn't stand up. I crawled into the corner and lay there. I started to see things that I don't think were really there. That scared me. I felt like I was floating on a cloud. A voice was calling me to dinner. I couldn't move. Uncle Jake came over and put his hand on my head.

"The child is boiling up!" he shouted.

He scooped me off the floor and carried me to the bedroom.

He lay me down and went outside. I could hear some grumbling noises outside my door. I think it was Uncle Jake and Aunt Edna. I had almost fallen asleep when Aunt Edna turned on the lights. She was carrying a cold towel. She put it on my forehead. Uncle Jake was behind her holding something. It smelled like chicken soup.

"Sit up now, Molly." She plumped up my pillows.

She looked friendly again.

"I'm sorry honey," she said. "I'm sorry that I made you sick. Now sip on this warm broth and let's get you well again. What does that grumpy old doctor know anyway?"

I was glad to taste the warm salty flavor on my tongue. I tried gulping it down. Aunt Edna told me to slow down or I would throw up.

"We won't be going back to him again," she said.

In the morning when I got out of bed, Aunt Edna had a big pile of my favorite pancakes on the table. There was bananas and whipped cream on top. My cousins were not happy eating their porridge. The pancakes were just for me.

A Visit to a Bad Place

It was Sunday morning. It was my favorite day. I liked having everyone home instead of just being with Aunt Edna all day. We had just got home from church. Ricky couldn't wait to get his white shirt off. He pulled his football shirt on over his head. He grabbed his football and ran out the door. Lenny got a book and blanket and went to sit under the apple tree in the backyard. Elizabeth said that she was going to bake cookies. She was getting things ready in the kitchen. I was expecting to be Sally's dog, or whatever else she wanted me to pretend to be. I was starting to unbutton my dress so I could change into my pants and t-shirt. Aunt Edna stopped me.

"Don't change just yet, honey. We're going out for a visit."

I was surprised. Everyone else was doing other things. Why was I going for a visit alone with Aunt Edna? I saw out the window that Uncle Jake was sitting in the car. I wanted to ask her where we were going. I tried. Sometimes I forgot that I couldn't make a sound.

"Watch your little sister while we're gone!" she yelled to Elizabeth.

She held my hand and led me outside. She still did not tell me where we were going. We drove for a very long time. We were on a busy road full of cars and then we were on a smaller road. I saw empty fields everywhere. There were no houses. Uncle Jake and Aunt Edna did not say anything, not even to each other. I thought maybe we were going on a picnic, but if that was true, the others would have come with us too. There was no picnic basket. Maybe they were taking me back to the farm where I used to live. The road did not look like anything I'd seen before. I usually liked surprises. Aunt Edna and Uncle Jake were not smiling, so this was not going to be a fun surprise.

I saw nothing for a long time. Then I saw a great big house very far away. I thought maybe it was a schoolhouse. It had a really big fence around it. We got closer. The giant house looked old. The people who lived here did not like to see out, because it had no windows. Uncle Jake parked the car by a large gate. It was taller than the roof of my farmhouse. What was this place? I got out of the car with Aunt Edna. Uncle Jake stayed in the car. He took his pipe out of his pocket and tapped it. He got his newspaper and started reading. It looked like he was going to be waiting here for a long time. Aunt Edna and I stood outside the car looking at this very strange house. Aunt Edna knelt down beside me. She straightened my dress. She licked her fingers to pat down my hair. I hated the smell of her spit in my hair and pulled away. She had a look on her face that was no nonsense. I thought about the stories I'd heard about children who lost their parents. They were called orphans. They were sent away to places like this to live. Was this going to be my new home? My bottom lip started to shake.

"We're going in that building to visit your father," she said.

I pulled in my breath. A big smile was all over my face. I was so excited that I thought I was going to blow up.

"Now don't get too worked up just yet child. This is not a very nice place where your daddy is living right now. There are strict rules here and our visit will need to be short. You will be able to see him and talk to him, but you won't be able to touch him. Do you understand?"

I didn't. I nodded anyway. My smile got smaller. I wondered why I could see him but not touch him.

Aunt Edna grabbed my hand and led me up to the large gate. She rang a bell.

"Identify yourself," I heard a voice say. It was coming from a box beside the gate.

"This is Edna Stone and I'm here to visit my brother Billy, I mean William Mulgrave. I have his daughter with me as well."

"Just a moment," the voice in the box said.

I heard a buzzing sound. The gate opened like magic all by itself. We walked up to a great big door. It was bigger than any door I'd ever seen before. I stared up at it. If I stood on Uncle Jake's shoulders, I would still not be able to reach the top. We waited there until a man opened the door. He was wearing clothes that looked like the ones the bad men who took my daddy away wore. I was scared of men who wore those clothes. We went inside. I held on to Auntie's hand very tight. The door slammed shut really loud behind us. We stood in a dark hall. It smelled like the barn at home when it was raining. He took us to a room with no windows. There were only benches to sit on in the room. It was not a very cozy room. "Wait here!" he said.

Why did this man sound so mean? Maybe it was because he was wearing those clothes. They were ugly clothes. If I had to wear those clothes, I wouldn't be happy either. I looked around the room. Mommies with children were sitting on the benches. They did not look happy. The bench was really hard and hurt my bum. Why was my daddy living in such a scary place? He liked being outside on the farm. I remembered him in the sunshine. It was a nice picture in my mind. He told me that being outside during the day was good for me.

"The four walls of a house are there to eat, sleep, keep the rain off and the cold away," he used to say. "Otherwise, being close to the earth, below the sky, and breathing the fresh air is where we belong."

This place was very different from that. I was worried that he must be feeling very sad right now. We waited for a long time. I watched other families go into another room. They looked excited going in but sad when they came out. Mommies wiped their nose and eyes with hankies. The children were crying. Why were they so sad when they just saw their daddies?

I needed to go potty. Our names were called so we had to go with the man. I followed Aunt Edna down a long hall that echoed as we walked. It reminded me of the sounds in church. We were in church that morning and this did not look like or feel like church. We went into a room the size of my closet. We were told to sit and face a wall. It had a small window with bars on it. We sat there quietly. I was worried that I was going to wet my pants. I pulled on Aunt Edna's sleeve and pointed to where I needed to go pee. Aunt Edna tapped on the door and asked where the toilets were? A man pointed down a hallway. Aunt Edna hurried me along. I looked in the cracked mirror to make sure that I was extra pretty for my daddy.

"Don't fuss child." Aunt Edna scolded. "We don't want to miss whatever precious time we have with your father."

We went back to sit on our bench. Aunt Edna took a tissue out of her purse and patted her eyes. She looked sad, like all the other mommies who had just left. I hadn't seen Aunt Edna cry since the day they took my daddy away. I could tell she was trying to hide it. I was confused why everyone was so sad. I was going to see my daddy and that was a good thing.

There was a clicking sound behind the window with the bar on it. Then a door opened. In walked a man who looked like my daddy. He wasn't like I remembered him. I had a big lump in my throat. I tried to swallow but couldn't. This man had a beard. My daddy shaved every morning. I would stand on a stool beside him and pretend I was shaving too. I'd put that marshmallow cream on my cheeks. Daddy would laugh. This man's hair was messy. My daddy always combed his hair back neatly. This man didn't have rosy cheeks like my daddy. He looked smaller than my daddy. Maybe because he was hunched over. This man's eyes were puffy. My daddy's eyes sparkled. But it was still my daddy. I jumped out of my seat and ran to the bars.

I tried to say "Daddy", but only a hissing sound came out. I tried again and a gurgling sound came out of my throat. I pushed harder to make a sound. Here was my daddy at last. I didn't know what had happened to him. I didn't know why he was taken away from me. Now I had found him. I wasn't scared any more. My throat did not feel so tight anymore.

"Daaa," I tried again. I tried again and again until I could make a sound. It came out louder and louder.

"Daddy!" I finally cried. "Daddy, Daddy!" I stood on the bench, reaching my arms out to him. I had to reach through the cold bars. I couldn't stop saying "Daddy" over and over again. His face started to get a sad smile on it. I was wondering why he wasn't reaching to touch my hands. I was reaching out for him. I was aching for him. I needed to feel him hold me again. I noticed then that his hands were behind his back. They were like that the day they took him away. Did they never take those rings off? I started to cry. He leaned towards the window and I rubbed his cheek. His eyes got wet like mine.

"D-d-don't be sad, Daddy," I cried. I tried to be brave.

"I miss you so much, angel," he said. He leaned his head into the bar.

"I miss you," I said with my new voice. How could I not speak to my daddy when I finally had the chance? "When are you coming home, Daddy?"

He looked into my eyes. He looked so tired, like he hadn't slept for a long time.

"Not for a while, honey. I have some things to sort out first. But I promise you I will come home."

I reached my other hand through the bars. I held both of his cheeks in my hands. They felt rough ... not like I remembered them. I held on tight. I was afraid that, if I let go, he would disappear. I didn't know when I would see him again. I felt the crinkles in his face with my fingers. I wanted to remember everything about him. More than anything, I wanted to be in his lap again. I wanted to feel his arms around me. I did not understand why my daddy was here. Why was he being punished?

"Why are you in this bad place, Daddy?" I asked. "Why can't you come home now?"

He started to say something. Then he stopped and let out a big sigh.

"You are too young to understand," he said. "Just remember that I love you very much."

"I love you too," I said, and started to cry again. I now understood why all the other families were crying when they left. I didn't like seeing my daddy in such a bad place.

Aunt Edna came up behind me. She rubbed my back.

"Oh my Lord Jesus, she hasn't spoken a word since she last saw you Billy. If I'd known that seeing you would get her talking again, I would have brought her sooner. I was just afraid that this was not a good place for a little girl and all."

"I can't thank you enough Edna, for taking care of her."

"Oh, she's no trouble. Fits in just like another member of the family."

Aunt Edna started squeezing her purse, just like she did when she was in the doctor's office.

"I'm more worried about you, Billy. Are they treating you okay in here?"

My daddy didn't answer. The man standing behind him stared at us.

"I guess that's a stupid question," Aunt Edna said. "Has the lawyer been by to see you yet? Are things getting cleared up?"

"Yes, yes, not to worry yourself about that. I've met with him twice now. Seems like an eager young man. Has given me lots of encouragement. He's collecting information and then we go to court again. These things take so long you know. I'm sure that things will get all cleared up eventually."

I let go of my daddy. I crawled into Aunt Edna's lap. I needed the feel of a warm body next to mine. I leaned my head into her chest and watched my daddy through the bars. I wished it was his lap that I could have been on. His voice sounded shaky.

"In the meantime, all I can think about is Molly. I miss her and Dora so much."

Aunt Edna reached her hand through the bar for his. Then she must have remembered that it was not there. She pulled her hand back quickly.

"Don't you worry! She's being well taken care of and so is Dora. She wasn't well, as you know, and we had to bring her to the hospital. That's where she is still. She's getting better every day though. So you just keep working on keeping as strong as you can and we can put this awful mess behind us."

"Time's up, Mulgrave. Say goodbye," said the man standing behind my daddy.

I got out of my Aunt Edna's lap. I leaned my head on the bar again. Daddy leaned forward to give me a long kiss on my forehead. I wanted to stay like that forever.

"You have to be a big girl, my angel. Remember the story of Cinderella? She had to live through some bad things, but at the end she was happy."

I nodded. I remembered when he used to read to me at bedtime. I wished we were there now. I kept my eyes closed tight and listened to his voice.

"This is a bad thing that's happened but it won't be forever, I promise you that... Things will get better and we will be a family again. You have to be strong like she was."

"I will Daddy," I said. I swallowed the lump that was stuck in my throat and wiped away my tears. The big scary man came to take my daddy away. I hung onto the bar. Daddy stopped and looked at me over his shoulder.

When our eyes met, I cried out, "I love you, Daddy!"

"I promise," he said again, and then quickly turned and left the room. The door slammed hard behind him. I heard another clicking sound. Then nothing.

Aunt Edna squeezed a tissue in her hand.

"Let's go back home," I said, patting her shoulder. I guess home was going to be Aunt Edna's house for now. I had to try to do what my daddy told me to do. I had to be a brave girl.

Got My Voice Back

I didn't know why my daddy couldn't be with me. I didn't understand why the bad men took him away. But now I did know that he was going to come back. He promised me he would. He always kept his promises. Like magic I had my voice back again. I don't know how that happened. I just know that I was so happy to see my daddy that I had to tell him. When my daddy got taken away, I became invisible like Casper the friendly ghost. Now that I know my daddy is coming back, I'm not so scared. I just wish he wasn't in that horrible place.

"Come!" Sally said in her bossy voice.

She tried putting a collar around my neck. She wanted to pull me around the room.

I snarled.

"Bad dog," she scolded and raised her hand to hit me.

I jumped up and barked at her, loud and fierce. She ran from the room and hid behind Aunt Edna's skirt. Making sounds again felt good. When she came back, she had a cookie in her hand. She held it out for me. I took it and ate it all up. She patted my head.

"Good dog."

"I'm not a dog!" I shouted.

Sally's eyes got really big. I think she was surprised that I yelled at her.

"You're my pretend dog." Her mouth got pouty, like she was going to start to cry.

"I'm tired of that game," I said. "I'll play if you be the dog."

Sally moved away from me.

"It's okay if you don't want to," I said, feeling just a little bit sorry for Sally. "I don't need a pretend dog. I have Rex." I went over and wrapped my arms around his neck. He lay on the floor with his head on his paws. He was always watching me. I was so happy I had Rex. I gave him lots of kisses.

"Do you want to play house then?" Sally asked. "I'll be the mommy and you will be my baby."

"I'll only play if I can be the mommy," I said.

Sally put her hands on her hips. She stood over me.

"But I'm bigger than you. Who ever heard of a mommy that's smaller than her baby?"

She folded her arms across her chest. She had a smirk on her face.

"Then I don't want to play. I already have a mommy."

"But your mommy is not here to take care of you. I heard she is in a nut house and never coming out."

I felt very hot. My throat got tight. I didn't know what a nut house was. The way she said it made it sound like not a nice place.

"My mommy got sick and is in a hospital. When she's better, she'll take care of me again. I don't need you to be my pretend mommy."

"She's never coming back," she said.

I made my fists really tight and stomped my feet.

"She is too!"

"Is not and neither is your daddy! You're an orphan!"

"I hate you!" I screamed.

I threw myself at her and started hitting her.

"Mommy! Mommy!"

In ran Aunt Edna. She was drying her hands on her apron. She saw me on top of Sally. I kept hitting her with my fists. The room was a blur. I had a red hot feeling all over. Then I was sitting in the corner of the kitchen on a stool. Sally was nowhere around.

"We can't have that kind of behavior in this house," Aunt Edna scolded. She was busy cleaning pots and pans. "What on earth brought that on?"

She paused and looked down at me.

I still felt very shaky. My lip was sore from where Sally had punched me. Maybe I had punched myself.

"Sally said my mommy and daddy are never coming home. She said that Mommy is in a nut house."

Aunt Edna stopped cleaning pots and wiped her hands. She gave me the look that she always gave me when she felt sorry for me.

"Sally never should have said those things. They're not true. Your mother is in the hospital and when she's well, and when your daddy has things ..." she paused and cleared her throat, "... resolved, they will come for you. In the meantime, fighting is not going to solve anything."

I kept looking at my feet. I was embarrassed that I had been bad.

She held my shoulders.

"Look at me," she said. "I've put Sally into her room for now, but I'll have her apologize later."

"What's a nut house?" I asked, not sure if I wanted to know.

Aunt Edna looked away, like she did when she didn't know the right answer.

"There is no such thing as a nut house," she said. "Those were just some bad words that Sally made up."

I didn't know if I believed her. The bad shaky feeling was starting to go away. My tummy still didn't feel right. I still didn't understand anything.

"Can I go and visit my mommy in the hospital?"

Aunt Edna sighed. "I don't know, honey. She may not be well enough yet."

I didn't want to cry, but I couldn't stop it. She patted my knee. I wished she would hug me like my mommy used to do when I was upset. Aunt Edna was not a huggy mommy. I never saw her hug Sally or the others. I was smaller and needed hugs. Even her hand on my knee felt good. So that was better than nothing.

"Let me find out how she is doing and whether we can go for a visit, sweetie," she said. She lifted my chin. She wiped the wet stuff away from my eyes with her fingers.

"Now cheer up, little one." I could tell she was putting a pretend smile on her face.

Hoping that I might see my mommy again helped me stop crying. The bad feeling in my belly was not knowing where I would go to see her. I wondered if it was a scary place like where my daddy lived. I wondered if people in hospitals all wore the same clothes. Places where people dressed the same were bad places. But in hospitals they were supposed to make sick people get well again. Where my daddy was, they weren't taking very good care of him. Maybe that was because he wasn't sick. Remembering where my daddy was made me worried about my mommy.

"In the meantime," Edna continued, "you have to promise to try to get along with your cousin. I know she can be bossy at times, but I also know she's quite fond of you. Will you try?"

Hoping she would take me to see my mommy soon, I nodded.

The Nut House

The lawn didn't look like real grass. It looked like a large green carpet as far as I could see. Pink roses had dropped their petals along the wobbly path. It was hard to walk on the stones in my new shoes. This place didn't look like a hospital. At least not like the one where my grandpa was. This place had a large porch. It was even bigger than the one we had at home. People sat on rocking chairs. I wondered why they stared at me. No one said anything. No one smiled.

A lady in a white dress and white shoes came to the door. She was smiling. She wasn't grumpy like the man at the big house where my daddy lived.

"You must be Mrs. Stone." She shook Aunt Edna's hand. "My name is Lilly."

"Pleased to meet you," Aunt Edna said.

"This is Molly, Dora's daughter."

Lilly knelt down. She had pretty blue eyes. They were the color of the sky. Her hair was the color of our wheat fields. Her hair was piled on top of her head. She wore a white cap that matched her white dress. She smelled like clean sheets. She smiled at me. Why was she happy to see me when she'd never seen me before?

"Aren't you just the cutest thing?" she said. "And what a pretty dress you have on!"

I had picked my clothes carefully. I wanted to look nice for Mommy. Aunt Edna had tied a white bow in my hair. It matched the lace around the sleeves of my dress. The sleeves felt itchy on my arms. I wore my favorite white shoes and knee socks. Mommy didn't like me looking like a tomboy. I wanted to make her happy.

"You are probably tired from your long drive. Would you like to come inside and have a soda?" she asked.

All I really wanted was to see my mommy, but I nodded politely. Lilly took us into a room with big chairs with big cushions. She told us to sit down. I climbed up on a chair. My feet couldn't reach the floor. I folded my hands in my lap and crossed my ankles like mommy had taught me to do. She said it was polite when we were visiting. Lilly brought us two glasses of fizzy soda, one for me and one for Aunt Edna. Aunt Edna sat in the big chair across from me. She had her purse on her lap. She didn't hold it tight, which made me think things were going to be okay. She took her gloves off to hold the glass.

"Thank you," I said, and tried my best to drink slowly. I didn't want to spill it on my pretty dress. I looked around the room. There was a tall fireplace. On top of it was a picture of a woman. She looked important. I wondered who she was. The walls were gray. I thought the room would look prettier if it was pink or yellow. I looked up and the ceiling was the highest I'd ever seen. I thought how hard it would be to clean spiderwebs up that high. Mommy was always mopping spiderwebs from the ceiling at home. Mommy told me that spiders eat other bugs. This place was so clean that there probably were no bugs and spiders wouldn't have a reason to live here. There was a big light in the middle of the ceiling. It had many sparkling pieces of glass. They made rainbows dance on the gray walls. There were two glass doors that were open. I had never seen glass doors before. Outside were plants in large pots. I stared at a chipmunk burying a nut in one of them. He looked at me sideways and quickly ran away. The chairs that we were sitting in were placed in a circle. In the middle was a table with plants on it. They looked like they were picked from the garden. In the hallway, I saw people walking back and forth. Sometimes they stopped and stared at us. I wondered if they were sick people like my mommy. Why were they not in their beds? Why were they walking around in their clothes if they were sick? Whenever I was sick, I had to stay in bed and wear my pajamas. Lilly sat with us and talked with Aunt Edna. My drink was finished. I didn't know what I should do with the empty glass. I kept looking at the door. I was waiting for my mommy to walk in. I stayed still, looking perfect in case she came. "Now I bet you are anxious for your visit with your mother," Lilly finally said.

I nodded hard.

"Well let me take your glass and we'll go to where she is."

I handed her the glass. She stopped and sat back down again. She took a deep breath and looked at me. I liked looking at her sky-blue eyes. Her eyes were saying things to me before her mouth said anything. Something about her made me think she was nice.

"Now you know your mother has not been well."

"I know," I said. "Me and Aunt Edna and Uncle Jake took her to the hospital and she slept the whole way."

Lilly made a little smile.

"Well, this is a different kind of hospital. This is the kind of hospital where she can rest until she gets better. Her visits need to be short. We don't want to upset her."

I didn't understand. Why would my visit upset her? I thought that she would be happy to see me. I sure was going to be happy to see her again.

"So if you're ready, we'll take a walk out to the garden and see if we can find her."

I hopped down from the chair when Aunt Edna stood up. Lilly took my hand. It felt soft as a kitten. I walked beside her out to the garden. There were people sitting on benches. They were staring at the lawns. I didn't know what they found so interesting about that. Some were walking slowly. They were having trouble lifting their feet. They stared at us when we walked by. Some didn't notice us. Aunt Edna followed us. Lilly stopped behind a bench. There was a woman sitting there. I could only see her back. She wore a hair clip with a butterfly on it. That was what my mommy always wore. This was my mommy. I was so excited I wanted to run to her. Lilly held onto my hand very tightly. I pulled ahead but she wouldn't let go. "You have a visitor Dora," Lilly said quietly. We walked around so that I could see her face.

She moved her head suddenly. The rest of her body stayed still. She watched us come around the side of the bench. Aunt Edna stood behind, watching us. I couldn't stop staring up into my mommy's face. Something was different. It looked like she had her eyes open but was sleeping. Her face didn't move. There was no smile, even though I had a big smile from my one ear to the other. Did she not know who I was? How could my mommy not know me? My smile went away.

"Your daughter Molly is here to visit you Dora," Lilly said, still holding onto my hand. I wondered if she wasn't going to let me go.

Mommy looked down at me and blinked. I think she was trying to remember who I was. She didn't move and she didn't speak. I pulled away from Lilly and crawled up on the bench and into her lap. I put my arms around her neck and pressed my cheek into her chest.

"I missed you, Mommy," I said.

She said nothing. Her arms were at her sides like a rag doll. Her eyes wouldn't look at me. I breathed in the smell of her hair and skin. It was the only thing that still reminded me of her. I was afraid to squeeze her too tight. I could feel her bones through her clothes. Why were they not feeding her? I held onto her. I liked the rocking motion of her breath as it went in and out. Everything around me disappeared. There was just me and my mommy, like we were the same person. I snuggled even closer. I felt an arm circle around me and then another one. I could feel her chin resting on my head. We sat together like that for a long time. We did not say anything. I wondered if the reason she didn't speak was because she had not seen my daddy. Maybe if she saw Daddy again, her voice would come back like mine did. Maybe she was frightened like I was and wanted to be invisible. I stayed still, not wanting to open my eyes. I wanted everything else to disappear so that I could stay like this forever. I thought that the longer I held onto her the more she might come back to being the mommy I knew. I thought about the nights back at home, when I would wake up feeling scared from a nightmare. I would crawl into her bed and snuggle next to her warm body. This felt like one of those nightmares. Aunt Edna sat down beside us on the bench. Lilly was talking to someone else.

"Dora, it's me Edna, Billy's sister. I just want you to know that Molly is being taken care of by us. We've seen Billy and he's doing fine. I'm sure everything will be cleared up real soon."

Mommy kept looking ahead, not saying anything. Her hug was not as tight anymore. I wished Aunt Edna would go away. She was upsetting my mommy by talking.

"This seems like a nice place," Edna continued. "I'm sure with the good care you're getting, you'll get better soon."

Still she didn't say anything. I continued to hold her, but it started feeling like holding my doll who was not alive. I wanted to ask her so many questions, but I knew it would be like talking to myself. So I sat quietly, just holding her. Her body was all I had to hold onto. The rest of her was gone somewhere else. Nurse Lilly came over and stood beside us. I knew my visit was over. I reached up and kissed Mommy's cheek. She blinked.

"Say goodbye now Molly," Lilly said.

Aunt Edna had stood up and turned her back to us.

"I miss you, Mommy," I said.

I couldn't think of anything else to say. I crawled off her lap and ran my han down her arm to her fingertips. I was about to let go when her fingers curle around mine. I looked up at her and saw that her eyes were wet and shiny. I kne she was sad. I wanted my visit to make my mommy happy. I didn't understand wh it was making her upset. I turned and ran away as fast as I could. I didn't want he to see me cry.

Summer 1955

BILLY

The Day I Met Nell

The day Nell strode up our pathway, I recognized her as our neighbor's kid. I remembered her biking by on her way to the lake with her brother. She always waved when she rode by, while her brother never gave me any notice. *Friendly kid,* I'd thought. I felt sorry for them. Rumor had it that their father was slogging back booze from morning to night and then hollering at the wife and kids. Their farm was in shambles and couldn't have been making much money. The day she came by, she had holes in her runners and her clothes were hand-me-downs of the sort the poor folk picked up from the Goodwill. She was as lanky as a yo-yo. Her hair hung across one eye, while the other eye squinted up at me. Her hands rested in her jean pockets, as she stood awkwardly before me. I put my pitchfork down and wiped the sweat from my brow.

"Hi, I-I-I'm Nell, your n-next door neighbor," she stuttered.

She pointed her long thin arm in the direction of their farm. All that was visible were fields between our homes. I stood there in the hot sun, a little irritated by the intrusion.

I reached out my hand and she politely shook it.

"What can I do for you Nell?"

The sun was shining on her face. She covered her eyes with the back of her hand while looking up at me.

"Well, I'm off for the summer holidays and needing to earn a bit of pocket money to help out. You know," she added awkwardly, "with family expenses and such. I was wondering if you might be looking to hire someone to help with farm chores for the summer."

I wondered why she wouldn't be working on her own family farm, but realized that her father had probably thrown in the towel on maintaining his crop. I'd noticed that her brother had a job pumping gas at the local corner gas station, and I'd seen her mother packing groceries at Ted's Food Mart. I sized her up and decided she was too scrawny to be of any value to me.

"I don't think the kind of work around here would be suitable for a girl like you," I said. "I know that they're looking for help at some shops in town. Have you tried there?"

She looked away for a bit, hesitating before taking a deep breath and responding.

"I couldn't work cramped up behind some ice-cream counter or cash register all day. I want to work outside. You should see the vegetable garden I've put in for my family. I know I don't look like I can do much, but if you give me a chance, I'll show you."

She pushed back a strand of hair that was hanging in her face and made solid eye contact for the first time. I saw a determination there that I liked.

She could see me hesitate and added, "Just give me a week to prove myself, that's all. I can do whatever work you give me."

Molly came up from behind, curious about who this new person was. I picked her up and introduced them. Nell tickled her tummy and she giggled with delight. I looked around the farm and thought that maybe it wouldn't be such a bad idea getting a couple months of help. If she didn't work out with the hard labor, at least she could mind Molly while Dora took her afternoon nap. Dora had been frail with her headaches and dizzy spells lately. Sometimes she'd stay in bed all day long with the curtains drawn. Doctors couldn't figure out what was wrong. They just gave her more pills, which just made her sleep more. Meanwhile Molly would follow me around like a lost puppy dog. I just didn't have the time for her. "Would you be willing to help with house chores and minding Molly as well if needed?"

"Yes, anything," she replied eagerly. I sized her up again. One hand rested on her hip, while the other dangled at her side. She shuffled her foot in the dirt, eyes squinting up at me and almost pleading, but still seemed confident, challenging me to not turn her away.

"One week," I said. "I'll give you one week, okay? Then we'll see."

A big grin grew over her face, revealing a perfect row of white teeth. She jumped up in the air.

"Terrific! You won't regret this!"

"I start early," I added.

"What time do you want me here?"

"Five a.m.." I expected that she'd quit right then.

"I'll be here!" she said. "Thank you so much. See you tomorrow."

She turned to leave. I realized she probably didn't even know my name.

"It's Billy Mulgrave by the way,"

"Thank you Mr. Mulgrave!" she shouted. "Bye Molly! You won't be sorry Mr. Mulgrave!" Then she ran off with her limbs flying in all directions.

I stood there grinning as I watched her run off. What had I done? She was just a kid, but she needed a break. I liked her spunk and her appreciation of the outdoors. And hey, what were neighbors for?

NELL

The Day I Met Billy

I stumbled and fell up the gravel pathway leading to our neighbor's house. I wiped my scraped knee off and pushed back my hair.

"What a klutz," I said to myself. These were words I often heard at home. I could do nothing right. If there wasn't enough milk for cereal in the morning, it was my fault. If the beer mugs were not washed and re-stacked in the cupboard before my father reached for another drink, it was my fault. I was the lazy one, the useless one, the burden to the family. Even though my brother had quit school and couldn't hold down a job, nothing was expected of him. I was learning from my mother that the only way to avoid fights at home was to avoid home altogether. She did just that. She worked ten, sometimes twelve hours a day at Ted's Market, and often did a double shift if someone didn't show up. Any excuse to avoid home. She came in when my father was already passed out and left before he awoke. As much as I missed not having her there, it was for the best. Those rare occasions when they were together, the battles would start. I would run out and hide behind the woodshed, where the voices became a droning sound like the rumble of a distant train. I'd then slink in and pretend I was invisible. Now that it was summer, I couldn't escape to school anymore. I felt like a trapped animal.

It dawned on me to try to find work somewhere other than town when I saw the neighbor across the fence tilling his fields in preparation for the late crop plantings. He always tipped his hat when he rode his tractor by and saw me staring into space, as I often did. He seemed friendly enough.

There wasn't any hired help on the farm, and if he had any children, they were obviously not old enough to help—at least not from what I could see.

It took me a lot of courage, but here I was stumbling up the pathway to his door. Just as I was about to knock, I caught sight of him around the side of the house. He was loading something into his truck and hadn't noticed me. He looked younger than Pa. His muscles flexed as he thrust his pitchfork, and unlike dad (who was bald), his hair was blowing wildly in the breeze. His shirt was open in the heat and his overalls were covered in mud. I didn't want him to see me watching, so I ran down the front pathway and re-entered along the driveway, making sure I was noticed. He stopped what he was doing and stared at me, his gloved hands resting on his hips.

When I was within earshot, I shouted a greeting and told him who I was.

Of course, I stuttered my words, which I often did when I was nervous. Who was I to come here hoping he'd hire me? He paused and took off his gloves, then reached out a hand to greet me. I shook it, feeling awkward. He was looking at me impatiently so I got to the point and told him I was there for work.

I glanced up at this face, trying to read him. He appeared a mere shadow with the sun shining into my eyes. I squinted to try to bring him into focus. He had a rugged look about him. Maybe it was the suntanned skin with dirt marks where he'd rubbed his glove across his forehead. His eyes were soft though, hazy like a dew-covered morning. I had a sense that he was a kind man. I realized I was staring and quickly looked down at my feet. I knew he was sizing me up, probably thinking I was crazy for being here.

A part of me was ready to run away in embarrassment. What was I thinking to have come here? Another part of me (a more determined one) spoke instead. It was the part that dreaded returning home. I tried to convince him that I was a hard worker. I was pleading with him to give me a chance. He glanced over in the direction I'd come from. I'm sure he was wondering why I wasn't working on my own farm. Our place was nothing but a bunch of overgrown weeds. I knew he was expecting more of an explanation, but I just didn't want to talk about my family. A little girl of about four or five wandered up beside him, looking up at me curiously.

"This is Molly." He picked her up, and asked me if I liked kids.

I didn't have to pretend there. I could be myself around kids. They accepted me. No one else did. I gave Molly's tummy a little tickle. She giggled and turned to bury her face in her father's shoulder. She peered out shyly at me but couldn't hide the grin on her face.

After I agreed to doing household chores and babysitting from time to time, as well as the farm work, he agreed to give me a week to prove myself.

I had been prepared to walk away and accept that coming by was a silly idea. Now I couldn't contain my excitement. I think I might have been jumping up and down like a two year old, and hardly even blinked when he told me we'd be starting work at five in the morning. I thanked him profusely as I headed back towards the road.

"It's Billy Mulgrave, by the way," he said, smiling at me in amusement.

"Thank you Mr. Mulgrave!" I caught a glimpse of the little smiling face, still peeking out at me. "Bye Molly!"

Molly waved at me shyly. I turned and ran down the driveway, calling back over my shoulder, "You won't be sorry Mr. Mulgrave!" I could feel their eyes on me from behind as I headed off down the road towards my home.

DORA

Disappearing

When did I first stop believing? I believed in "the dream" ... the dream of having a home, a kind husband, beautiful children who would love me, and the happiness of being together. I had all of that—at least the home and husband. A baby was growing in my belly back then, as I knitted blankets and booties in anticipation of its arrival. Everything went as planned. I was hoping for a girl and there she was, all pink and wrinkled, fists clenched, and a healthy holler in defiance of her entry into the world. I had never experienced the pure love and adoration that I felt the moment I gazed into her sea-blue eyes. I couldn't believe that I had created something so perfect. I stroked the softness of her cheek and held her tiny body next to my skin. It was a moment that I keep going back to, trying to relive it and feel it again. That perfect moment has been like a dream I'm desperately trying to remember and hold onto, but the harder I try the more it eludes me.

I don't know if it was days after giving birth or weeks, but I suddenly felt like I had dropped into a deep dark hole that I've been trying to crawl out of ever since. The lights hurt my eyes, sounds resonated in my ears, and food became tasteless. I felt hollow. It didn't help that people came to see me and exclaimed what a beautiful baby Molly was and how lucky I was. It just made me feel worse. I wasn't able to feel what others expected of me. It was all I could do to get through my daily chores, let alone meet the never-ending needs of my baby. My overflowing breasts cried out for her in the early morning hours. I couldn't bring myself to lift my head, my arms, or my legs to go to her as she wailed for me in her hamper. Billy would get up and bring her to me, and she'd coo at my breast. I felt like she was draining the life out of me. My breasts were no longer my own. My body was there to meet her demands and my soul was sucked out of me. I'd lie there day after day, observing the coming and goings of the household, void of energy, and void of any connection to any of it. "Take her," I called out to Billy from my bed. She had just finished suckling and was drifting off to sleep. "Billy!" I called again, feeling that the weight of her was making it difficult for me to breathe, even though she was no larger than a doll. She woke up and started to cry. She grappled for my breast again. They felt sore and I resented her for that. I needed to rest. Billy came into the room. The baby was crying louder now.

"Why did you wake her?" He scooped her out of my arms and tried soothing her with a rocking motion.

"I'm sorry. I feel so weak. I need to sleep. Please just take her away." I was crying now. Billy had managed to calm Molly down and brought her over to me. "Look at her Dora," he said. "She's such an angel." He leaned towards me so that I could see her eyes staring up at him. Her mouth was moving in a sucking motion, and her tiny hands were grappling with the air. Her innocence made me feel so inadequate as her mother. I had nothing left to give her.

"Please just take her away." I rolled over in the bed and pulled the blanket over my head. Darkness surrounded me.

The few mornings when I managed to get myself dressed and push the pram around in the market place, the friendly smiles of other women had changed to averted eyes and whispers behind my back. I felt like I was no longer part of their social circle.

"You're just imagining things," Billy would say. "If you'd only speak to these women when you see them, you'd find there is nothing wrong. Honey, you have to make the effort."

These were empty words. Making an effort meant putting one foot in front of the other to get through the day. It seemed that doubt always turned to fear no matter how I tried to convince myself otherwise. Everything was just too much effort. I was merely going through the motions, numb to feelings as I attempted to appear normal in a world that seemed hostile and unforgiving to me. Billy looked at me with those eyes that I'd always felt safe in. Sometimes those eyes appeared pleading, sometimes angry. The worst were the eyes of disappointment—disappointment in me. He didn't understand where I'd disappeared to. Neither did I. I would look in the mirror and wonder who the woman was that was reflected back at me. I had always been considered pretty throughout my high school and college years. Now my once rosy complexion looked a sickly milky white. My eyes were lifeless. I had always meticulously curled my shoulder-length hair, brushing it multiple strokes every night and taking pride in its luster. It now hung limply without any shape. No wonder, as I had stopped caring how it looked. Did I really appear as bad as I saw myself or was it just my perception? Billy still tried to be affectionate with me and told me how pretty I was, but I didn't believe him. It didn't even matter. I felt I'd somehow vaporized, become invisible.

At one time, I thought Billy was much simpler than me. I was the one who attended college and had career plans. I'd thought of going into nursing before I met him. I was attracted to his wholesome good looks and his earthy nature. His passion for living in the countryside overpowered any idea I had of living and working in the city. I gave that up to be with him and to have the children we dreamed of together. This dream had now turned into a nightmare. I failed to be the kind of wife that he deserved.

I went along with him when he insisted that I see the doctor. I wished a doctor had the power to make it all better. He gave me pills: pills to go to sleep, pills to wake up, and pills to kill the feelings that were already nonexistent. My life began to revolve around my pill schedule. I took them hoping for a miracle that never came. Now, five years after Molly's birth, the black hole still remained deep and invasive and my life was a mere puppetry.

A Helping Hand OR Am I Being Replaced?

I was initially apprehensive when Nell started working for us. Billy tried to convince me that it was a good idea. "I've hired the neighbor girl to help out," he announced over dinner one night.

I gazed up at him, surprised.

"Help out with what?" I asked. We'd always been self-sufficient. We'd talked about getting help with the farm, but Billy liked being a one-man operation. He took pride in his work.

"A bit of everything. I could use a hand with some of the farm chores and well ..." he hesitated a moment before continuing, "maybe she could help with some of the household chores."

I felt like he'd slapped me. Was I really that inadequate in his eyes? I remained silent.

"I just thought it would give you the time you need to rest. Molly is needing someone around more. She's been talking to the animals as if they were her friends."

"Well maybe Molly needs some friends her own age."

"You know that there *is* no one her age for miles around. When would I have time to drive her anywhere? This would be like a built-in big sister for her."

Billy's eyes pleaded, waiting for a response. I continued playing with the food on my plate. Molly had been rather clingy lately. Maybe having a young girl with lots of energy to play with her was not such a bad idea.

"When does she start?" I asked.

"Tomorrow morning at sparrow chirp. Molly's already met her and she was excited. You'll see that it will be the best thing for her. For all of us."

What harm was there in having another helping hand available? As I started to clear the dishes away, Billy grabbed my arm and looked up at me intently.

"We don't have to hire her if you don't want. I wasn't looking for anyone. She just came around and seemed desperate for work. I figured it was the neighborly thing to do, to give the kid a break. I think you'll like her, Dora."

I forced a half smile, offering him some reassurance. It didn't really matter. I felt my life was out of my control and things just happened around me. This was just another one of those things.

"I'm sure she'll work out fine," I mustered in response, and turned towards the soapy sink to immerse myself in doing the dishes.

NELL

First Day on the Job

I didn't sleep well that night. I'd tried to talk to Pa that evening, to tell him I'd found a job. He stared at the wall while he listened to the radio show he'd had on all day long. He took a sip of his beer and grunted. Ma didn't get home until I was in bed and wasn't up yet when I had to leave for work. I left a note on the kitchen table. I knew that they'd all laugh at me if I said I was going to work as a farm hand, so instead I wrote "babysitting next door." I made sure that the dishes in the sink were washed before I left, even though I had not left the mess. I ran the half mile to the neighbor's farm. A red glow was appearing on the horizon. When I arrived, Mr. Mulgrave was already in the barn finishing with milking the cows. I looked at him, searching for direction. He looked surprised to see me, as if he hadn't really expected me to show up. He looked at what I was wearing, overalls and a plaid shirt borrowed from my brother.

"I hope you're ready to get dirty," he said. "The pigs are going to need their slop and the chicken-feed needs to be scattered. If the rooster gets in your way, you need to show him you're tougher than him. Understand?"

I stood there nodding my head, not having a clue what I was doing.

He looked down at my feet. "Those shoes won't do," he said. "Let me get you Dora's boots. They may be a bit big for you, but you won't get through the pig pen with sneakers on."

I slid the boots that he handed me up over my overalls.

"You may want to tie back your hair as well, if you don't want it falling into the manure."

I was fine until then but froze with the suggestion. I liked my hair down and felt naked without it. It was what I needed to hide behind when I didn't want others to see me.

"It's okay," I muttered. "I can wash it when I get home."

"Suit yourself," he said and handed me a bucket. "Now go to it. First the pigs and goats, then the chickens. While they eat, you collect their eggs. Don't forget to watch out for that rooster. If you have any questions, just ask. When you're done, let me know. There's lots more to do out in the fields."

He turned to walk away, as I stood there feeling overwhelmed with what I had taken on. He turned back around and winked at me. "I'm sure you'll do fine," he said with a smile, and then left.

That helped. I took a deep breath and started my first day of work. I sloshed through the pig pens, pouring heavy buckets of slop that looked like thick gravy into the food stalls. The smell of the sows made me feel faint as they snorted and kicked manure up my trousers. The piglets let out piercing squeals, annoyed that their mothers had gotten up to feed. One little one hung on to its mother's teat and got dragged along as she made her way to the stalls. The hens scattered when I appeared. I got a basket and started collecting their morning offerings. The eggs felt warm and smooth in my hand, which was somehow comforting. Accidentally, I let one fall and watched in horror as it splattered on my boot. In a panic, I found the water tap and rinsed off my boot, fearing that my new job would soon be over if Mr. Mulgrave saw what I'd done. I collected the shattered shell, piece by piece, and put it into my trouser pocket. Leaving the coop with the eggs, I walked directly into the dreaded rooster that Mr. Mulgrave had warned me about. He gave me the evil eye, puffed out his chest, and flapped his enormous wings, ready for a fight. I wasn't sure what Mr. Mulgrave expected me to do, but I knew that if I appeared weak, I was doomed. I quickly lowered the eggs, raised my arms up in the air and flapped them in a similar way, howling at the top of my lungs. The rooster took one look at me and fled, shrinking in size. Mr. Mulgrave came running and laughed as the ferocious rooster skittered under a fence and out of sight.

"Well done, Nell!" he exclaimed. "I knew you had it in you!" He picked up the eggs and motioned me to follow him. "Before I take you out to the fields, there's someone I want you to meet."

I followed him dutifully, in a similar manner to the brown mutt that wouldn't leave his side. He led me to the farmhouse and motioned me in.

"You may want to leave the boots outside," he said, looking down at the muddy mess under my feet.

Embarrassed, I sat on the front steps and pulled them off. I suddenly felt the tiny arms of Molly around my neck.

"Hi there," I said. I turned and we were eye to eye. All her shyness had disappeared.

"Want to play?" she asked, beaming at me.

"I do, but I think I need to get some more work done first."

I loved kids and they seemed to gravitate to me. I felt an instant connection with Molly. However, I knew that Mr. Mulgrave had not brought me here to play with her. I got up and pulled open the screen door to the kitchen, Molly following me close behind. "Nell, I'd like you to meet Dora, my wife."

Dora was not what I had expected. She was a pretty woman but frail looking—not what I imagined a farmer's wife would look like. She stood in front of the stove, drying her hands on her apron. She looked like she had just gotten out of bed, with her hair messy and no makeup on. Unlike Mr. Mulgrave, who was jovial, she didn't smile. She looked at my mud-stained overalls. I felt uncomfortable.

"Pleased to meet you," she said, very formally.

Mr. Mulgrave cleared his throat, breaking the silence between us.

"You'll be doing some work in the house when needed. Dora will instruct you on what needs to be done. I hope that's okay with you?"

Although house chores were not what I'd hoped for, I needed work and any work outside of my own home would do.

"Of course," I said.

"Now I'll take you out to the fields and get you started out there. You can check back with Dora later."

Molly clung to my dirty pant-leg and Dora beckoned her over to the stove. She hesitantly obeyed. I thought that Mr. Mulgrave watched with a hint of sadness.

"Molly, you'll get your turn with Nell soon. See how popular you already are, Nell?" he asked with a warm smile, putting his hand on my shoulder.

I returned his smile. "Thank you Mr. Mulgrave."

"Please, it's Billy. No need for formalities here."

Without a word, Dora turned and walked out of the room, dragging Molly behind her. Molly looked over her shoulder and waved with her other hand, but Dora gave her a sudden jerk. They disappeared into the next room.

Protecting My Brother, Sacrificing Me

I got home feeling exhausted that night. In the kitchen, the note still sat on the table. I wondered if anyone had bothered to read it.

"Is that you Nell?" boomed Pa's voice from the living room.

The radio was blaring as usual on some sports station.

"Yeah, it's me!" I hollered back.

"Get me another beer, will ya?"

I knew to do as he ordered. Avoiding arguments was something I'd learned. I looked in the fridge. It had been full of beer this morning, but only a few bottles remained. I brought him the beer.

He glanced over and did a double take. "What the hell have you been up to? Wrestling with hogs?"

"Sort of," I said. "I'm doing some farm work for the neighbor."

Pa grimaced and lit a cigarette. "Well you smell like shit."

I wondered how he could smell anything with all the smoke in the room. I grabbed the overflowing ashtray and headed for the kitchen.

"Get those smelly pants off and then get me some dinner."

I had been looking forward to sinking into a bathtub. Every muscle in my body ached.

"I'll get changed and wash up, and then I'll see what I can cook you. Okay Pa?"

"Well be quick about it. My dinner is late already. From the smell of ya, I'll have to wait or I may just gag."

Andy, who was slouched on the couch opposite Pa, was staring blankly at the floor. He'd obviously just lost another job or he wouldn't be home yet. It looked like he was spending the last of his wages on beer as well. He was becoming just like Pa.

I sank into the tub and let my head slide under the water, luxuriating in the warmth. As I emerged, I was shocked to find Andy standing there. I scrambled to cover up under the suds.

"Do you mind?" I hollered.

"Don't mind at all." He walked over to the toilet and took a leak.

"Couldn't you wait till I was done?" I asked. "Or at least have knocked."

"I knocked but you didn't answer."

"Well maybe you should have considered that I was underwater and couldn't hear you."

"Hey you're my sister, so what's the big deal?" His eyes scanned my body.

"Get out!" I yelled.

He lifted his hands up in the air and staggered drunkenly out of the room. I'd noticed before that he'd appear unexpectedly just as I was either getting ready for bed or getting dressed in the morning. He'd linger outside my door if it was cracked open. I'd slam it shut. One time I had felt hands groping me in the middle of the night. I thought I was dreaming and then woke up startled. The room was dark and I couldn't see anyone.

"Who's there?" I cried out in fear.

I could hear someone breathing. I reached for my light, but by the time I turned to scan the room, there was no one there. I lay there for the rest of the night, afraid to fall asleep again ... not trusting that I was safe.

"Stay out of my room!" I yelled at Andy, as I entered the kitchen in the morning.

"What are you talking about?"

"I know you were in my room last night, pervert!"

Ma turned from the kitchen sink and gave me a scornful look. "That's enough now. I won't listen to name calling like that."

She was always ready to come to Andy's defense, but not mine.

"Tell Andy to leave me alone then!" I said, a desperation in my voice. I wanted so badly for her to protect me. I felt like nothing I said mattered.

"I'm sure you were having bad dreams. There's no need to accuse your brother now of something he didn't do."

I stared at her, challenging her not to ignore what was becoming obvious. I'd seen him peering at her as well, through the bathroom keyhole the other day. When she opened the door to see him standing there, I knew she was flustered, but had said nothing. She was good at pretending to not see what she didn't want to see. Andy was two years older than me. He was never good at school, repeatedly being sent home for causing trouble. My parents would have to go to the school with him if he wanted to return. My father had called the school a "bunch of assholes" and opened another beer. "I went through the same shit that Andy's going through," he'd said. "I didn't put up with it and neither should he."

"Do you want him to end up like you then?" my mother would screech. "We have to try to keep him in school or what will become of him?" Ma would do what she had to in order to get him back in. She'd make up excuses for him. I knew they were all lies. Our grandfather may have just died, but Andy didn't grieve his death as Ma claimed. He'd never liked him. My mother told the school that he was devastated and needed sympathy. In fact, I was the one who had loved Grandpa. I cried for a week, but no one took notice. Life just went on and I was expected to do my chores and get myself to school no matter what. Grandpa had been my last hope for a home that I wanted to return to. Without him, there was no feeling of comfort here. My parents were relieved that they no longer had his disapproving eyes watching them. Now they could behave as they liked in the home that had been his.

Yes, there was always an excuse for my brother. In their eyes, he could do no wrong. Perhaps it was because they couldn't face what they really saw. In the end, he dropped out anyway and was on the road to becoming a drunk like my pa.

BILLY

A Ride to Town

Nell was true to her word. There wasn't a chore she wasn't willing to do, from milking the cows to hauling the hay. She'd be there right at five, full of energy and ready to put in a hard day's work. Her endurance amazed me, given her thin frame, but I guessed it was pure determination to prove herself. When the midday sun sent even Rex to the shade of the orchard trees, Nell continued to push herself along. When she was hot and filthy, she would stick her neck under the water pump and let the cold water soak her face and hair and drip down the rest of her.

"What next Mr. Mulgrave?" she'd ask.

The formality seemed unnecessary, since she'd earned her keep and was gonna stay.

"Call me Billy, if you would. And I wouldn't send my workhorse out in this heat. Why don't you take a break with Molly for a while and let me finish up."

Molly was crayoning beside Rex under the apple tree. I expected that Nell would go lie down beside her to cool off, but the next thing I knew she was playing tag with her in the yard, with squeals of laughter echoing across the lawn. Molly so looked forward to time with Nell that I didn't mind giving up the help I needed for an hour or two. With Dora resting most of the time, Molly was left alone. She never complained, but having Nell around was like a big sister, which she needed so badly.

"Can Nell stay for dinner with us Daddy?" Molly asked as I came in for a glass of water. I had just loaded the wheat into the truck to take to town.

I looked at Molly's pleading eyes and glanced Dora's way. She was at the stove preparing a stew.

She turned to look at me. "There's plenty of food for everyone," she said. "I don't mind."

Nell sat in the kitchen playing cards with Molly, whom I hadn't seen so excited for a long while.

"I don't see why not," I said, "but first I got to do a delivery in town."

"I'll come and help." Nell jumped up eagerly, while Molly frowned.

"We'll finish the game when I get back," she reassured Molly, and gave her a little squeeze.

"You don't need to come," I said, but she insisted. I appreciated the help. The truck kicked up the dust on our way to town. I glanced over at her as she hung her one arm out the window, holding her hair in a ponytail with the other. The truck bounced her like a rag doll along the bumpy road.

"I just wanted to say that you're doing good, Nell. You've been a great help."

She grinned and glanced over at me. Then the grin faded.

"I'm just so glad to be out of my home all day. You have no idea." She shook her head.

I didn't know what to say. Didn't want to pry into personal matters. I could tell there was something driving her, as if she were getting some devil feelings out with the energy she put into her work.

"Molly is taking a real liking to you," I said, wanting to lighten things up.

"She's so cute and really smart too. Can beat me at cards every time."

She spit her gum out the window with some force.

"Are you and Mrs. Mulgrave planning on having more children?" she asked casually.

I was a bit taken back by her directness.

"Well, I think we'd like to, but Dora hasn't been well lately and having another one wouldn't be good for anyone just now."

Nell turned to look out the window again.

"My parents never should have had me."

I glanced at her several times, not sure what to say.

She didn't look at me.

"Dad was starting to drink back then, and they were fighting lots after my brother was born." She paused for a moment before continuing. "My auntie told me, when she was a bit tipsy, that Ma tried to get rid of me while I was still in her belly, but it didn't work. I wish it had."

What an awful way to feel, I thought. I needed to cheer this poor girl up a bit.

"Well such a lovely lady wouldn't be sitting beside me right now if she had." I offered her what I hoped was a reassuring smile.

She looked my way, with a faint smile in return.

In some ways she seemed years beyond her age, but she was still a child in other ways, needing the reassurance she obviously wasn't getting at home. When we got back to the house, Molly ran into her arms.

"Come to the barn," she said. "Fluffy just had her kittens. Come see!" She pulled Nell out the door.

Dora was setting the table as I went into the pantry to wash up.

"You sure you don't mind Nell staying now, do you?" I yelled to Dora, who was in the kitchen. "I don't think she gets much to eat back home."

No answer. Dora was sitting at the table and didn't look up when I returned. I came up behind her, put my hands on her shoulders, and bent down to kiss her neck. She shrugged me away.

"Not now," she said. "The kids could walk in at any time."

"There's nothing wrong with a hug is there? I don't think Nell sees much of that between her parents." I felt like adding that Molly didn't see much of it between us either. Dora pushed me aside and went to the stove to stir the stew.

"Smells good, honey."

Silence.

Losing Dora

It had been years since Dora had let me touch her the way she once did. The birth of Molly changed everything. A child was what she wanted, but after Molly was born, Dora cried for days. I tried my best to comfort her, and to take care of the baby for her, but nothing helped. There were times that I thought I had my Dora back. We would go for Sunday drives and have a picnic at the lake. Molly would busy herself picking up stones or trying to eat blades of grass. Everything was fascinating to her and we would laugh together while watching her. These were the moments that gave me hope.

When Molly cried, it was me who she wanted for comfort, probably because I had been the one to go get her at night when she was a baby. I tried to hand her over to Dora, but she'd only cry harder. Dora saw this as rejection. Her mood would drop and she'd want to be alone again. She would weep and say that she wasn't a very good mother or Molly would love her more. As far as I could see, Molly wanted her mother badly but was never sure if her mother wanted her. She was so rarely available to her that she learned to count on me instead. I didn't want to take anything away from Dora. I just wanted to help. It was hard running a farm and taking care of Molly. Hiring Nell was a blessing. I was free to take care of my farm and not feel badly for Molly. Molly took an instant liking to Nell and giggled and laughed around her more than I'd ever seen before. Dora was also relieved that she didn't need to be responsible as a mother all the time. But I could sense resentment growing.

"Molly is more attached to Nell than to me," she cried one night.

We had just finished dinner, with Nell once again staying for the meal. Molly and she had run outside to play while I helped Dora clear away the dishes.

"Don't be silly, honey. She finds Nell fun to play with, like a playmate. It has nothing to do with the kind of love she has for you."

"I didn't say love," she snipped. "Love is duty bound. I said 'attached'. She prefers Nell to me."

I was thinking that if Dora was a bit more playful with Molly, she would want to be with her mother more. I wouldn't dare say that. I'd learned to be very careful with what I said to Dora.

"I do everything for her. I sew her dresses; I cook her meals. I take her to the doctor. I don't feel I'm appreciated for all that I do," she sniveled.

Her thinking was ludicrous.

"Molly's only five years old! For God's sake, Dora! How is she supposed to show appreciation?"

"Maybe a thank you once in a while would do. We haven't taught her proper manners."

Dora turned away, banging dishes loudly in the sink. There was no doubt in my mind that Dora tried to be a good mother, but she just wasn't enjoying being a mother.

"Maybe you could sit in the evenings and read to her or do a puzzle. Have some fun with her. Maybe that's what she needs more."

Dora turned around abruptly to glare at me—wet hands on her hips.

"I'm tired by the end of the day!"

I wondered whether I should go further. I knew that this would not end well but had trouble holding back.

"Well then have the fun time during the day. You both need that time together. Can't you see how much she wants her mother?"

She turned back to the sink, shaking her head.

"You don't understand. During the day I'm busy. You have no idea how much work is involved in my day."

I felt like saying that my day was full as well, but I always found time for Molly. I felt like saying that if she didn't sleep her afternoons away, she'd have more time. I felt like saying that I loved her and wanted my Dora back—the fun side of her that was there before Molly. I said none of that. Something had died between us and I didn't know how to get it back.

DORA

Observing Nell

It was difficult for me to read Nell at first. She seemed very young and very old at the same time—a contrast within herself. She was young in the playfulness she shared with Molly, as if she'd somehow missed out on something in her own childhood. Watching them together was like seeing two playmates of the same age. The mature side of her came out when she was working, focused on the task in a no-nonsense way. I wondered why she failed to ever look at me when she spoke. It was as if she didn't want anyone to really see her. She had what it took to be very attractive, but it was as if she were trying to hide it. Her hair was an unremarkable shade of light brown, but thick and long. If she'd just rinsed some henna and lemon juice through it, it would have sparkled with highlights. She always wore it covering half her face. When I caught glimpses of her face from behind this veil, it was a face with fine features. Her eyes were a striking turquoise with long lashes. Her nose had a slight upturn and her lips looked like she was pouting all the time. On those rare occasions when I caught a smile, she had the most perfect white teeth. She was tall and lanky and a little awkward. She concealed her thin frame with baggy shirts and pants, as if she didn't want the world to know she was female. I found it odd, given that most girls her age in town were flaunting themselves with tight-fitting tops and streamlined skirts, wobbling around on their first high-heel shoes. I remembered the excitement I felt when I discovered that my body was a fine tool for attracting boys. But none of that was apparent with Nell. She seemed to want to remain as obscure as possible. "What can I help with today, Mrs. Mulgrave?"

Nell startled me, standing in the doorway looking at me, her clothes smeared with grime from the farm chores. She looked hot and out of breath but still full of energy. The times when I'd notice her slow down, she would quickly pick herself up again as if she were avoiding any idle moments. A gloominess would come over her when things slowed down. I still wasn't quite used to having her around in my home. It wasn't like I was incapable of doing the household chores. I just needed to do them on my own time schedule, which was slower than Billy expected. I resented her exuberance and wished I could have a fraction of it.

"Nell, why don't you take a break for a while? There's nothing pressing."

She looked disappointed and rejected.

I sighed. "All right, you can help me fold the laundry, if you like."

Her energy re-emerged.

"But first go and wash up and put an apron over your clothes. I don't want any dirt touching the newly washed linens."

She scurried off to the kitchen to wash her face and hands. I decided I would take this time with her to get to know her a little better. She returned and started eagerly separating the laundry.

"So Nell, other than working, are you enjoying your summer vacation?"

She shrugged and thought about it for a minute.

"I'm glad I have a job. Other than working, there's not much going on."

I thought this strange for a fifteen-year-old girl.

"What are your friends doing for the summer?"

She shrugged again. It dawned on me that she may not have any friends. *How can that be?*

"I guess with working all day, you don't get to see them much?"

"That's okay," she said, while neatly folding pillow cases into rectangles. "I enjoy working. I like being busy, and Billy, I mean Mr. Mulgrave, has been great to work for."

It occurred to me that he was probably the only person that she spent time with other than her family, which got me curious about them.

"How are things at home?" I asked. "Do you do things on the weekend with your family?"

It was as if a brick wall came between us. She let her hair fall over the side of her face, as she often did, and looked away. The sudden silence was unexpected.

"We don't do much," she finally muttered.

Billy had talked about her father having a drinking problem, but there was a mother and a brother as well. Surely she spent time with them. I was about to pursue it further with her, hoping to break through this wall that seemed to surround her, when the screen door opened and Nell ran towards it like a wild animal escaping a hunter.

"Do you need me for anything?" she asked Billy, almost pleadingly.

"No, it's fine," Billy replied. "You go ahead and finish what you were doing. Just came in for a cold drink."

"Let me get it for you," she said, and ran to the fridge.

I folded the last of the laundry on my own, wondering what I had said.

Drifting Apart

"You know better than to ask Nell personal questions," Billy said that night as we sat together after dinner on the veranda. "Her personal life is none of our business."

I disagreed with him. We had this girl virtually living with us and we knew nothing about her.

"It wasn't like I was prying. I was just asking her very general questions about her family. What's wrong with that?"

"What's wrong with it is that she obviously doesn't want to talk, so why push her?"

It made me angry that Billy was so passive about this. How could he spend his days working with a girl who was so odd? There were so many pieces of the puzzle missing, and yet he chose to just ignore it and carry on working with her without knowing anything about her.

"I'd like to know something about her. She has a family. They are our neighbors. We should know who they are. It's odd that she doesn't have any friends and no interest in making any."

Billy looked impatient, as he often was with me lately.

"What difference does it make? She's a good worker. I hired her to work on the farm. That's all that matters."

It frustrated me that he didn't see the bigger picture.

"It matters to me who is spending time with my daughter. Did you ever wonder what kind of influence she may be having on her? Or don't you care?"

Lines of anger emerged on his face. He pushed his chair aside and stood up.

"Of course I care about Molly. That was part of the reason I hired Nell, because Molly adores her."

He walked to the railing with his arms folded across his chest. I knew I was pushing it with Billy, but I wasn't letting go.

"Molly adores anything or anybody who gives her attention. She'd follow a stray dog wherever it took her if we weren't careful."

Billy stared out into the dark night.

"Well if she doesn't want to talk, how can I force it? What, for God's sake, do you want me to do about it?"

I resented him in that moment. If something was a challenge, he'd just give up and pretend it didn't exist. No matter how bad my moods got, he acted like there was nothing wrong. Life just went on for Billy. He wouldn't try to talk about it or try to understand. He'd ignore what was staring him in the face and walk away, burying himself in his farm work.

"Oh come on, Billy! You spend all day with her. You have the perfect opportunity to talk to her. You need to ask her some questions."

It was obvious that we weren't getting anywhere. Suddenly I felt very tired. Billy and I were like orbits spinning around one another but never connecting. I stood up to walk away, but wearily hesitated.

"You are just so naive, and someday you'll pay the price. Life is not always how it seems Billy, and someday you'll learn that the hard way."

I went inside and headed for the bedroom, the one place where I could crawl under the covers and pretend that nothing mattered.

BILLY

A Scream from the Barn

Nell had been working for me for a month when she showed up two hours late. This was not like her, so it had me worried. I thought about calling her house but decided against it, in case her father answered. She had made a comment that her father didn't like her spending so much time away from home. I didn't want to cause her any problems with him. When Nell did finally appear, her hair was uncombed and she looked like she'd been up all night.

"I'm sorry Mr. Mulgrave. I mean Billy," she said rushing into the barn. "I promise it won't happen again. I know I've missed milking the cows, but tell me what I can do."

She looked at the ground while she spoke.

"Is everything okay?" I asked.

"Yeah, everything's fine. I just slept in."

Her eyes were red and puffy. Obviously she wasn't okay, but I let it go. She worked harder than usual that day, maybe trying to make up for her lost time. However, I noticed that her mood was low. She was solemn, withdrawn, and avoided any conversation. She wasn't playful with Molly like she usually was. At the end of the day, she neglected to say goodbye. Instead she just ran off after finishing her last chore. I figured maybe she had boyfriend problems or something—the usual teenage stuff. The next day she was on time, and although she wasn't her usual self, she didn't look as upset. I couldn't help but notice a bruise on her left cheek. She tried to hide it by pulling her hair forward over her face.

"Is everything okay?" I found myself asking, even though I'd promised myself to keep out of her affairs.

I passed a stack of hay over to her from the back of my pickup. She paused for a second and looked away.

"Yeah, fine."

"It's none of my business, but that's quite the bruise you got yourself there."

"I'm fine, really," she said, not very convincingly, and turned her back to untie the barrel. "I fell, that's all. I'm kind of clumsy sometimes as you probably noticed."

I thought about that and couldn't disagree more. She was the most nimble and coordinated kid I'd ever seen.

"Well I just wanted to let you know that, if you ever have any problems, feel free to talk about it with me."

I couldn't help but feel protective of her. She was a good kid and didn't deserve someone hurting her if that was what was going on.

"Thanks," she muttered and carried on with her chores. About a week later, something else came to my attention. Nell seemed to favor her left hand while carrying buckets from the well and pitching hay. I thought this odd, as I was sure she was right-handed. Her right arm rested limply at her side. She grimaced whenever she moved it. I tried my best to ignore it, thinking that even though this was slowing her down, as long as she got her chores done, it was none of my business. It wasn't until late in the afternoon that I heard a bloodcurdling scream from the barn. I rushed in from the yard to find Nell on the floor.

"Nell, what's wrong?"

She was down on her knees, rocking back and forth, grasping her arm.

"My shoulder. It really hurts," she cried, and suddenly began gagging. The contents of her stomach spewed out onto the hay.

I rushed to her side and felt her shoulder. Sure enough, it was dislocated.

I remembered the time I had relocated a calf's shoulder after a difficult breaching. There was no reason I couldn't do the same for Nell. "Okay, I can fix this," I said. I had her lie down on her side and lay down diagonal to her. "Now this is really going to hurt Nell, so hold on," I said. "It'll be fast." I placed one foot against her back and the other under her armpit, and then I grabbed her arm.

"Ready?" I warned, and then pulled her arm in a quick jerk.

She screamed so loud that it got Rex barking and brought Dora and Molly running out to the barn. Nell lay on her side, massaging her shoulder while I lay beside her stroking her hair, trying to comfort her.

"It should be okay now," I reassured her. "You should be able to move it again without pain."

"What's going on?" Dora shouted.

Molly stood at the door, sucking her thumb.

"It's okay now. Nell dislocated her shoulder and I helped realign it. She'll be okay now."

Dora rushed to Nell's side and looked down at the quivering girl.

"Is that what happened?"

Nell was curled up in a fetal position moaning quietly now, more in shock than pain. Dora stood looking at me in an accusatory way, as if I'd been the one who had hurt her. I couldn't believe she would even think that. I looked away in disgust. I could hear Molly whimpering at the door.

"Why don't you go and look after Molly. I'll take Nell home," I said, refusing to look at her.

Dora stormed to the door, grabbing Molly's arm. She half dragged her back to the house.

What is wrong with her? I thought.

"I'll take you home, Nell. You need to rest that shoulder."

"I don't want to go home," she protested.

"I'll pay you for the rest of the day, but you're of no use to me here. You've got to get some rest. Now try to get up."

"I feel weak," she muttered as she struggled to her feet.

"Put your good arm around my neck and I'll carry you to the truck. I'm going to drive you home."

She looked too tired to protest and reached out for my neck as I hoisted her up and walked to the truck. I gently placed her on the passenger seat. I noticed that she was trembling, so I placed an old burlap blanket I had in the back seat around her shoulders. As I got into the driver's seat, I couldn't help but notice Dora at the window watching my every move. I felt like I didn't know the woman I was married to anymore. I drove off.

DORA

Peeking out from a Dark Hole

I wasn't sure if it was just my imagination, but I noticed something in Nell's eyes when she spoke to Billy. Perhaps it was a growing fondness. That would have been expected, given that he was like the father she didn't have. But perhaps it was something more. There was a certain flirtatiousness in her voice. The same tone wasn't there with me. I also noticed that Billy was responding to it. He seemed flattered by it. The Billy that I knew when we were dating came out when he was with her. But I wasn't sure. I was never sure of my perceptions anymore. I was peeking out from the dark hole I was buried in and everything appeared uncertain to me. My self-doubt was clouding any sense of what was or wasn't real. All I knew was that there was an uneasiness growing inside me when I saw them together, and I was watching more closely for signs of something ... but I wasn't exactly sure what.

It was well into the second month that Nell had been working for us when I was startled out of my afternoon nap by a gut-wrenching scream. At first I thought it was another bad dream. Was it the sound of my own voice? Then I very clearly heard it again. I threw the sheets aside and got out of bed as quickly as I could. I was worried that something might have happened to Molly and ran down the staircase. I was feeling a little unsteady from my pills, so held tight to the railing. Molly was standing at the bottom of the stairs looking up at me wild eyed.

"Are you okay?" I cried, as I grabbed her to check her over.

She nodded but remained rigid.

“I heard Nelly crying,” she said. “She must be hurting.”

I went to the door to look outside. Molly pointed towards the barn. I ran out through the yard and Molly followed close behind.

“Nell!” I cried. “Billy?”

There was no answer. I heard sobs as I approached the barn. The doors were slightly ajar. I looked around to find Billy, but couldn’t see him anywhere. Rex was whining at the entrance to the barn. I wondered if Nell had fallen off the loft and hurt herself. I quickly swung open the doors and took in what I saw. It took a moment for my eyes to adjust from the bright sunlight to the dim shadows of the dark barn. Nell was lying on her side sobbing and rocking herself. What I had trouble grasping was that Billy was beside her. He was lying on the ground and stroking her hair. His face was close behind hers, and he was whispering to her. I froze. It seemed like forever before Billy noticed me standing there. He seemed to be annoyed by my presence.

“What is going on?” I managed to get the words out.

His response was a jumble of words. Something about a shoulder he was helping her with. None of it was clear. Nell continued to whimper. Her shirt was partially unbuttoned and the top of her breast was exposed. I cried out, asking her what had happened, but she didn’t respond, just curled up further into a fetal position. Billy commanded me to go look after Molly, so he could take Nell away. He wanted me gone.

Everything swirled around me. I felt faint. I didn’t want to believe what I was seeing. I was wondering how I could have been so naive. There was nothing more to say at that moment. I didn’t know the monster who was my husband anymore. I turned and grabbed Molly, who was standing near the barn door whimpering, and pulled her towards the house. This was not a sight for our young daughter to see. By the time I got to the house, Molly was wailing and clinging to my skirt. I took her into the rocking chair by the window with me and soothed her in my arms. I was in shock, still not fully comprehending what I had seen. Moments later, Billy walked by the window towards his truck, carrying Nell in his arms. He placed her in the passenger seat, then gently wrapping something around her. He may have given her a kiss, but I wasn’t sure. As he walked over to the driver’s side, he saw me in the window. In that moment, we locked eyes like two strangers, not recognizing each other. We both looked quickly away.

BILLY

Tractor Mechanics

Nell stopped me when I tried to drop her off at her door. She preferred I let her off at the entrance to the driveway, which was hidden from view of the house. She disappeared behind the ragged hedge, which had not been trimmed for some time. She turned and raised her arm, waving me away more than saying goodbye. I stared at their run-down work shed and the overgrown fields beyond. What a waste of good land. From what I understood, her father was home all day. Why would he not make an effort to work this place? There was a fleeting moment when I almost stepped out of the truck. I wanted to go and introduce myself to Mr. Dickson. After all, we were neighbors. I wanted to see for myself who this man really was. In the end, I let go of the door latch and stayed in the truck. I didn't want to upset Nell. She was very private about her family, and I had to respect that. Instead I started the truck and drove into town. I couldn't help but think that someone in town must know something about Nell's family. The best person to ask was Ken Norton, who ran the bookstore. He'd been there for twenty years, and knew everyone by first name. His wife had passed away a dozen years ago and his bookstore was his life. I wasn't much of a reader myself, but thought I'd go in and browse through the section on tractor mechanics. Maybe if I chatted to old man Norton, I'd get some questions answered. It would be a start.

"Billy! Haven't seen you much in town." He looked up at me over his reading glasses.

"Been pretty busy Ken, with the farm and all. 'Specially this time of year. Not much time for anything else."

"How's the missus?" he asked.

I wondered at the question. Was there gossip in town about Dora? She had lost touch with most of her women friends lately. She spent most of her time alone.

"She's well, thank you for asking," I replied in a matter-of-fact tone.

"What can I help you with today?"

"Just thought I'd do some browsing through your mechanics section. Tractor's been acting up on me lately. Not sure what the problem is."

He pointed to the second aisle without getting up.

"Over there you'll find lots of material. Feel free to look around."

I picked up a book that looked relevant and started flipping through the pages.

"So I've hired young Nell Dickson to help out on the farm this summer. Hard working girl, that one."

"Ah, Stan Dickson's girl. She's probably the only normal one in that family."

I turned the page, pretending to be reading the book. I paused.

"What's that?" I asked, as if I hadn't heard.

"Dickson family. Old man drinks like a fish. Gambles too. The missus is a hard-working woman but Dickson and his son?" He shook his head.

"I thought the boy was working at the gas station?"

"Nope. Got fired after a week. Came to work drunker than a skunk, just like his old man. Seed doesn't fall far from the tree."

I wondered why Nell hadn't mentioned anything about her brother. Then again, she never talked much about her family at all.

"Seems strange that they still have that farm. Gone to seed and all. Why don't they sell the place if they don't want to work it and need the money?" I asked passively, putting the book back and scrolling the shelves for another.

"The farm belonged to the grandpappy. Couldn't wait for him to die fast enough. He was a hard worker, that senior Dickson. Shame that his son turned out like he did. What a waste of a good farm. Stan's too lazy to do much of anything 'cept use all his pappy's money on drink. Damn shame."

"I never knew about the elderly Dickson," I said. "Probably was gone before we bought our place."

"Well as soon as the old Dickson's wife died, the son and his family moved in on him. Old man went downhill quickly after that. Stan's not exactly the kindest folk in town."

I put the book back on the shelf, feeling guilty for not buying something. My curiosity was somewhat relieved though, and it was time for me to go.

"Time to go and try that old tractor again. Picked up some tips from them books. Thanks Ken."

Ken remained on his stool behind the counter and pushed his glasses up the bridge of his nose.

"No problem. Always enjoy the company." He nodded to me. "Good to see you again. Say hi to the missus."

The bell clanged as I opened the door. I paused and slowly looked over my shoulder.

"Do you know if Dickson has a temper when he's drunk?"

Ken gave me a puzzled look, and I quickly explained.

"Just wondering. Nell sometimes seems a bit frightened of him. Not wanting to go home after work."

"Don't know, but I guess it would go with the drinking now wouldn't it? I know the wife works a lot of hours here in town. Keeps to herself. Poor kid. Doesn't get to pick the family she's from. You're fond of her, are you?"

I turned back towards the door, feeling slightly embarrassed by his last comment.

"She's a good kid. Deserves better. That's all. Thanks again."

I turned and left.

DORA

I'm Being Poisoned

My world grew even darker. The hole I had slipped into grew deeper and deeper. I was no longer a part of my surroundings. I didn't want to be a part of them. I had nothing to live for. My husband was lost to me—a stranger in my own home. My daughter didn't need me. She had Nell replacing me. I was of no use to anyone, including myself. Billy insisted that I go see the doctor again. He pretended to care. The doctor increased some of my medications, changed some of the others. My days started with an irritation of daylight shining through my window. I'd push myself to rise from the safety of my bed and face the day on Billy's insistence. I'd eat without any appetite. I'd sleep again without feeling tired. I'd walk around as if I were floating. My body felt detached from the rest of me, like a foreign appendage—something I had to take care of but not really a part of me. Billy would remind me that it was time for me to bathe. Otherwise I'd forget. He'd place food in front of me that I'd stare at, wondering what I should do with it. He'd feed me if he had to. Molly would cling to me, still trying to wake something up in me that was no longer there. I'd hold her when she'd demand it, but my arms had no feeling in them. Neither did my heart. I was as good as dead. Nell continued to work with Billy after that awful day, as if nothing had happened. It seemed like everyone around me was pretending to care, but I knew they didn't. I pushed away the tray that Nell brought to my room and screamed, "Get out!" She pretended to look hurt.

"I'm just trying to help," she said. "I thought you might be hungry after not eating all day."

Molly peered at me from behind her ... as if I were a stranger to her. I worried that the food was poisoned. I'm sure they wanted to be rid of me.

"Take it away. I don't want anything."

She cautiously removed it as if she were fearful of me. Molly came and tucked the blanket around my neck and gave me a kiss on the cheek. *This is backwards,* I thought. I couldn't remember the last time I'd tucked her in. About a week after 'the incident', Nell failed to show up for work. Billy was frantic.

"It's not like her," he said. "She's always been so dependable."

He was probably worried that his affair was over. I had a glimmer of hope that, without Nell around, our lives could go back to what it had once been. I got up to put the kettle on as Billy paced around the kitchen.

"I'm going to try harder," I offered. This was going to be my last plea. "I'm going to try to look after things. I know I've been a terrible wife and mother. But I want to try."

I knew these promises must have sounded empty. I didn't feel I could make a proper cup of tea anymore. I poured us each a cup that looked far too weak. He didn't seem to be paying much attention.

"I'm worried about her, Dora." He hadn't heard a word I'd said. "This isn't like her. Something is wrong"

He put several lumps of sugar into his tea and took a sip. I tried to make eye contact with him, to get some acknowledgment for what I had just promised. He looked a million miles away. He looked through me as if I were invisible. He jumped out of his seat suddenly, went to the door, and grabbed his hat.

"I'm going for a drive." I stared at the two full cups of tea in front of me. I felt the loneliness pump through my bloodstream like a vial of poison. I no longer mattered.

BILLY

Trying to Protect Nell

I drove past the Dickson farm, debating whether I should go and knock at the door. Things were eerily quiet. Perhaps she'd had a rough night and was sleeping in, but that wasn't like her. I decided to return to the farm. There was work to be done, with or without her. Even at our farm, a ghostly eeriness hung in the air. Dora was shutting me out, and I was trying hard not to feel angry with her. She'd look at me as if I were the enemy. Meanwhile, all I'd ever wanted was for her to get better and come back to me. For her to think there was anything going on between Nell and me was ludicrous, and only proof that she was getting sicker. Caring for her was getting beyond me.

Ken's words lingered with me somehow, and bothered me: "You're fond of her, are you?" I'd never thought of myself as fond of Nell. Perhaps caring for her in a fatherly kind of way. Wouldn't anybody if they saw a young girl so distressed? What frustrated me was that I felt helpless to do anything about it. Unless she confided in me, I really didn't know what her life at home was like. Even if I knew, I wasn't sure what I could do about it. I wasn't one to meddle in other folks' business, but I felt a responsibility towards Nell. She seemed to trust me, and if someone didn't help her, what would happen to her? She deserved better. Nell did get to the farm later that day. She started to apologize, but I stopped her. I could tell how upset she was. I was just glad to see her there.

The summer was getting on now. The sun wasn't as hot any more, and the leaves were beginning to change. The days weren't as long. The ducklings were mature now, almost ready for market. I was just beginning to see the rewards for my hard work. I was feeling uncomfortable about Nell leaving at the end of the summer when school began. I decided to broach the topic with her that afternoon. Molly had just brought us some cool lemonade.

"Let's take a break," I said.

We sat down under the old apple tree and sipped our drinks.

"Do you have any relatives Nell? You know uncles ... aunts?"

She looked up, appearing surprised by my question.

"Not that I know of. If there are, my parents aren't speaking with them anymore. Grandma died about two years ago and Grandpa died soon after. He was the only one I used to talk to. Why do you ask?"

I wasn't sure what to say. I knew that, even though she used our farm as an escape from home, she tried hard to disguise it. She wasn't open about herself. Maybe it was pride or fear or both.

"Just wondering if you have anywhere else you can go and live when school starts?"

She paused and took a long sip of her lemonade.

"If I did, I would. But I don't."

This was the most open she'd been with me yet. I wasn't sure whether to go any further with it. I tried being as tactful as I could.

"Nell, you just seem so unhappy at home. Is there anything I can do to help?"

"You're helping me already," she responded. "I have a place to work. I have my own money now."

"But that's going to come to an end in the fall. I'm just trying to think ahead."

She shrugged.

"What about your brother?" I asked. "Is he someone you can talk to?"

She looked up like a mouse trapped in the corner of the barn. If I wasn't mistaken, she started to tremble.

"No, no. I can't go to my brother. I don't want to talk about him." She suddenly stood up.

Her reaction left me wondering. Ken had mentioned that her brother drank just like her father did.

"What would you like me to do now Billy?" she asked, ready to end our conversation and get back to work. There was nothing more to say for now. Another word and she would have bolted. I felt like offering her a place at our house if she needed it. I knew that Dora would be furious if I did. Besides, I didn't know how her father would react to something like that. We walked in silence towards the barn.

"You can start cleaning out the stalls if you like," I told her.

A lump was forming in my throat as I watched her get the shovel and start scooping the manure from the stall. I wasn't one to express my feelings, but I felt choked up.

"Nell," I said, clearing my throat.

She paused and looked my way.

"I care, you know?"

Someone has to care, I thought.

"I know," she responded, and went back to work.

NELL

A Safe Haven

As the weeks of the summer went on, my only escape from my nightmare life at home was my work on the farm. Molly ran out to greet me with open arms in the morning. She'd give me drawings she'd worked on as gifts. She'd chatter away excitedly. She was like the little sister I never had. Even Rex greeted me with a wagging tail every time I arrived. He smiled up at me as I stroked his head. Billy always had a kind word to offer.

"You're doing good Nell," he'd say.

Something I never heard at home. The only one who remained hard to reach was Dora. She watched me suspiciously, like an unwelcome intruder in her life. I really wanted her to like me, but the harder I tried to please her with housework and by babysitting Molly, the more resentful she became. She acted like she didn't want my help, and yet it was so obvious that she needed it. She rarely got out of bed to do anything anymore. When I tried to be helpful, she would snap at me. I learned to keep my distance. Home was becoming more and more unbearable. Andy was prone to fits of rage for no reason. The drinking made it worse. He would suddenly lash out or throw things, then pass out and not remember any of it later. Pa ignored him and Ma was rarely there. It was me who took the brunt of his anger. He started sounding more like Pa when I was home in the evenings.

"Get me a beer," he yelled, as I walked in the door from work.

I ignored him. He came into the kitchen and took a swing at me. He was too tipsy to aim properly and missed.

"What did you bring me to eat?"

"Why don't you get your own food?"

"Bitch!" he screamed. "Gimmie the money you made and I'll go and get something."

He staggered toward me stinking of booze.

"You're in no shape to drive. I'll make us sandwiches," I offered, fearing that he'd run the truck off the road. Besides, I was trying to save my money for school clothes. He held me down hard and searched me for money. He groped my breasts while I was on the floor. Then he dragged me to my room and pushed me on the floor.

"Get the money," he commanded.

He towered over me. I scrambled through my drawers to find him what he wanted. I watched from the window as he staggered to the truck and screeched off down the road, swerving from side to side. There was a part of me that hoped he would drive into a ditch, never to return. But before long, sure enough, I could hear the tires grind to a stop in front of the house once more. I ran to the door to see what he bought, feeling hungry for dinner myself. He staggered in with another case of beer.

"Where's the food?" I asked, fearing the worst.

"You're looking at it." He plopped the case onto the table and handed me a beer.

I left the kitchen in tears and hid in my room. I hated him. I wished that I could just run away—live in the stalls next door if I had to. Anywhere but in this house. I started barricading my door at night to make sure I'd get some sleep. The work was tiring and I needed to be rested. I couldn't let Billy down by coming in late. I wasn't eating much, and without food in the house, I'd show up in the mornings tired and hungry. I'd sneak a cup full of the fresh cow's milk from the bucket when Billy wasn't watching or eat one of the raw chicken eggs I collected. I had to stop my stomach from growling. I tried hard to remain cheerful and to work hard so that Billy wouldn't notice anything. I could see him watching me at times. I didn't want to be seen. I'd let my hair fall forward over my face, trying to hide behind it like an ostrich with its head in the sand. It didn't work. "Is anything wrong?" he'd ask. "You know you can talk to me, if there is."

His words sounded so reassuring. I wanted to soak them up and believe that someone really cared about me. I didn't dare let on though about my home life. My parents had always protected Andy. We all knew that he wasn't all there in the head. Even though I feared him, he was my brother and I wasn't going to turn on him. My parents would never forgive me if the word got out and someone took him away. I had to keep my head low and my mouth shut.

"Everything's fine," I'd say and turn away.

I knew that he was noticing the blue marks on my arms where Andy had grabbed me, and the swelling on my face where he'd swung at me. I was grateful that Billy never asked anything more so that I didn't have to lie.

DORA

A Surprise Return Home

When I was Molly's age, I worshiped my father. I still remember the scent of his skin, with his aftershave full of exotic spices. It was the smell of strength and safety for me. The power of his arms swung me up in the air and made me fly free. I always trusted that he would catch me and I'd let myself go limp in his embrace. I'd giggle until I hiccupped when he put his whiskered mouth on my belly and blew noisily, making my whole body vibrate. I liked stroking the rough stubble on his chin and feeling the smoothness after he'd just shaved. He'd carry me on his back if I was tired and I'd wrap both my arms around his neck and bury my cheek against his back, feeling like we were one. I could never get enough of him. The times when he wasn't there my world felt hollow. Mother explained that he was away working in the forest. I understood that his job was cutting down trees. I savored the smell of pine needles on his clothes when he returned. He was bringing his adventures from the fresh forest air home with him. He'd tell me tales of what he saw and what he did. I knew that some of them were make believe, but I loved to listen anyway. Sometimes there were other smells that he brought home that I didn't like—unfamiliar ones that somehow aroused a sense of danger. I smelled it after he had been out for a night of drinking. It was not only the smell of the alcohol and cigarettes but of other people. These smells made my mother angry with him. I hated to hear them fighting.

One time when my father was away, my mother and I went to visit my aunt in another town. Our trip was cut short when my aunt was called away to some family matter she needed to attend to. We had to return home sooner than planned. To my delight, my father's truck was parked in the driveway. My disappointment about cutting our visit short at my favorite aunt's house was replaced by my excitement at seeing my father sooner than expected. I ran ahead of my mother to the house and bounded up the stairs, two at a time. The door to the bedroom was closed, so I assumed he must be napping. I slowed down and thought I would tiptoe in quietly and snuggle up to him. I cracked open the door and froze. My father was naked on the bed with Anna, the girl who looked after me when my mother was busy and my father was away. Anna was naked too and was lying on top of him. He was stroking her face and hair the way he did with me. I swung the door open and screamed, "Get away from my daddy!"

Anna jumped up, grabbed at the clothes strewn around the bedroom floor, and ran into the bathroom. My father sat up abruptly, covering his privates with the sheet.

"What are you doing home?" he asked, with the voice of a stranger.

I stood there in tears.

"Ah honey, come here," he said, beckoning me with his hand, unable to stand because he was naked. I'd never seen my father naked before, not even with my mother. I was unable to move. I saw a blur of Anna with her clothes on running down the staircase. She didn't even look at me or say anything. I heard a shrieking squabble at the bottom of the stairs, between her and my mother, before the door slammed. I remained frozen in my tears. I didn't feel safe with my father for the first time. I could smell him from the doorway and he had those unfamiliar smells to him that I didn't like. My mother came up behind me and picked me up. I turned and buried my face in her shoulder, pretending that none of this was happening.

"Get out!" she yelled. "Get out!"

My father babbled and protested, but finally threw on his clothes and swept past us. As he ran down the stairs, I reached my arms out to him across my mother's shoulder.

"Daddy, Daddy! Please don't go! I'm sorry! Please don't leave me Daddy!"

I didn't know why he was so angry with me that he wouldn't even turn around. I didn't see my father again for a long time. When I did see him, it was not together with my mother. He didn't have the same familiar smells to him anymore and I didn't feel the safety with him that I had once felt. I never saw Anna again either. It was not long after that my father introduced me to Amelia, and then to Kendra, and soon I lost count of the new girlfriends that replaced what I once felt I had with my father.

NELL

Floating

I thrashed around in my sheets. I was suffocating. A heavy weight lay on me. My breathing was blocked. I let out a silent scream that raged through every vein in my body. I was hurting so bad. My muscles contorted, trying to fight off the burning sensation that penetrated me. I felt like my body was being ripped apart. There was no use fighting. I was trapped between my bed and the weight and no one could hear my screams. I could smell the heavy scent of alcohol—that familiar smell that I despised. I could hear the guttural groan that accompanied each thrusting motion. I glared at the dark ceiling and felt myself float up there, as if I were leaving my body and watching it from above. I wondered if I was dead. I hoped I was. I couldn't feel anything anymore. I watched as the dark figure got off me. It threatened me, saying that I better not scream when it let go. It left me there gasping for air. I couldn't move. I was frozen in fear. I wet my bed and remained in the stench and dampness, too afraid to move until the morning light slowly penetrated the darkness, entering through the window and defining the room. My body ached with every movement. In the bathroom, I gasped as I saw dried blood stuck to my thigh. I washed my tear-stained face under the shower, and stayed there until the water ran cold.

I was late for work again.

"I was worried about you," Billy said.

If only he knew how difficult it had been to get there. I had to though, in order to return to some sense of feeling normal. The routine of my workday was what I needed to keep myself sane.

I held back my tears. "I'm sorry—"

"Not to worry," he interrupted. "Are you sure you're not ill? Perhaps you need to stay in bed today."

"Please no ... please don't send me home," I gasped in a state of panic. Then I realized just how alarming I must have sounded. "I'm fine. Really I am. It was just a hard night. I had some bad dreams. I'm fine now. Just tell me what still needs to be done. I'm sorry I'm late."

Billy wasn't convinced. He tried to make eye contact with me, but the harder he tried the more I avoided him. I just wanted to be invisible. I had waited until my mother had left that morning. I made sure that Pa and Andy were still asleep as I slipped out of the house. I couldn't face anyone. I couldn't look at Billy now. I felt like I had somehow not quite re-entered my body yet. I was merely going through the motions—and only barely at that.

I could tell that Billy sensed he couldn't push me any further.

"Just remember, you can talk to me anytime. I'm your friend. Anytime now." He looked at me with that concerned expression that was becoming so familiar. Appearing uncertain as to what to say or do next, he pointed to the pitchfork in the corner.

"You can start stacking the hay in here. Just don't overdo it. Take it a little easy today, Nell."

With that, he left me to myself.

When I was sure that he was well out of range, I collapsed on the barn floor. I put my head in my hands and sobbed. I cried so hard that I threw up in the hay and then cried some more. Why did I feel safer here with strangers than with my own family? It was a mixed-up world and I didn't know how to deal with it. Why couldn't my life just be simple? How was I going to spend another night at home? I wanted to trust someone like Billy to help me, but I knew that I couldn't trust anyone. If I told him, things would only get worse. I would be an orphan. Homeless. My mother would hate me. Andy, as much as I hated him in this moment, would be sent away somewhere scary. It was safer to say nothing.

I grabbed the pitchfork and thrust it into the hay, over and over again as hard as I could, until my arms ached.

DORA

The Dream We Once Shared

I had just broken up with my third or fourth boyfriend after high school. Nothing seemed to be working out for me. Nothing until I met Billy.

"You've got to meet him; he's different," my best friend Shelly claimed.

"They're all the same," I said. "Just a bunch of big babies when things don't go their way. I'm convinced of that. I think that I'll just have to stay in college and become a spinster teacher or maybe a nurse. I've given up on silly dreams of happily ever after."

"I'm not asking you to marry him," Shelly persisted. "I just think you should meet him. No harm in that is there?"

We had been spending a lazy Saturday afternoon together, Shelley and I, trying to study, but all we'd managed to do was fix each other's hair.

"Okay, what makes this guy any different?" I asked passively.

"I don't know," Shelly said, looking up from the toenails she'd just painted.

"He's a friend of Tommy's that I met for the first time last week. If I wasn't with Tommy, I would have been interested in him myself."

"Well, tell me. What's so special?"

She reflected for a moment.

"Hmm, I guess he's just a little different. Seems to be more serious, in a sexy kind of way. Maybe a little shy or something. Just more interesting than the everyday boring ones."

"It all sounds a little vague. Most importantly, what does he look like?"

We both giggled.

"*Very* handsome. Curly hair, on the tall side, strong muscles. I could see them bulging under his t-shirt."

When she mentioned curly hair, my heart twanged. I always had a soft spot for men with unkempt hair. My father had curly hair that I used to love running my fingers through as a child.

"Anyway, you should meet him. Tommy and I are going to the movies next Saturday. Why don't we ask him to come along? Kind of a double date."

"Let me think about it," I said, still feeling a bit bruised from my last break up. I knew she had my curiosity piqued though, and I couldn't take a pass on finding Mr. Right.

I hadn't believed in love at first sight. When I met Billy, the feeling that surged through me was instant, and I knew that this would be the man I married. He would take control of situations but wasn't pushy. He was chivalrous but not condescending. He was old fashioned but also open to new ways. He was interested in me as a person. I was moody, at times melancholy but other times spirited. He seemed to be able to flow with my moods rather than resist them. I prided myself on my independence and he seemed to like that about me. We shared similar values and dreams of home and family. He said that he always wanted to own his own farm, till the earth, and produce life through working the soil. I wasn't a farm girl, but I had romantic notions of living in the countryside, baking my own bread, collecting fresh chicken eggs in the morning, and learning to make fresh cheese. We talked about having children—lots of them—with room to play. I was in love with the way we dreamed together. We talked passionately about the future. It all looked so promising. I could have burst with happiness back then.

NELL

The Downward Slope

Life had not always been this hard at home. I thought we were a normal family, just the same as my friends' families. My father went to work every day. My mother braided my hair for school in the morning, sewed me pretty dresses, baked cookies, and read to me and my brother at bedtime. We'd go to Sunday school and then take a drive to visit my grandparents in the country. We'd bring home fresh vegetables and eggs from the farm. Sunday was always my favorite day of the week. My grandpa treated me special. He called me the apple of his eye. Grandma baked fruit pies with sugar on top and sent them home with us. I had friends at school that I played with. I even had a best friend. I never saw myself as being different in any way.

Then things changed. Pa was always a drinker and I remember Ma yelling at him to stop. Instead of things getting better though, they got worse. He started to drink until he was drunk every night, and Ma had to go to work to help pay for the extra he spent on booze. They were fighting all the time now. Ma wasn't there anymore, not only physically but emotionally too. She stopped smiling and never listened to anything I said. Andy was getting into trouble at school. I'd see him fighting in the schoolyard. His face would be smeared with blood while his so-called friends urged him on. Pa used to whip him when he got home, for whatever reason he managed to find. If he fought he was in trouble, and if he didn't fight he was a sissy. Andy became miserable to be around. He started bullying me, calling me names, and hitting me. Ma tried to stop him, but when he started getting more angry and not going to school, she backed down. I was told to be more understanding, because Andy had special problems. The word 'special' was always said about him and never about me. I resented him for that.

Pa lost his job. He was not getting to work on time. He tried finding other work without any luck. That same winter, Grandma died suddenly from a fall. At first we thought she was going to be okay, but things took a turn for the worse while she was in hospital. They said it was a blood clot that finally killed her.

My poor grandpa was devastated without her. He stopped working the farm and sat staring at the walls most of the time. We'd go and visit less often. He'd light up whenever he saw me. I'd sit on his lap and stroke his cheek.

"Don't be sad, Grandpa," I'd say, and sometimes he'd smile.

Ma and Pa were having trouble paying their bills without my father working. We packed up and moved in with my grandpa. I was told that he needed us to take care of him. But when we got there, no one but I took care of him. They took over the house and moved him to a room in the basement. They didn't even invite him up for dinner. I'd go down with the left-over scraps from the dinner table and sit with him. He'd tell me stories about Grandma and him when they were young. He would stare at the picture of her that was always on his dresser. One night he died in his sleep. I always thought it was from a broken heart.

By then Pa had stopped looking for work and Ma was working all the time. Andy had quit school and found odd jobs. He started drinking with Pa in the evenings and couldn't get up in the morning to get to work on time. He'd lose jobs regularly and got such a bad reputation in town that no one would hire him. He was angry about everything and I became his punching bag. I stopped seeing my friends, because I was embarrassed by my family. They thought my brother was weird and wouldn't come and visit. Their parents didn't want me in their homes, thinking I'd be a bad influence.

I'd never felt so alone, but then I started working for Billy. There I felt like I belonged. I knew I was just the hired hand, but sometimes I was invited to stay for dinner. Molly couldn't get enough of me. I know that she longed for her mother and I guess I was the next best thing. I craved the mother that I once had as well, and somehow being there with this family who needed me helped. Billy was everything that my father wasn't. I knew he was lonely with Dora not being well. He treated me as someone he could help, unlike Dora who shut him out every time he tried. He looked so hurt when she'd leave and shut the door to her room behind her. He had so much to give and no one to give it to. I didn't want him knowing the truth about my family, but just being in his presence gave me comfort. He made me believe that some good still existed in this world. He offered me hope.

DORA

Peering Through Distorted Glass

Nell became less consistent with turning up every morning, but when she did, Billy would light up like a torch. He hovered over her throughout the day. I watched passively, drained and void of emotion—a twisted preoccupation. They'd work side by side, eat lunch side by side, ride into town side by side, and they would talk and talk. Sometimes they would laugh, but at what I couldn't imagine. I wasn't in earshot to hear any of it. I was invisible, in the shadows. I did not exist.

There was also something different about Nell. At first I wasn't sure what it was. She wasn't quite as scrawny as she'd appeared when she first started working for us. I couldn't figure out how she had changed. I wrote it off to maturing. She'd taken on more responsibility than most fifteen year olds, which must have made her grow up a little faster. Perhaps it was more of a self-assurance. Having the attentions of an older man I'm sure had something to do with it. She talked more than she used to. She even came late some mornings, obviously knowing that Billy wouldn't fire her. She avoided me whenever possible. I guess I couldn't blame her after the last few times I'd yelled at her to get away from me. I couldn't hide the disdain I felt at her taking over my place in the household. I hated her for seducing my husband. But for some morbid reason, I couldn't give up the curiosity of watching her from afar. It was as if I needed to torment myself with her existence—the presence that never went away.

Even when she wasn't there, Billy would talk about her incessantly. He was smitten with her. He was oblivious to how I felt, my inner demons.

I could feel his pity at times, as if I were a wounded animal. I think he'd given up any hope that things would get any better. That only magnified my own self-doubts. I was sure that I was just someone in his life who he felt obligated to care for, and his heart was elsewhere. He reveled in the attention of an infatuated teenager. He was weak, seeking what I was no longer able to give him. Lusting for the attentions of someone barely into puberty. He said that he was concerned for her wellbeing, but that didn't explain all that I saw.

I observed and I put the pieces together. I finally recognized the subtle changes in Nell as only one woman can notice in another, if she looks closely enough. Nell was in the family way.

BILLY

The Accusation

It was getting on towards the end of the summer. The corn crop stood high in the sun-drenched fields. I took pride in my hard work. It was close to picking time—the closure to the season.

Nell was late most mornings for work now. She was always apologetic, trying to work extra hard to make up for it. It was only a couple weeks away from the start of school and the end of her work with me. I let it go. I was more concerned with what she must be going through at home than any help I needed for the farm.

The times when Nell was there in the mornings, I couldn't help but notice her running to the back of the shed, looking queasy.

"Stomach's just a bit upset. Probably the leftovers we ate for dinner last night." She wiped her mouth.

She went over to the well and splashed water on her face, then looked over at me, hoping I wasn't watching. She rinsed out her mouth and took a moment to collect herself. Then she came back to help me load the barrels into the truck.

"So you getting ready for school?" I asked.

"I ain't going back to school."

I stopped and stared at her in disbelief.

"Why ever not?"

"Just taking a year off, that's all."

My fatherly instincts kicked in.

"You're far too smart to not continue," I said. "What grade are you in? Ten? Eleven? You need to finish high school if you want to get anywhere in life."

Nell didn't respond. Just handed me another barrel to load, avoiding looking at me.

"Is your father making you stay working?"

"Nope," she said. "Just won't be going for a while."

"You know, by September, I won't have much work here for you at the farm anymore."

Nell strained to pick up another load, but collapsed in tears. I took off my work gloves and knelt down beside her.

"What's wrong, Nell? Talk to me."

She struggled to get herself under control. She pushed her wet hair back, and as I sat close to her, I couldn't help but notice the swelling over her eyebrow. She'd concealed it well with her bangs.

"It's okay. I didn't expect to keep working for you," she muttered.

"Then why on earth would you not want to be back at school with your friends?"

It had occurred to me that Nell didn't seem to care much for friends. I wrote it off to the long hours of work, but what kid wouldn't mention a friend or two over an entire summer that was full of conversations?

"I can't talk about it," she said, trying to compose herself. "I shouldn't have even mentioned it."

Again, I felt shut out, with questions left unanswered. My concern for her was growing. During the following weeks, Nell was ill regularly in the mornings.

"She's pregnant, you fool," Dora said. "I know it when I see it."

I was stunned, as we sat together on the porch after dinner—Dora with her needlepoint and me with my paper. I put the paper down as Dora kept her eyes focused on her work. She seemed so matter-of-fact with what she was saying. Nell's vomiting did remind me of Dora's early months of pregnancy, and I must admit that the thought had occurred to me as well, but I had dismissed it as ridiculous.

"But how is that possible?" I mumbled to myself more than to Dora. "She works long hours for us, *including* weekends. There's never been any mention of a boy."

Dora stayed intent on what she was doing. I could tell she was trying to avoid looking at me. A vein started bulging on her forehead, as it often did before she'd explode with emotion.

"That's right," she said. "She's only spent time with you."

There was an undeniable tone of anger in her voice and I wasn't sure why it was there.

"Dora, I hired her to help her out. Help us *all* out. Why are you so cold towards her?"

Her hand movements became more intense.

"The kid's a mess because of her home life," I continued. "I've just shown her some compassion."

Dora threw her handiwork down and stormed towards the front door.

"Take the first three letters out of that word! *That's* what you've shown her!" She slammed the door behind her.

Molly, who had been playing on the corner of the deck, came and crawled into my lap. She buried herself into me as if she wanted to block out the anger that surrounded her. I hated her having to see any part of this. I rocked her in my arms, wondering what had gotten into Dora.

"Sweetie, can you please take Rex for a walk. Mommy and I need to talk."

Molly reluctantly lowered herself from my lap. She called Rex and wandered away. I'm sure she was more than familiar with what was to come.

I stepped inside the kitchen expecting Dora to be there, but she was not. I went upstairs and called, but there was no answer. I went into the bedroom to find her lying down with her back to the door.

"What were you insinuating out there, Dora?" I asked, trying to control my anger.

Silence.

"For God's sake, talk to me!" I went over and tore the covers off her.

She turned farther away from me, burying her face in her pillow. I grabbed her arm and pulled her back towards me hard. She spun around, her eyes glaring with a look of utter disdain.

"What do you want me to say? Oh good for you for saving the poor waif. I'm not as naive as you think, Billy. You're a man and she's a pretty young girl. I've seen the way you look at her."

I felt outraged.

"How could you *think* such a thing?" I spat out at her. "I have had nothing but the purest intentions with Nell. It would be nice if *you* could have also shown her some kindness. And to accuse me of . . ." I wasn't even able to utter the words. "I can't believe you would even *think* that!"

Dora pulled away from me and rolled over, pulling the sheets over her head. She was blocking me out like she'd done so many times before, like I didn't exist. She was shutting down.

"Two more weeks Dora! Then she'll be gone. Or do you want me to fire her now? Just tell me and I'll do it. I want to put an end to this absurdity!"

"I don't care what you do," she said, her voice muffled by her pillow. "What difference does it make now?"

NELL

The Surrounding Fury

I didn't know what was wrong with me when I first started throwing up every morning. It wasn't like any flu I'd had before. As soon as I woke up, I'd feel sick and have to throw up. As the day went on, I felt fine, only to wake up sick again. I put two and two together when I missed my period. I didn't know what to do. Andy was after me every chance he got. I'd scream and kick and punch but he was strong. I knew Pa must have heard, but he'd just turn up the TV. I thought of telling Ma, not sure what she would do about it. She saw my bruises, but never asked how I got them. She didn't want to hear any complaints about Andy.

"I'm not going back to school," I told Ma as the summer got near the end.

She had fought so hard to keep Andy in school, I thought she'd react the same with me. She always said that school was our only hope to make things better. Ma looked at me with lifeless eyes.

"Why would you do that?" she asked in a vacant tone.

I didn't know how to get around the truth.

"Because I'm pregnant." The truth hit me hard as I said it, bringing tears to my eyes.

She shook her head and looked away. It couldn't have been a surprise to her. She had seen me bent over the toilet in the mornings. I suspected that she already knew. She looked at me with disgust.

"Did I not teach you anything? Did you not realize that this could happen when you let boys take advantage of you?"

I looked at her in amazement. Did she really not know?

"Ma, when is the last time you saw me with a boyfriend? I work all the time. When would I ever have time for a boyfriend?"

"Well you sure ain't no Virgin Mary."

I felt like blurting out the truth, but restrained myself. I would lose her right then and there, if I hadn't already.

"Ma, what am I going to do?" I looked at her pleadingly, wiping the stream of tears that were dripping off my chin.

"Well, you should have thought of that before you let this happen," she said.

Before you *let this happen to me,* I thought, but did not say a word.

I tried my best to hide my condition from Billy. Dora was looking suspiciously at me as she watched me eat soda crackers and drink ginger ale, refusing the meals she prepared. Feeling so awful in the mornings, it was getting harder to get to work on time. I couldn't do as much as before, getting exhausted easily. Billy was noticing the bruises more often and would shake his head in frustration when I refused to answer his questions about them. After a while he stopped asking.

Dora out and out hated me. She had never liked me, but it got much worse after the barn incident. Although I'd learned to put up with pain, when Billy pulled my wounded shoulder, I couldn't control my screams. I saw the shadow of Dora in the doorway looking down at me, speechless. I was used to seeing anger on the faces of my family, but couldn't understand the look of disgust on Dora's. Was it that I had brought my troubles on them? That was not my intent. All I know is that she never spoke to me again after that.

BILLY

The Joy of Ice Cream

Late September was here, with its long shadows and golden hues. The work days were no longer so tiring. The harvesting was done and the livestock sent to market. I enjoyed spending the extra time I had with Molly. She was such a joy in my life, always so curious about everything—in some ways almost years ahead of herself. Molly came into the field and sat down beside me. "I've tucked Mommy in." I hated that she had taken on the care of her mother. It didn't seem right for such a little girl. We sat there looking out over the pasture, watching two monarch butterflies flutter over the wildflowers. Their grace was mesmerizing. I took a blade of grass between my palms and played her a tune. Her face lit up and she clapped her hands.

"Will you teach me how to do that, Daddy?"

I thought that what she needed most was to play, not worry about her mother or be so alone. Now that Nell wasn't coming by to help anymore, she missed her company. I had to admit that I kind of missed having her around as well. Dora had become even more withdrawn lately. Most of the time she stayed in her room with the door closed. When she was up, she barely spoke.

"I'll drive you to see Dr. Anderson honey," I'd offer. She was complaining that she always had a headache. "I think you really need to have that pain in your head looked at. You need some help."

"All I need is to be left alone," she'd say.

I'd given up on trying to get through to her. I had thought not having Nell around would make a difference, but her mood didn't change. It was worrisome to me, but I felt helpless to do anything about it.

I found a long blade of grass and showed Molly how to hold it. She blew and blew until she made it squeak.

"I made the grass sing," she said, all excited.

I took my big straw hat off and put it on her head to protect her eyes from the afternoon harvest sun. She loved wearing anything that belonged to me. Unlike other little girls, who copied their mothers by dressing up, she copied me. She wore her mud boots and over-sized shirts and didn't seem to care if she got dirty. I gazed at her. Her blonde curls hung down to her shoulders. Her pudgy cheeks still had baby fat she hadn't quite lost yet. My heart melted as I watched her.

"How about you and I go into town for an ice-cream cone, cowboy?"

"Oh boy!" She jumped up, clasping her hands. "Can I get my favorite?"

"You can get anything that you like, honey."

We sat on the bench outside of Mike's Parlor, eating our cones and watching the sun dip into the horizon. Rex lay at our feet. Molly loved watching people and this was the place for it.

"I want a pair of boots like those," she said, pointing to the knee-high cowhide boots worn by a man strutting by.

"Honey, those are men's boots. What about a pair like those red shoes Mrs. McKinney has on over there?" I gestured to the lady on the opposite side of the street.

She looked at them curiously and considered it, then shook her head as she slurped up another mouthful of ice cream.

"I like the boots."

Molly's favorite shows on TV were *Rin Tin Tin* and *The Roy Rogers Show*. She wanted to be like Dale Evans when she grew up. She sometimes mimicked the way she walked and talked. She had pleaded with me for a pony, but I didn't need another animal to take care of right now. I knew it would just make her want to be a cowgirl even more, and Dora wouldn't approve. Dora would dress her in crinolines and lace and Molly would put up a fuss, saying that she found everything itchy. Dora would be stern and say that she needed to learn to look like a young lady.

"But why can't ladies be comfortable like men?" she would ask.

"That's just the way it is," Dora responded.

Molly did whatever it took, trying to keep her mother happy. Unfortunately keeping Dora happy was very difficult for us both.

"Look Daddy!" Molly was pointing across the street excitedly. "There's Nell."

My heart skipped a beat. I made out a girl leaving the grocery store who did resemble Nell. She placed the groceries into her bicycle basket. Molly jumped down from the bench and waved her arm in the air.

"Nell!" she called. "Nell! … Hi Nell!"

The girl mounting her bike glanced over briefly and then looked away. She turned her bike in the opposite direction and quickly rode away.

"Why didn't Nell come and say hi, Daddy?" Molly asked, taking the last bite of her cone.

"Maybe it wasn't Nell, honey."

"It sure looked like Nell," she said. "I miss her."

I knew it was Nell, but had an inkling of why she had ignored us. She wasn't the same lanky kid who had appeared on our doorstep last June. She was much more filled out now. I realized that she would not have wanted us to see her that way.

"I miss her too, Molly."

NELL

The Failed Rescue

A chill was in the air. I was at home feeling sorry for myself. Work on the farm was over now, school had begun without me, and I was stuck at home every day with Andy and Pa. I felt like their slave, expected to serve their every whim. Andy's abuse was routine now. I no longer fought back. I felt that maybe I deserved it.

I hadn't seen Billy or his family for several weeks, and I so missed the little bit of normal life I'd had there. I also didn't have school, or friends to talk to. The schoolmaster had called to ask why I wasn't returning. Ma told him that I was needed at home. She was good at lying. I was to stay in the house until the baby was born. Then they would take it away and put it up for adoption. That was as much as they would say about the matter. I felt like the walls were closing in on me and there was no escape.

Andy was in a foul mood. I don't think it was my imagination that he was getting worse.

"Maybe you should go and see a shrink," I suggested. "You need help."

Andy looked at me. His eyes had become frightfully empty of any emotion. I'd read somewhere about people who lacked feelings, and how they cause others pain without any sense of guilt. I was starting to suspect that Andy was this way.

"The only help I need is for you to get me another beer!" He lay sprawled out on the couch. It was one of those rare days when Pa wasn't around. He occasionally went out for target practice.

I would normally do what Andy commanded to avoid a fight. I was foolish enough this time to think that I could reason with him instead.

"Andy you don't need another beer. Look at you. I can't go out because of this," I pointed to my stomach, "and that's thanks to you. But you can go out. You can do whatever you want. You need to do something with your life or you'll end up just like Pa."

I realized that he already was like Pa. "You can at least *try* to get a job or something. It's not too late."

His eyes glazed over. It was the look that I feared the most.

"Don't talk to me about my life, you whore. You think you're just so perfect, don't you? Working all summer, getting perfect marks at school. Well look at you now. Who are you to talk?"

"I'm just trying to help," I said, slowly backing away, like an animal sensing their predator.

"Well, don't!" he screamed, getting up and hovering over me with a raised hand. I ducked and hid my head with my arms, anticipating a blow. He grabbed my hair and pulled my head back hard.

"You know you're only good for one thing, don't you?"

I knew what was coming and tried kicking his legs out from under him as he started undoing his belt buckle. He tumbled sideways and I managed to run for the door and out of the house. I ran as fast as I could up the driveway. He staggered up behind me, and before I could escape, threw his weight on me, pushing me to the ground. I thrashed and screamed for help as he dragged me across the gravel towards the shed. That's when I noticed a truck pulling into our driveway. Andy quickly got up, grabbed me, and pushed me into the shed, latching the door behind us. I tried calling for help. His large hand covered my mouth and held it shut. I wasn't able to breathe and tried to fight for air under his grip. Andy leaned close to my ear.

"You don't make a sound or I'll kill you, understand?"

I was struggling for my breath, and for the first time, had the terrified thought that my life was going to be over. There was no doubt in my mind that Andy was capable of doing what he threatened. I desperately nodded as I felt myself grow weak from lack of air. He released his grip but stayed on me. I could hear shuffling outside.

"Open the door you coward! Nell speak to me!" It was Billy.

Andy watched the door, ready to pounce if necessary. He reached for a nearby shovel, still holding me on the ground with his other hand. I prayed that Billy would leave. I feared for his life.

Billy kept banging on the door and demanding to be let in.

"You tell him to go away," Andy hissed. "I'm going to open the latch. One wrong move and he's dead. Understand?"

He let go of me and hid in the shadows. The door opened. I didn't want Billy to see me like this. A blast of daylight appeared, surrounding Billy's silhouette.

"Please go away," I cried.

He ran toward me and tried to help me up, but I resisted. I was frightened for him. I needed him to leave before Andy hurt him bad.

"Go away!" I screamed.

"Where's that bastard?" he shouted, as he looked around. "Come out here you prick!"

Andy hid in the shadows holding the shovel.

"Billy go," I pleaded. The caring eyes I remembered so well looked surprised—hurt maybe.

"But I can't leave you here! Not like this."

"Go!" I screamed. "Please just go." I was sobbing now.

It was enough to make him take a few steps back. He looked confused.

"I'm gonna get you help, Nell!" he cried. "I'm going to put an end to this. I promise!"

Thankfully he turned away. He took a step outside and Andy slammed the door back shut.

After some excruciating silence, I heard Billy's footsteps walking away and the start of an engine. I was not afraid for myself. I had been through this before and survived. I was just relieved that Billy was safe. But I was also fearful of what he might do next. He knew for sure now, and I knew he wouldn't let this go.

BILLY

Coffee with the Neighbor

I had a restless sleep that night. I fought my covers as I thrashed around. I didn't speak to Dora about what I had seen, and she was too much in her own world to notice my distress. I debated going to the authorities but decided I would go and talk to Nell's mother instead. Surely she would want to know that her daughter was not safe. I thought it best if I approached her at work, rather than anywhere near the house.

I drove into town that morning after giving Dora and Molly an extra-long hug. I looked over my shoulder before I left. "I love you." They were sitting together at the breakfast table.

"Love you too, Daddy," Molly said with a little wave.

Dora looked at me with surprise. I guess it had been awhile since I'd spoken those words. Too many other things had gotten in the way. I felt very lucky to have them in my life. Seeing another person in distress made me appreciate just what I had.

I pulled into the parking lot of the grocery store and thought about how I would deal with this. I decided that talking to Mrs. Dickson about something this serious wasn't appropriate with people around. I would need to arrange to meet her elsewhere. I went inside and looked around for her.

"Do you know if Mrs. Dickson is working today?" I asked a clerk, knowing full well that she worked every day.

"She's just stepped out back. I'll go get her for you," she said with a smile. She paused. "Can I tell her whose asking for her?"

In all the time we had lived next door to one another, we'd never met and she wouldn't know who I was.

"Err, just tell her I'm a neighbor. Billy's the name."

She nodded and turned the corner.

I waited at the register, scanning the magazines on the shelf and trying to look inconspicuous. A few minutes later she appeared, tying an apron around her waist. She walked up to me with a quizzical look on her face. She was a small woman, gaunt and pale as if she had not seen sunshine for a long time. Her posture was slightly stooped. She looked like someone who had been burdened with a heavy load on her shoulders for years. She looked far older than I would have expected a mother of teenage children to be. She had Nell's eyes though, deep and penetrating.

"Can I help you?" she asked.

I offered her a smile. It was the last thing I felt like doing.

"I'm your neighbor Billy Mulgrave." I extended my hand in greeting. She hesitantly took it. "Your daughter Nell worked for me this summer."

A puzzled look came over her, as if she didn't know much of what her daughter had been doing. She crossed her arms as if preparing for battle.

"Did she cause you some sort of trouble, mister?"

"No, no, not at all. In fact she worked really hard. You're lucky to have such a lovely girl."

She didn't seem to relax.

"Do you have a few minutes to talk?" I asked. "Somewhere private?"

She looked around.

"Doesn't look like it here, now does it?" She was growing impatient. "Look, mister …?"

"Mulgrave," I said. "Billy."

"I'm already late getting back to work here. What's this all about?"

"I'd rather speak to you in private. I can come back and meet you on your break if you like."

She paused, sizing me up, not sure what to do. I think she knew I wasn't going away too easily.

"I have a coffee break in two hours. I could spend a few minutes then if you insist."

"Great!" I said with relief. I glanced outside. "Perhaps you could meet me across the street at the diner. I'll have a coffee ready for you."

"Okay then," she agreed hesitantly.

I tried to do a few errands in town but had trouble concentrating. I went to the café half an hour early with a newspaper and pretended to read. I couldn't concentrate. There was something about Mrs. Dickson that didn't feel right. If anyone had come to talk to me about Molly, I would have been eager to hear anything they had to say. Somehow she was dismissive, uninterested, and perhaps even uncaring. She treated me like I was nothing but an unpleasant thorn in her side that she was anxious to be rid of.

I was on my second cup of coffee when Mrs. Dickson appeared at the door. She had that same distrustful look on her face. I stood up and took my hat off in greeting.

"I only have a few minutes, Mr. Mulgrave." She slid into the booth. "What is it you want to speak to me about?"

She pulled out a cigarette and I lit it for her with the matches that were on the table. She took a deep drag off it, with a look of agitation on her face. I signaled the waitress to bring her a coffee and pushed the cream and sugar towards her. I watched her stir in three large spoonfuls of sugar and take a sip, glancing up at me rather dismissively.

"Now what is it about my daughter?" she asked.

"This is difficult for me to tell you," I paused and looked beyond her, out the window at passersby. I was feeling very uncomfortable with this woman.

"I came upon something rather disturbing yesterday as I was driving home."

I could see her eyes were frozen upon me. Her jaw tightened.

"I saw your boy beating up on Nell. I saw him drag her into the shed and I believe he may have ..." I couldn't say the words, couldn't find them. They were lodged deep in my throat.

"Mr. Mulgrave, what are you implying here?" she asked. She pushed the coffee aside.

"What I'm saying is just what I saw. He hurt Nell and did things to her against her will. I tried to help but ..."

Mrs. Dickson was on her feet now. She crushed out her cigarette in the ashtray.

"I won't listen to another word of this." Her voice was hushed in an angry snarl. "How dare you come here and accuse my son of such things. I won't listen to such nonsense. This conversation is over!"

She turned abruptly and marched out the door. I sat there staring after her. Why would she not want to hear what was happening to Nell? How could she not care? I looked down at the two cups of coffee sitting in front of me, still full, and the destroyed cigarette butt smoldering in the ashtray. Then I felt an awful certainty in my stomach: Mrs. Dickson already knew.

When I got to the parking lot, I looked in the window of the grocery store but couldn't see Mrs. Dickson at her usual stall. Then I noticed that her pickup truck was missing from the parking lot. Could she have left to actually deal with the matter? I hoped so, but somehow doubted it. I got behind the wheel of my car feeling heavy hearted.

When I got home, Molly was busy playing with Rex on the veranda. I sat with her for a moment and gazed over at the Dickson farm. What was I going to do now? It seemed like going to the police was the only option. I thought about Nell ... about those bruises, the twisted arm, the secrecy. This had been going on for some time. Then the vomiting and late mornings. Then it hit me like a thunderbolt. It was her brother who impregnated her! I felt the vomit in my throat and ran to the toilet.

When I had collected myself, I came back into the kitchen. Molly had come in from the veranda.

"Daddy, look!" She offered me a drawing.

The sky had a big yellow sun. Three people stood under it holding hands and smiling. A dog sat beside them. *If only life could be that simple,* I thought.

I rubbed her head affectionately. I wondered where Dora was and called for her.

No response.

"Mommy has her door shut," Molly said, putting her finger to her lips to silence me.

Not again, I thought. I had to get her back to a doctor soon.

Molly started placing plates on the table for lunch. The last thing I wanted was food, but I knew that Molly needed to eat. I was reaching in the cupboard for glasses when I heard a rumbling noise in the distance. Molly ran to the window.

"Daddy look!" She pointed.

I came up behind her. A car was throwing up dust and gravel as it approached rapidly. *Who could that be?* We rarely had visitors and never ones who came unannounced. We stood there together at the window, hand in hand, watching the car approach. It screeched to a halt sideways in front of the house. That's when I noticed the word "POLICE" written on the side.

NELL

Twisted Minds

Ma came home early from work. She slammed the door when she came in.

"That man who you worked for in the summer, he came to talk to me at work today."

My heart started thumping in my chest. He knew about Andy. What had he said to Ma?

"He accused Andy of some awful things. I should have known sooner," she continued.

"Known what?" I asked, with a sense of doom oozing over me

"You say you had no boyfriend all summer and yet you spent all your time with that man. Now he's trying to cover his own wrong."

Pa had staggered into the kitchen.

"What's this all about? What are you doing home?"

"Our neighbor, Mr. Mulgrave, had the audacity to come in and accuse our Andy of some horrendous things," she said.

Pa wiped his chin with the back of his hand, where beer was dribbling through his whiskers.

"Well, what did he say?"

My eyes paced between them. No one looked at me.

"He says he saw Andy attack Nell. I think he might just go to the police."

Both my parents finally looked at me. I wanted to be invisible.

"What do you know of this Nell?" Pa asked, his brow furrowed.

"I haven't said anything to him about Andy, honest."

"Well then, what would make him say such awful things?" Ma asked.

I'd had enough of protecting Andy. My life was falling apart and everything was still all about protecting Andy.

"Because he raped me!" I screamed. "He rapes me every day! Billy saw it! He's the only one who cares about me and is trying to help me!"

I thought I was going to pass out when the blow struck my face. My father then grabbed me by the shirt collar.

"How dare you!" he yelled. "How dare you utter such nonsense?"

My mother was crying now.

"I knew it," she said. "I knew we shouldn't have let you spend so much time with that awful man. Especially a man who has a wife everyone says is crazy! Of course he would take advantage of a stupid girl!"

I was stunned. Did they really *believe* this? Were they blind to what was really happening right in front of their noses? Or was it easier to create a lie?

"It wasn't like that Ma!" I cried. "He never laid a hand on me. He was nice to me."

"I bet he was," Pa piped in. "Now look at you. If you think we're going to look after his kid, you have another think coming."

"Stan!" Ma cried. "What are we going to do? He's going to call the police! They're going to come and take our Andy away. We have to do something!"

"Don't worry. I'll be calling the police before he ever does." He gave me a hateful look.

"And you, young lady, better not deny what he's done to you! Not if you know what's good for you."

I felt like the lid had been lowered on the coffin and any light of hope extinguished.

The Constable

I quivered like a rabbit in a trap when Constable Harris came to take a statement from me that day. My parents had threatened to throw me out in the streets if I didn't cooperate. They said that my life wasn't worth more than a stray dog in the condition I was in. They said that we were family and needed to stick together, and couldn't let someone try to tear us apart. The part about family, and looking out for one another, made no sense to me. When did *I* ever matter? All I knew was that I was helpless. I needed them and I was at their mercy.

"So young lady, is it true that Mr. Mulgrave has been doing things to you that he shouldn't have?" The constable cleared his throat, looking uncomfortable. "Perhaps certain indiscretions occurred?"

I remained silent, looking at my sweaty hands folded in my lap, feeling numbed by what was happening. I felt like screaming, *Billy has been nothing but a saint to me!* He was the only one who tried to come to my rescue. I should have realized that no one could rescue me.

"The poor girl is traumatized," Pa said on my behalf, pretending like he cared. "As if it wasn't enough what he did to her this summer, he came by again yesterday to have another go at her."

"Is this true?" Constable Harris asked.

"You can check the tire marks in the driveway yourself if you like," Pa piped up again. "Those aren't our truck tires."

He gave up on getting any words out of me and looked up at Pa. "We certainly will look at all evidence. Meanwhile, did anyone witness any of this?"

"I did," said Andy. "I saw him grab her and drag her into the back shed. She has the scrapes on her knees and arms to prove it," he grabbed my elbow to show him.

I pulled my arm away from him.

"If I hadn't shown up in time, who knows what he would have done to her. He sure took off in a hurry though."

I gave Andy an incredulous look. He stared back at me as if he were daring me to argue. He knew that he had won. How could he not, when everyone was always on his side?

"Nasty wounds you have there." The constable wrote some notes on his pad.

"How did you know Mr. Mulgrave?" he asked.

"I worked for him." These were the first words I could utter.

"What kind of work did you do?"

"Farm chores."

"A young lady like yourself got hired to do farm chores? Now, now," he said, shaking his head and making more notes.

"How often were you there?"

"Every day," I answered.

"So from what I understand, you were there every day this past summer?"

"Yes."

"Were there other farm workers present?"

"No."

I somehow knew I was digging Billy's grave with my truthful answers. But what else could I do?

"That's a lot of time alone between a man and a young lady like yourself, now isn't it?"

"I was working for him," I protested.

Ma started to sob. Giant crocodile tears rolled down her cheeks. The constable patted her shoulder.

"There, there now missus. I know that you've been through a lot here," he said.

"You don't know the half of it," she said in between sobs. "You may not have noticed constable, but poor Nell is in the family way because of this man. There was no one else that Nell saw but Mr. Mulgrave when this happened. She had to quit school and we have to support her and a new baby, all because of this awful man."

"Is that true Nell? You're pregnant?"

I nodded. "But..." I glared at Andy. He was leaning against the wall with a smirk on his face, daring me to say another word. I looked away.

"How old are you Nell?"

"Fifteen," I said.

"My, my," he said, shaking his head and slamming his notebook closed. "I think we may have a case of statutory rape!"

DORA

The Lights Go Out

The first signs of fall were upon us. They were subtle: leaves starting to curl at the edges, a blast of cool morning air, and a lack of intensity to the sun that blazed directly into my eyes as it hung low on the horizon. I didn't care for the sun much. I felt that I should be happy when it was sunny and happiness continued to elude me. I even looked forward to the rains so that the weather would match my mood. Today the winds made the house creak and bang, startling me from my afternoon nap.

"I'll be going into town this morning," Billy said on his way out the door. "I'll try to make it back for lunch but might be later."

I never bothered to ask where he was going or what he was doing anymore. It didn't seem important. We passed each other by like strangers living in the same house. I had noticed a restlessness in Billy the night before. Usually he slept like there was no tomorrow, but he'd been up several times. I could see the light through the crack at the bottom of the door and his feet pacing back and forth. I thought it odd since he usually slept hard. I didn't pay much attention as my medication quickly lulled me back to sleep.

For whatever reason, he gave Molly and me a long hug that morning. I heard the words "I love you," for the first time in as long as I could remember. They rang hollow in my ears. I didn't say anything back. I was glad he wasn't going to be around for the morning. I preferred the silence of the house. Occasionally it was disrupted by Molly's chatter, but for the most part she was used to playing on her own. Sometimes she'd pretend to read her story books to Rex under the kitchen table or she'd dress him up in her clothes. I watched her in wonder. I didn't deserve her. I didn't deserve anything.

When I heard Billy's truck pull up the road that afternoon, I disappeared into my room for a sleep. Molly would have her time with her father while I'd escape under my covers. I heard him call for me, but didn't answer. I wanted to be left alone. As I was drifting to sleep, I heard the sound of another car pulling up the road. The driver was coming fast. I heard the gravel churn under his tires. *That's odd,* I thought. *Who could possibly be coming for a visit uninvited?* I rolled onto my back and listened. There was the muffled sound of men's voices. Who could they be? I mustered enough energy to rise from my bed, even though my medication was taking effect. I pulled the curtain aside. My knees grew weak. I clutched my chest as I thought my heart would stop beating right then and there. A police car was parked outside and two officers were pushing Billy into the car. His hands were clasped behind his back as he looked up at the window with terror in his eyes. I could hear Molly wailing in the background.

"What have you done?" I mouthed, but no sound came out.

I wondered if Billy could read my lips. I knew what Billy had done. He'd done the unspeakable and now he was paying for it. We were all paying for it. The wailing got louder as I watched the car pull away. Rex ran barking after it until he realized that he couldn't catch up. I watched the dust in the distance as the car grew smaller and disappeared. I thought momentarily about Molly and that I should go to her but I couldn't walk. I fell to the floor like a rag doll and then crawled on my hands and knees to my night table. There was only one thing for me to do. I grabbed my medication and poured the bottle of pills down my throat. I collapsed on the floor. The wailing faded and the daylight turned to darkness.

Part Two

BILLY *1955*

The Nightmare Begins

I shivered in my cell, the dark nightmare surrounding me. I didn't know if it was from the cold fall air or from fright or both. No one had told me why I was there or what I had done. I knew that this was a terrible mistake and surely it would get cleared up if someone would just come and speak with me. No one did that first night. I'd fall into a restless sleep on my metal slab, exhausted by my thoughts, only to be awoken to the slamming of iron doors, the cussing or screams of other inmates, or just my own nightmares. I'd bolt upright with the faint hope that I'd wake up and none of this would be real. But as sure as the cold floors and windowless cement walls surrounded me, my hell hole was real.

It was hard to tell whether it was day or night without windows. My watch was taken from me. On the second day a young man came to see me. He was lanky, with a nose like an eagle's beak and thick-rimmed glasses resting midway down the bridge of his nose. He kept pushing them up so that they wouldn't slide off. His hair was thin and plastered tight to his head. He smelled of pungent cologne. His tweed jacket, tie, and briefcase made it obvious that he was here on business. The guard opened my cell door and ushered me to a waiting room. It was windowless with pale green walls. The guard remained standing at the door with his arms crossed. He looked like he was prepared to come to this man's rescue in case I were to make any sudden moves.

"Hello, my name is Kenneth Mitchell. I've been appointed as your lawyer," he said. No handshake was offered. From his pale and sanitary appearance, it would be no surprise if he were afraid of germs. Who could blame him in a place like this? I felt a rush of relief that I finally had someone there I could get some information from. I wondered why I needed a lawyer though. This was obviously just some sort of mix up. Maybe I needed a lawyer to sue for this obvious error. Kenneth sat tentatively on the edge of his seat.

"Please tell me why I'm here," I pleaded. "No one is telling me anything."

He stared at me, expressionless. "You have been accused of statutory rape, Mr. Mulgrave," he said plainly, as if he were telling me what the weather was like outside. "This is a very serious offense and I'm here to get your side of what happened. I am here to defend you the best that I can." He hesitated for a moment before proceeding. "That is, unless you choose to plead guilty."

I sat there feeling stunned. I rested my head on my clenched fists, trying to compose myself. Kenneth Mitchell jabbered on but his words became a drawl and I no longer heard them. Then it seemed to hit me all at once, and I suddenly stood up and lurched over him. I must have startled him as he leaned back, glancing over his shoulder to make sure the guard was still watching.

"Wait a minute!" I yelled. "Statutory rape? Don't you realize that this is a terrible mistake! They've got the wrong guy!"

Mr. Mitchell cleared his throat in an annoying way and shuffled some papers.

"Did you have a young lady named Natalie Dickson work for you this past summer?"

I wasn't sure at first who Natalie was.

"You mean Nell? She worked at our farm."

He cleared his throat again. "I have a written, signed statement by the defendant, accusing you of statutory rape."

This hit me like a fist and I staggered.

"What are you talking about? That poor girl was being molested by her brother. I was about to call the authorities when I found out. Did she not tell you?"

He looked at his notes and shook his head.

"No mention of a brother. Your name appears on the file, signed by her parents who have legal authority over her."

"Just let me talk to Nell. We can get this cleared up quickly."

"I'm sorry, that's not possible," he said. "You are not allowed any contact with her prior to the trial."

"The trial! What trial?"

"That's why I'm here," he continued. "I will do what I can to defend you. Now if we can get started."

Get started? With what? I was not grasping any of this. Why was this happening?

"Who hired you?" I asked, not sure where this malnourished, sun-deprived man came from.

"A Mrs. Edna Stone gave our office a call. I'm apprenticing with Dean Colts, the defense attorney in town, and he sent me for the preliminary meeting with you."

"So you're not even a lawyer yet. My whole life is on the line, and I'm talking to a law student? Well tell Mr. Colts that I need to talk to him now! Do you not realize what a grave error this all is? I need proper representation."

"Let me assure you, Mr. Mulgrave, that you are in good hands. I will have Mr. Colts look over your preliminary statement and advise me accordingly. Now if we could just get started."

A fire was building in my gut, ready to explode.

"Get out!" I screamed. "Get out!" Fury rang in my ears.

He jumped to his feet nervously, collecting his papers, and couldn't get out of there fast enough. When he got to the door, he paused.

"I will let Mr. Colts know you prefer to speak with him, but he is a busy man and you will have to wait. I was merely trying to expedite the process, but if this is your choice, so be it."

"Get out!" I screamed again like a mad man.

I was left there with my thoughts once more, wondering if I was losing my mind. A shock wave ran through me. How could this be? Accused of rape when I was the only one trying to help Nell? Why was someone not coming forward to clear this up? I now wished more than anything to have Mr. Mitchell or anyone there to talk to. In the midst of my gloom, I wondered where Dora was. Why had she not come to see me? After looking after her all these years, why was she not here when I needed someone to help *me?* Where was my Molly? Oh God, what would happen

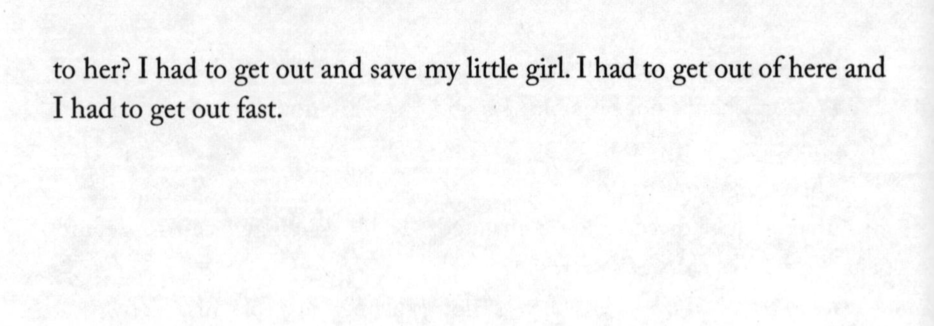

to her? I had to get out and save my little girl. I had to get out of here and I had to get out fast.

DORA *1955*

The Lost Child

Green grass. Lots of green grass. Not like the meadows at home. Those had yellow and purple flowers growing wild. The sound of crickets. I missed the sound of crickets. The echoing crescendo in the heat, like a string quartet warming up before a concert. No sound. Here it was silent. The green lawns smelled freshly cut. It looked like my mother's carpet when I was a child. She loved that carpet—said that green was her favorite color. I thought green was kind of a sickly color. I'd roll my marbles on that carpet, watching them collide. I loved the kaleidoscope of colors in the glass. I also liked the shiny black one and white one. They felt cool and smooth in my palms.

A voice sounded from behind. It took me a while to hear the words, to shift my thoughts from my childhood. I did not turn my head. Words were not important. They had no meaning. Nothing did. It was a familiar voice in this place with the green lawns. It came from the woman with the starched white hat. She reminded me of myself when I was young. She had color in her cheeks and smiled a lot. I wanted to be a nurse once. Now I was a patient instead. I heard it again. Her voice. Something about a visit maybe... I wished she would be quiet. Her voice sounded so loud in the green silence.

A young child stood before me. She looked familiar. She looked very sad. I should have comforted her, but I couldn't move. She was wearing a white bow in her hair. She must have had a good mother who brushed her hair and tied it with pretty bows. She must have lost her mother. She crawled into my lap and put her little arms around my neck. She smelled of soap and baby shampoo. She was saying something in a small, innocent voice, her breath sweet as a fresh spring morning. My focus was drawn beyond her to a hummingbird suckling on a red flower. I gazed in wonder at how fast its little wings flapped, just to suck some sweet nectar. The little girl started crying and squeezed me more tightly, and I found my arms going around her, almost like they had a mind of their own. She felt so familiar. But how could that be?

Someone sat down on the bench beside me, a woman with a large hat, and started talking as if she knew me. Did I know her? Why couldn't I remember? I tried to hold on to the little girl on my lap, but my arms felt like lead, their weight slowly loosening my grip even as my mind wandered back to the green grass, searching for yellow and purple flowers that weren't there.

The familiar woman with the white hat suddenly appeared at my shoulder, muttering something I couldn't make out. The little girl reached up and kissed my cheek. I blinked. What a sweet child she was. Surely her mother must miss her terribly.

"I miss you, Mommy," she said.

I'm sure she misses you too,

I felt her crawl down off my lap and slide her hand down my arm to my fingertips. My fingers moved. I suddenly wanted to grasp that small hand, and managed to curl my fingers around it. For a moment, I looked right into her lovely sea-blue eyes...

Wait.

I felt my eyes mist over as she moved away from me.

Molly?

She flitted away out of sight like a hummingbird … gone like a dream, so elusive ... as if she never was...

I sighed. It sounded deafening in the silence.

What a sweet child. I do hope she finds her mother.

I could feel the metal grate of the bench I sat on and ran my fingers along it. It felt like a cage and I was the bird who was housed within it. My wings were clipped and I could no longer fly. I could only watch as the world passed me by.

NELL *1955*

Frozen

"I hate you!" I beat my stomach. "I want you dead! I want you gone, now!"

No matter how much I wished my pregnancy away, my stomach continued to grow. I had no choice but to have this baby and then be rid of it quickly.

Life at home was intolerable. I hated them all. I had stopped speaking to them. Sometimes I fantasized them dead and felt nothing but relief at the thought of them gone. It wasn't long before my wish came true, at least in part. Pa seized his heart after a night of heavy drinking and never moved again.

"Call an ambulance!" my mother screamed at me. She held him as he lay hunched over against her chest. I curled up in the corner of the room and stayed there, frozen, unable to move. I was hoping, as every minute passed, that he would never stir again. My mother continued to scream hysterically, "Do something!"

Andy staggered out of his chair and stumbled for the phone. He cussed under his breath. "Damn it Nell, you bitch! Don't just sit there. Do something!"

I knew he needed me to make the call, but in that moment I was in control and wasn't coming to their rescue. I sat there in a ball, watching the scene unravel before me. Ma let go of my father and came up behind Andy, slapping him in the head. It was the first time I'd seen her raise a hand to him.

"What's wrong with you? Why can't you just get one thing right in your life?"

She grabbed the phone away from him and dialed. Andy came towards me, shaking his fist. I curled farther into a ball, anticipating the blow. He staggered sideways and grabbed onto a door to steady himself, then fell towards the kitchen. I continued to huddle there as the sirens got closer and men in uniforms rushed in the door. They fussed over my father, who was now laying on the floor. They kept pushing on his chest hard, but he lay lifeless. My mother stood beside him, wringing her hands and moaning. I watched as if it were a movie. They finally brought in a stretcher and three men struggled to lift him onto it. They covered him with a white sheet and pulled it over his face. Ma sobbed louder and followed them out. In that moment, I felt a tinge of pity for her. She looked pathetic to me. Her whole life had revolved around a useless husband and son and a now-pregnant daughter. It was a life that I hoped I would never have to live. I heard the sirens start up again and fade into the distance. I didn't know where Andy was, but I guessed he'd passed out on the kitchen floor. I stayed curled up in that corner listening to the silence, which was complete except for the beating of my heart. Then I felt a gentle movement close to my heart. That's when I had my first sensation of being no longer one person, but two people—together as one.

BILLY *1955*

A Bird in a Cage

Each day crept by at a snail's pace, the days flowing into night. A constant rage ate away at my insides.

I was finally taken to court without having had any further contact with counsel. I waited for a visit from Mr. Colts, or even the assistant I had frightened away, but it was as if I'd been forgotten. Here I was with my life on the line, standing alone.

"You are accused of the following crime," the judge read, while taking glances at me over his reading glasses. "Statutory rape of a minor."

The tone of his voice made me feel like I wasn't worth the ground that I stood on. I felt already convicted of something I hadn't done, before I was even heard. I wondered why I was being punished in such a way. I'd always been a man of integrity and peace. I was a farmer, a simple man of the earth. I agonized about how the farm was doing without me. My insides were in knots at the thought of all my hard work just wasting away. And my daughter! What had become of her? Not knowing tortured me.

"Given the nature of your crime, the bail will be steep. Do you or anyone you know have means to pay?"

"Your honor, this is all a terrible mistake."

"Please answer the question," he said without looking up.

"I am a farmer. I own the house that I live in, but I have no money to spare."

"Very well. You will stay in custody then until the property has been sold or you have some other means of payment. A trial date will be set and I suggest you make sure to arrange for proper representation."

"I have been waiting to see a lawyer. An apprentice came to see me. I asked to see a proper lawyer."

"In that case, the State will assign you legal counsel. Dismissed!"

"But Your Honor, I have a farm and a family to support. They're depending on me. I need to get back to my daughter. She's only five years old! My wife is not well and cannot care for her."

The judge furrowed his brow as he shuffled his papers.

"Mr. Mulgrave, this is a very serious crime. You should have had a lawyer speaking on your behalf today. I have no other choice but to keep you in custody. In the meantime, I suggest you speak to the public defender we assign you so that you are properly prepared. Now please remove the defendant!"

With that he rose and turned his back to me. I was led out of the courtroom by two guards, hands bound in front of me. I felt like a wild animal being taken back to his cage. Back to the damp smell of blood and urine, in the midst of men who had committed monstrous crimes. What had I done to deserve this? I couldn't believe that Nell had done this to me, when all I'd offered her was kindness. I cursed her under my breath. I ached to know how Molly was. The helplessness to do anything about my situation ate away at my core.

I didn't have a clue how to survive in a place like this ... how to be with men who would taunt others for entertainment. I tried to keep my head low and avert eye contact to avoid confrontations. I tried to remain as invisible as possible. But confrontation was in the nature of the environment and inevitably it happened.

"Hey Slick. What are you in for?" a man with a chest the size of a gorilla grunted at me. I wouldn't dare mention the accusation. I would have been diced meat in no time. I learned to lie.

"Armed robbery," I said, thinking that was the safest. I noticed that when others made this proclamation, it seemed to get instant respect from fellow prisoners. But one of the guards must have blabbed something because barrel chest came within inches of my face the next day, offering me a toothless grin.

"Hey Slick, so you said robbery but I heard otherwise. I heard you like little children. You sick fuck!"

I took the blow to the chin and ended up on the ground. I was surrounded by the others. I realized that, in their eyes, I was the worst scum in there. I lay on the ground terrified. This was going to be the moment of my death, and it was going to be a painful way to go. A guard beat his way through the circle with a club, threatening to use it if they didn't back off. I was pulled off the floor by my shirt and yanked away from the gang. Men shouted profanities at me and threats to my life.

"I'm putting you into solitary," he said. "It's for your own good."

I was grateful to be away from the others. As difficult as it was to be constantly alone, exposed to my tormented thoughts without distraction, I wanted to survive. I needed to prove my innocence. I knew I wouldn't survive living with men with hateful minds and fists to match. I needed to get back to Molly ... to Dora. Where were they? Why had no one come to see me? Those questions kept haunting me. I felt so devastatingly alone. All that had once defined me was gone: my home, my family, and my work. Who was I now? I wasn't even sure I existed anymore.

DORA *1956*

The Discharge

"So how is my favorite patient?" Dr. Holston asked.

He had such a warm smile and he smiled at me often. I didn't notice the same demeanor when he was with other patients. I smiled back. How good it felt to smile again.

"I'm doing much better, doctor," I responded. Was I even being a bit flirtatious? I had to remind myself that I was still a married woman (married to a man who was no longer in my life, but nevertheless).

"Your medications seem to have you stabilized. You are looking much more chipper these days. It's good to see such a beautiful smile on a beautiful woman."

Was he flirting back? He was a handsome fellow with gray-green eyes that seemed to reflect a kaleidoscope of shades. I wasn't sure if it depended on the lighting or his moods, but I found them fascinating. His hair was dark (except for the gray whisks on his temples that matched his eyes) and combed straight back. He wore his glasses on a band around his neck and put them on the end of his nose when he read my chart. I studied his hands when he was intently reading and admired how his fingers were both strong and delicate, and his fingernails neatly trimmed. There was no ring. I was grateful for the daily attention he'd lavished on me over my months of convalescing. I didn't notice him much at first, but over time, as I gradually healed, I looked forward to his visits with anticipation.

"I'd say that in another week or so we could be looking at a discharge for you. I must say, I'm going to miss our daily visits. It's been remarkable to watch your recovery. To think that we could have lost you back then, and look at you now! You are very vibrant, and thankfully, very alive."

I wanted to say that he had saved me, but I wouldn't dare. Back then, I hadn't wanted to survive. I couldn't face all that had happened. I was the wife of a criminal. I didn't have the strength to cope. Dr. Holston gave me hope. I started noticing things again. Colors became brighter; the clouds that shadowed my mind were lifting. There was a tomorrow, and Dr. Holston was there every small step of the way, cajoling and reassuring.

"I'm better all thanks to you, doctor." I looked up at him demurely.

"I'll check in with you again in the morning. Do get out of that drab nightgown and put on your clothes for me tomorrow. It's time to get ready for the real world."

"I'll do that, doctor." I said, and watched as he started for the door.

He turned before he left.

"By the way, do call me Collin."

I had a restless night. The word "discharge" kept playing in my mind. Discharge to where? Billy was in jail. The farm was gone and Molly was with her aunt. I had no home to go to and no relatives to stay with. How was I going to pay for a place to live?

I got dressed that morning in the only dress I had at the hospital: a green and pink floral print. I even dabbed on a bit of lipstick. The real world? What would that be like for me now? Collin was at the door as promised, holding his chart in one hand, with his lab coat open at the front revealing gray pants and a light blue shirt that was open at the collar. He smiled as we made eye contact and I thought, once again, how handsome he was. I was still Billy's wife though and felt like I was being deceitful to him. I didn't even know where he was or when I'd see him again. Right now I had to fend for myself and find my own way. The thought frightened me.

"Well good morning, Dora. You look very pretty today," he said. The grin on his face remained as his eyes lingered.

I sat down on the edge of my bed and looked down at my hands, which were twitching.

"Is something wrong?" he asked. He grabbed the chair beside the bed and sat down. His gaze lingered as he took my hand. I warm current ran through me.

"I don't know," I said. "I'm so grateful that I'm feeling better, but I'm also nervous. Ever since you said that I could be discharged from here in a week, I've been thinking about where to go. I haven't come up with anything yet."

Collin chuckled as he tightened his grip on my hand.

"Don't you worry your pretty head about that now. We're not going to throw you out on the street you know. We have staff here who will help to find a place for you and assist with funding until you are settled and able to work again. My guess is that, being as pretty as you are, you will be scooped up in no time by a man who will want to take care of you forever."

Did he not realize that I was still a married woman, without a husband to take care of me? What man would want someone like that? I blushed and looked away. He let go of my hand, as if he realized he needed to get back to being my doctor. He flipped through my chart.

"I think that we can lower the dosages of some of your medications now that you're doing better. You will find your mind will be clearer and you'll have more energy. I will need to monitor you closely though after you leave and would like to continue to see you in my office."

I let out a sigh of relief. It would mean not having to say goodbye to Dr. Collin Holston—something that I dreaded but wasn't willing to admit to myself. He made me feel safe.

"There is nothing that I would like more, Collin."

NELL *1956*

The Escape

My mother cried for days.

"What are we going to do? I have three of you now to take care of on my measly salary. Why has God cursed me like this? I don't deserve this! No husband and useless, good-for-nothing children to support."

Her sadness seeped through my hollowness. I felt nothing. I didn't console her. I didn't defend myself. I hated her for the crime that they had committed against Billy. In the name of protecting my brother, they had sacrificed him and threatened me to silence. I looked at Andy as he lay slumped over the arm of the couch, watching TV with a beer in his hand, and wished *he* was paying for this crime. His life was a waste anyway, while Billy was a saint. I despised them, and myself, for what this had done to him and his family.

I realized that not only was I of no value to my mother but she was also of no value to me. That's when I knew I had to leave. That was the pivotal point at which I mustered the courage to do so. At least in the streets I could fend for myself and do what I needed to do to survive. I would speak out about this despicable crime that had been committed. I was almost due to deliver and this burden would soon be gone. I would do whatever it took to make a life for myself away from this hell that I lived in. Continuing to stay was no longer bearable.

I had heard of a place on the other side of town: a church that offered food to those in need. I was now one of those people and that's where I headed. I hesitated at the door before I knocked. I had a hard time grasping that I was now a homeless person. The matron at the door looked me up and down. Her eyes lingered on my belly, and she made the sign of a cross.

"Where are your parents, child?"

"They're dead," I said, without feeling like I was lying. "Please," I continued, as she looked at me with doubt in her eyes, "I'm very tired and I need some food and a place to get warm." I put my hands to my mouth and blew on them.

She took both my hands in hers and rubbed them. It felt soothing, welcoming.

"Come in," she said. "Sit here." She motioned to a bench inside the door.

I looked around the church at the stained-glass windows. A picture of a mother and child was painted on the glass. The mother looked down at her baby with a peaceful glow on her face. A calm came over me as I sat staring at it. This is the way a mother should feel towards a child. I thought of the mother I had and felt sadness. I then touched my belly apologetically. The matron interrupted my thoughts as she entered the room carrying a gray blanket and a small pillow.

"You can rest on the pews for tonight. I will fetch you a warm broth from our kitchen. We can then discuss what to do with you in the morning." She offered me a kind smile.

"Thank you," I whispered.

I lay on the pew, resting my head on the pillow. I was fast asleep before the soup arrived.

I felt a gentle shake. I opened my eyes and took in the blue hue that the sunlight cast through the stained-glass windows. My first thought was that I had gone to heaven. Then I noticed someone's presence. A woman stood before me. She wore a buttoned-up coat that looked like it was choking her at the collar. Her hair draped to her shoulders from under a small, round bonnet. She had neatly cut bangs and red lipstick. Her gloved hands were folded and she had a frown on her face.

"I thought you would never wake up," she said.

I had to remember where I was for a moment. And who was she?

"What is your name?" she asked.

"Why do you want to know?" I responded.

"I'm from the social welfare office. You look like a minor and I'm trying to determine where you belong. Where do you live?" she asked.

"I don't have a home," I said.

My stomach grumbled and I felt faint as I tried to sit up.

"I need something to eat," I said.

"I can take care of that for you. First, I need to know who you are and where you belong."

"First, I need to eat before I can answer your questions," I responded, feeling annoyed.

She let out a heavy sigh. "Very well. There's a corner diner and I'll take you there for breakfast and we can talk."

I scanned the menu, wanting to order everything. I had never been to a restaurant before. The waitress came over with a pad and pen.

"What can I get you?" she asked.

"I'll have the waffles with syrup, and eggs with bacon, and the home fries and—"

"Hold on," the social welfare woman interrupted. "She'll have an order of toast and a tea for now."

She took the menu out of my hand with a stern look and handed it to the waitress.

"Who knows when you last ate so let's start slow. I don't want you getting sick."

I was about to protest but realized that she was probably right. I couldn't remember the last time I'd eaten. Then came the questions I'd dreaded: Who are you? Who are your parents? Why are you not at home? Why are you not in school? (Did she not notice my belly?) Do your parents know where you are? Are you receiving medical care for your pregnancy? Who is the father?

"My brother," I said, in answer to the last question.

She paused and stared at me, looking as if she wasn't sure what to do with this information. She took her napkin and patted her red lips, which became not so red.

"I can't go home," I continued. "My brother did this to me and he will continue to rape me. My father is dead and my mother doesn't want me. I am not welcome there and I have nowhere to go."

Her demeanor changed and she stopped treating me like a delinquent child.

"I will need to verify this information," she said. "In the interim, I'll find you a place where you can stay."

A sense of relief poured through me. I'd finally spoken the truth and someone heard me. Could it be that I'd finally escaped my home?

BILLY *1955*

The Promise

The walls were closing in on me, crushing me. I couldn't breathe. I'd scream sometimes just to make sure I still had a voice ... a breath. Sometimes I wished I didn't. There was no purpose anymore, merely empty time, which became the enemy. I was in the depths of despair when a spark of light flickered.

"You have a visitor, Mulgrave," the guard came to inform me. "You may want to clean up so you don't scare them off."

He took me to the shower room, which I was normally allowed to use only once a week. He threw me a rag. "Hurry up."

I didn't realize how bad I looked until I peered into the small hand-held mirror. I had always been so clean shaven and now a scruffy beard had grown. My hair was a frightful mess. They wouldn't give me scissors to cut it, probably thinking I'd stab myself. They may have been wise. My cheeks were sunken, making my eyes look bulgy and scared. I hadn't realized how much weight I'd lost. I couldn't stomach the tasteless mush they slipped through the crack in my door, infested with cockroaches. I hosed myself off and slicked down my hair and beard. I didn't really care what I looked like. I had someone there to see me and that's all that mattered. The guard handcuffed me and led me to a small room.

"Now sit here," he said.

I was facing a small barred window. The light was bright on the other side and I had to blink a few times for my eyes to adjust.

There, to my amazement, stood my angel. For a long moment, we just looked at each other, and then she started making sounds as if she were gasping for air. She was trying to talk but only whispers of air were coming out. She kept struggling to say something and then finally, there it was. "Daddy!" she cried, calling to me over and over with her hands stretching through the bars, reaching for me. I couldn't touch her with my hands cuffed, so I leaned my head towards her and let her touch my cheek. Such a gentle touch. At first I couldn't look at her. I tried so hard not to let her see me cry, even though tears were welling in my eyes. I had to be strong for her.

"D-d-don't be sad, Daddy," she stuttered. My little girl, always worrying about everyone else.

"I miss you so much, Angel." It was like a physical ache in my chest. I leaned my head against the bar, trying to focus on the cold steel so that I could keep it together in front of her. Molly told me she missed me and then asked me a question that felt like a punch.

"When are you coming home, Daddy?"

How could I possibly explain what had happened and why I was here? How could I offer her any comfort as her father? "Not for a while, honey. I have some things to sort out first. But I promise you I will come home." *God, please don't let me be lying to my little girl.*

She reached through the bars with her other hand and then held my face, with one palm on each cheek. As her soft skin met the bristles on my cheek, I felt ashamed. Then she asked me why I was there, and why I couldn't come home. What was I supposed to say to that? Never in my life had I been at such a loss. She was simply too young to understand, and I told her as much, before asking her to remember that I loved her very much. My words sounded empty, too small and heartbreaking to help my little girl in the least.

When she told me that she loved me too, I started to cry. I couldn't help it. While my words seemed somehow pathetic and hollow, hers seemed to fill me to overflowing. Before seeing her, I hadn't known how I would survive another day in this place. Now I knew. I would survive for her.

It was then that I noticed someone standing behind her. At first I thought it might have been Dora, but my sister Edna stepped forward.

"Oh my Lord Jesus, she hasn't spoken a word since she last saw you Billy," Edna said, rushing up behind Molly to stroke her back. "If I'd known that seeing you would get her talking again, I would have brought her sooner. I was just afraid that this was not a good place for a little girl and all."

"I can't thank you enough Edna, for taking care of her." My voice cracked. Molly was safe. She wasn't alone. Edna went on to tell me about how Molly was adapting to life at her new home, fitting in fine with their family. Then she started asking about me. She was worried about how I was being treated.

When I couldn't answer her, she didn't ask again. I could see the alarm reflected in her eyes. Was I as visibly destroyed as I felt on the inside?

She asked me about the case then—if I'd seen my lawyer and was he taking care of things. I reassured her that the case was proceeding well, not seeing any point in letting on just how desperate my situation seemed.

Molly gave my face a final squeeze and then pulled away, crawling into her aunt's lap and seeming to take comfort there, as she stared back at me with sad, scared eyes. It ate away at me that I wasn't the one who could comfort her now, but I was more grateful than I could say that she had Edna to love and take care of her in the meantime. I looked at my sister, who stared back at me with sympathetic eyes, and tried to explain to her how I couldn't stop thinking about Molly, and how much I missed her and her mother.

She reached out to me then, putting her hand through the bar for a moment, and then quickly pulling it back when she remembered I couldn't return the gesture. She consoled me once again that Molly was well cared for and no bother, and told me that Dora was in the hospital, not well but getting help. It was pretty much what I expected and explained why she hadn't been by to see me.

"Just keep working on staying as strong as you can and we can put this awful mess behind us." She wiped her eyes with her handkerchief.

I tried to listen, but all I could really take in was the lingering touch of my angel, and the precious moments I'd had with her. I had breathed her into every pore of my body as she stroked my cheeks. Oh how I longed to hold my little girl. *Damn these restraints!* It was torturous to be with her and not hold her.

"Time's up Mulgrave. Say goodbye."

I felt panic grip me at these words. Molly climbed out of Edna's lap and reached for me again, leaning her head against the bars. I squeezed my eyes shut, unable to bear the thought of that cold steel on her skin. I leaned close and kissed her forehead, savoring every second of our contact, knowing that I would dream of it every moment until I saw her again. She clung to my face, trying to will me through the bars. "You have to be a big girl, my angel." *She's so small!* "Remember the story of Cinderella? She had to live through some bad things, but at the end she was happy." I felt her nod ever so slightly. "This is a bad thing that's happened but it won't be forever, I promise you that."

In that moment I believed what I said. I had to. Seeing her gave me the strength to believe and to keep fighting. I had to get back to my daughter again. She needed me. I would do whatever it took to try to prove my innocence and be set free.

"Things will get better and we will be a family again. You have to be strong like she was."

"I will daddy," she said.

I held onto those thoughts as the guard came up behind me and pulled me away from the window.

I took one more glance over my shoulder before he ushered me out of the holding room.

My angel still held onto the bars, her tiny tear-streaked face pushing through them.

"I love you Daddy," she cried.

"I promise," I said once more.

DORA *1957*

The Toast

Mr. Porter sat behind a wooden desk, leaning back in his chair while he scanned through documents. I studied the top of his bald head, which glistened in the light that was streaming in from the window behind him. His fingernails looked like they had been chewed short and his knuckles were raw. I watched those hands stroke his mustache as he furrowed his brow.

"You are legally entitled to a divorce," he finally said. "You have had no contact with your husband since his incarceration, oh let's see ... two years ago now. Given the nature of his crime, he will remain incarcerated for many years to come, which gives you grounds to proceed."

Collin sat beside me holding my hand.

"That's good news, isn't it dear?" he said, giving my hand a squeeze. "It's incomprehensible that Dora should need to suffer any more than she has because of this criminal."

"I will need to inform Mr. Mulgrave, of course, of the proceedings, and hopefully this will go smoothly. I can't see him contesting given the situation. If he does, the divorce can proceed by default. No, I think this is a pretty straight-forward case."

"Thank you Mr. Porter." Collin stood and shook his hand. I was glad that he did not extend his chewed-up hand for me to shake and nodded instead.

"I think this calls for a celebration lunch, don't you Dora?" Collin asked.

I nodded in agreement and offered him a smile.

I wasn't quite sure why I wasn't feeling a sense of excitement ... of joy. Here stood a man who had shown me nothing but kindness. He helped bring me out of those dark days and helped set me on my feet again. I had managed to find a place of my own, but it wasn't in a very good neighborhood. Collin insisted that I spend more time at his beautiful home and soon after he wanted me there permanently. He declared his love for me and said he wanted to take care of me for the rest of my life. I knew I'd never have to worry about anything ever again. But what I felt in this moment was a sadness that I tried to hide. It may have been a new beginning, but it was also an ending. Why wasn't I overjoyed that my ties to Billy would be forever cut, after all he had put me through?

Collin took me to our favorite spot near the gardens by the river. I loved looking out over the pruned floral pathways with the trickling fountain in the middle. We got our usual seat by the window.

"Welcome Dr. Holston, Dora. Good to have you join us on this beautiful day," our familiar host said in greeting.

"Fine day indeed, especially since you will soon be able to greet Dora as Mrs. Holston."

Collin beamed.

"Congratulations, this certainly calls for a celebration. Let me get our finest champagne immediately."

Collin gazed at me over the table. I looked out to the garden.

"I told you it wouldn't be difficult," he said. "Aren't you glad that we saw the lawyer? And such splendid news! Now we can be together properly as man and wife."

He pulled on my arm so that I met his gaze. I offered a smile.

"That big house of mine has needed a woman to make it a home. I'm so glad you can finally leave your past behind, to be free to move on to what you really deserve. We can give Molly the family she deserves."

Oh yes, Molly. How I had dreamed of having her back with me. I knew that with Collin I would be a much better mother.

The champagne arrived and the waiter poured us both a glass.

"To us!" He raised his glass.

I looked at him. He looked so content in this moment, as if he'd just won a victory and I was the prize. I didn't consider myself to be much of a trophy. It gave me purpose though, to think that I mattered that much to him. If he felt this way, then I must be special. I raised my glass.

"To us."

NELL *1956*

Rubbish at the Bottom of the Heap

Finding a home for me was not easy. After all, a pregnant teenager was not something that appealed to many foster homes. What I ended up in was a girl's holding pen, or so it seemed. It was obvious that this was the place where unwanted children were sent. In fact, they were children I didn't want to be around.

I was put into a room with two bunk-beds, which I shared with three other girls. The room was windowless and cold. Clothes were strewn around the floor, leftover food was crawling with bugs, and the smell of sweat and vomit was pungent. My sense of smell was particularly keen with my pregnancy and the odor made me gag. I grabbed a garbage bag in an attempt to clean up and was met by a cold stare.

"What do you think you're doing?" asked a girl with jet black hair and matching heavy eyeliner. "This place not good enough for you?"

I ignored her and continued picking up the rubbage. I felt the weight of her boot on my hand and flinched in pain.

"She didn't hear me," the girl said, while she popped her chewing gum and motioned to the other girl, who had been laying passively on her bed.

The second girl, who had bad acne and yellow teeth, came and grabbed the garbage bag from my hand. She emptied it onto the bed that I was sleeping in.

"Let's get the house rules straight around here," the second girl said. "There are none. And we don't need little Miss Mommy trying to change that. Got it?"

"I was just trying to help," I muttered.

They both burst out in a menacing laugh. "Well don't," the dark haired girl said, while lighting a cigarette. She flicked her ashes onto the floor and rubbed it into the carpet with her foot. When I tried to remove the garbage from my bed, I got stopped again.

"Enjoy the filth, because that's all you are around here."

I pushed it to the foot of my bed and crawled under the covers.

Things were not much better in the morning with the other girls in the house.

"You've gotten around now haven't you," one of the girls scoffed, looking at my belly.

"We don't like dirty sluts here," another chimed in.

I looked around to see who was in charge. There was a woman with unkempt hair sitting at the kitchen table, chain-smoking. I looked to her for some support or guidance, but she didn't seem to take notice as she flipped through a magazine. I had not eaten since the day before and was feeling famished.

"Please, I need to get something to eat," I told the woman.

After a pause she looked up at me. "And what would you like me to do about that?"

There was a box of cereal a couple girls were sharing. There was some dried toast on the table and some murky water in a cup that may have been tea.

"Is there anything I could eat in the house?" I asked.

"Not my job to feed you," she said. "You need to wait for your worker to fork over some funds and then you can eat. You'll get fed when she gets here."

The social welfare lady who had taken me there the previous day arrived that night and handed the woman some money. That night I was allowed to eat a can of beans and stale bread. I later found out that these welfare payments were also paying for the woman's cigarettes and alcohol.

I learned to ignore the insults that were hurled at me routinely. I learned to accept that I was the newcomer and at the bottom of the pack. I kept my eyes averted and my mouth shut. I wondered why there was so much anger and hatred around me. What had happened to these girls to make them so mean? I realized that they were from similar backgrounds to mine. There were stories of alcoholic fathers, of rape, of beatings. I just knew that I never wanted to become like them.

BILLY *1956*

My Day in Court

They did appoint me a defense lawyer, a Mr. Cullen, who took a history of the events of the past summer. I told him nothing but the truth and trusted in that to set me free. He was a chipper and eager man, but young and inexperienced. I guess he wouldn't have been working as a public defender if he'd already been established. His freckled complexion, toothy grin, and reddish curly hair reminded me of a cartoon character. He was a pleasant enough chap, but he did not instill confidence. I had no other choice and had to put my life in his hands. He had advised me not to take the stand, but I felt I had nothing to hide and welcomed the opportunity to tell my story to the jury. After all, I was innocent and that would be obvious to everyone.

"Remember to not show your emotions in court," he advised me. "The D.A. will test you and try to break you down, but try not to let him get to you."

He was right. The district attorney had a pompous manner, strutting about the courtroom as if he was of sole importance. He had a protruding belly that only one button of his suit jacket could close over. He smelled of stale cigars and his face had the ruddiness of a heavy drinker.

"Why did you hire a fifteen-year-old girl to work on your farm, Mr. Mulgrave?" he asked.

"She was looking for work and I was trying to be a good neighbor."

"Quite generous of you, Mr. Mulgrave." I hated the way he addressed me in a derogatory tone. "Not many farmers would put being nice ahead of getting the help they really needed to run a farm."

"She turned out to be a good worker," I countered.

"Yes, I'm sure she was quite pleasant to have around to break the daily monotony."

He played with his cuff-links to keep the jury's interest on what he might utter next. "Court records show that your wife was not well at the time. Is this true?"

"Yes, she was under medical care."

"Were you sleeping with your wife during this time?"

I was taken aback by the question and my lawyer objected.

The prosecutor apologized and continued. "Let me then just ask you whether you were under some strain during your wife's convalescence?"

"Yes, but–"

"Just a yes or no will do. Were you in fact spending more time with the plaintiff than with your own wife?"

"Yes, because we worked for twelve hours a day together."

The prosecutor theatrically rolled his eyes at the jury.

"Twelve hours a day. My, my, that is a long time together. I've also been informed that she quite often came to work for you on weekends as well."

"Sometimes. But that was because she was having difficulty with her family."

"Oh, so she would confide to you about the intimate details of her life?"

"Not really. It was obvious that she was not happy."

"Aww," he said, with insincere sympathy. "So let me get the picture here. You had an emotionally distraught fifteen-year-old young lady working with you for twelve hours a day. That sounds like a situation that would be ripe for something to develop, don't you think? After all, you are a man and she's a pretty young girl."

My attorney again jumped to my defense, but the damaging inferences had already been strategically planted into the jury's minds. I hated this man. He was determined to make me appear guilty in any underhanded way he could. He would twist everything I said.

"Did you ever touch Natalie Dickson while she was your employee?"

"Absolutely not!" I stated emphatically.

"Let me present the jury with a documented incident that happened on August the eleventh, 1955, at approximately 1:30 p.m., in the barn on your property. Let me quote what was seen by an eye witness. 'She was screaming and I ran to the barn. What I saw was Nell lying on the ground crying and Billy,'" he looked up at the jury and clarified, "the defendant, 'lying beside her stroking her hair. He then picked her up and carried her to his truck and they drove off together.'"

Dora! How *could* she? I knew she had suspicions, but that was part of her illness. How could she have made a statement like that to the prosecuting attorney? How could she have sold me out like that?

"Nell was injured. I was just trying to help her."

"I bet you were. You just told the court that you had NO physical contact with the plaintiff and you lied. Stroking her hair, carrying her in your arms, that constitutes physical contact. I have no further questions, Your Honor."

I was shocked at how truths were twisted, suspicions aroused by a lawyer who was obviously much more experienced at manipulation than my own. I was totally taken aback by the witnesses that he found to come forward. I felt a rush of relief as I saw what I thought was a friend and neighbor take the stand.

"Please state your name to the court," the prosecutor instructed.

"Ken Norton."

"Tell the court how you know Mr. Mulgrave," the prosecutor asked.

"I run a book store in town and Billy Mulgrave occasionally dropped into the store."

"Please tell the court about his visit on September 23rd, 1955."

"Well he came in looking at books on tractor repairs. We talked for a while. He started asking me questions about the Dickson family."

"What kind of questions?"

"He wanted to know about Mr. and Mrs. Dickson. Said he was concerned about Nell, their daughter."

"Concerned about what?"

"He said that she deserved a better home than what they were offering her."

"Did it appear to you that he was overly involved with Natalie?"

"Yes, it was obvious that he was very fond of her. Never did buy that book on tractor repair."

"Thank you, Mr. Norton. No further questions, Your Honor."

Nell never came to court. Mr. Cullen said that sometimes, if it's too traumatic for a minor to testify, the court would not force them. This only made me appear more guilty. Instead her parents and brother testified on her behalf, which nailed the coffin on my case.

"We were quite concerned about the amount of time Nell spent on that farm," Mrs. Dickson testified. "I didn't think it was natural for my daughter to be with a man old enough to be her father all day long. Especially a man whose wife was no longer able to, you know…"

"Did you ever ask Nell about her feelings for Mr. Mulgrave?" the prosecutor asked.

"Yes. She said she liked him a lot. She said she trusted him. I tried to warn her about men, but she didn't listen. Now look at her." She started to sob.

My stomach churned as I watched the fake tears flow. She was a despicable mother and was putting on a performance for the court. She pretended to compose herself and continued.

"She was such a bright student at school and her whole future is wiped away now. She's having this baby out of wedlock and we have no means to support her and a baby." She looked at me with disdain. "And it's all because of you!" She spat her words out at me.

"How does your husband feel about what happened?" he asked.

"He's dead. All because of this. It was just too much for him to bear."

I felt like jumping out of my seat and choking her. *Show no emotion,* I kept repeating to myself. Mr. Cullen sensed my tension and rested his hand carefully on my arm.

Things got even worse for me when the brother took the stand. Out-and-out lies flew from his mouth.

"Yes, I saw her in his barn late in the days. Just the two of them in there. When she'd come home with her clothes on backwards, I was concerned and started watching them more closely. It was a regular occurrence. One time I banged on the barn door and demanded to come in. I was her brother after all and it was my responsibility to protect her. When I got the door open, Nell was lying on the ground, her shirt was ripped open, and Mr. Mulgrave was nowhere around, coward that he was. I said I'd come back with a baseball bat and kill him. Instead of taking the law into my own hands and getting myself into trouble for it, I decided to tell my parents. That's when they contacted the police."

He had taken what he had done to her and twisted it around to make me the guilty party. What I had to say came off sounding like a copycat story. I knew I was losing the jury.

The jury deliberated and I was returned to the courtroom a few days later. I stood before the magistrate for the final time.

"How do you find the defendant?" he asked the jury.

"Guilty as charged."

I saw black dots in front of eyes and felt faint. I thought I was going to empty my stomach.

"Mr. Mulgrave, please stand."

I struggled to my feet. My attorney stood meekly beside me, holding me steady. The courtroom spun as I tried to grasp this incomprehensible moment that would change the course of my life.

"You have been convicted of a most despicable crime. You took advantage of a minor who had put her trust in you and exploited her for your own benefit. The damage you have caused the defendant and her family is irreparable. You will be sentenced to twenty years in prison. You will not be eligible for parole before you have served a minimum of ten years in a state penitentiary, including time served. Your sentence will begin immediately."

I wished they'd offered me a death sentence instead. I was led out of the courtroom, the door slamming shut behind me.

DORA *1958*

Starting Over

There Molly stood in the doorway. My darling little girl. How I had agonized about meeting her again, my confidence as a mother shrouded.

"Oh my, you've grown so thin," were the first words I muttered. How long had it been since she had visited me in the hospital? I'd lost track. Had I really even seen her when she was there? Now the soft baby fat that I remembered had disappeared and before me stood someone taller, more confident ... or was it distant and unfamiliar?

"Come and give your mother a hug." I held out my arms to her. I had dreamed of the day I could hold her again, my baby girl, and here she was.

She held back shyly, rocking herself from side to side. Edna coaxed her forward. I knelt down and wrapped my arms around her frail little body and held on. She remained rigid.

"I know she's thin, but it's not that we've been starving her," Edna said. "I just can't get her to finish her meals. She says she's not hungry. What am I to do? Maybe she's copying her cousin Elizabeth, who eats like a sparrow so that she can be a feather puff ballerina."

The commotion in the house was distracting. With Edna's four children and their friends running around, we had to shout above the noise. I had grown used to the large empty hallways with acoustic walls at Collin's home. Edna didn't seem to notice, as she flopped back on her couch, her legs splayed under her mid-calf skirt. She wiped her brow with her apron intermittently or fanned herself with her hand.

"I keep asking Jake to get us a fan in here. The air sits on me like an overheated oven sometimes."

Molly had moved away from me and sat down close to Edna on the couch, watching me suspiciously. It broke my heart that she saw me as a stranger. Her own mother.

"Molly, sweetheart," I said. "I've missed you so." The truth was that I had not been able to think of her at all until recently—until I felt I was on my feet again. With my new home and a husband who could take care of us, I longed to fill the emptiness in my life. Collin worked long hours, leaving me to think about her endlessly. Although I still felt some trepidation, I so wanted to make up for the mother I had not been able to be for her.

Molly kept looking at me, expressionless.

"You know that mommy was very sick and I'm so grateful that Aunt Edna and Uncle Jake took such good care of you. I'm feeling much better now. I have a new home that I'm living in and am able to take care of you. I'd like you to come live with me. We can be together again. Isn't that exciting?" I was trying to muster up some enthusiasm. There was still no response, so I continued. "It's a really nice house, with a swimming pool. You'd have your own room." I felt like I was bribing her, which was not my intent. I was hoping that being with her mother would be enough, but that was naive of me. She was used to another life now. "I know this is difficult after not seeing me for so long, but I really want to try to be your mother again. If you'll give me that chance?"

Molly looked up at Edna, as if she were looking for some approval from her. Edna winked at her and rubbed the back of her neck affectionately.

"Just think, no more sharing a room with Sally. We'd miss you honey, but you need to be with your mother. You can come and visit us any time you like."

Molly looked far too sad, and it broke my heart. I should have realized that I'd be like a stranger to her now. She'd grown used to this new family. Why would she want to come with me?

"Why don't we just start with a little visit, okay? I know this is all so fast. We need to get reacquainted. How about, the first time, you come with Aunt Edna for dinner? There is someone very special I want you to meet."

Molly looked visibly relieved.

"How is next Saturday night for you and Jake?" I couldn't fathom inviting all the kids to come as well. I was better but didn't want any setbacks with overdoing things. Besides I wanted to concentrate on my time with Molly and introduce her to Collin.

I wondered how Edna would feel about meeting Collin, given that I had divorced her brother. She had been quite distant when I first contacted her, but she agreed to try to make the transition for Molly as easy as possible. I was grateful for that.

"That sounds wonderful, doesn't it Molly?" Edna replied, while grasping Molly's chin, offering her reassurance.

Molly nodded tentatively. It was a start.

NELL *1956*

A New Life Begins

I was still sleeping in the same bunk-bed a week later, and the other girls had stopped taunting me but now just shunned me. That's when I found comfort in the gentle movements inside me. Somehow I didn't feel quite so alone. There was someone else there inside me, also trying to survive. Each and every day it became more restless to enter the world.

On my way to breakfast, the pain hit me. I crumpled to the floor, clutching my stomach. I thought I had lost control of my bladder when I saw a puddle of fluid surrounding me. I felt humiliated and looked around for a towel or rag to wipe it up. Before I could find one, the pain started again, only this time it was stronger. I cried out.

Soon the hallway was full of peering eyes. One of the kitchen staff dropped the casserole she was carrying and rushed to my side. I didn't know what was happening to me, but her touch was soothing.

"Breathe deep, honey." She rubbed my back. "It will help you manage the pain if you do."

I'd never heard of such a thing. Breathing is what we do all the time, so how would that help? More than the pain, I felt the fear. I didn't know what was happening to me and no one was telling me anything. This fear was intensified as I heard a siren approaching. My father's death flashed before me—the last time I'd heard a siren. Was I going to die too? Was my baby going to die? A wheelchair was rolled towards me. A man in a uniform grabbed my arm.

"Can you manage to get up?" he asked, as he tried to pull me to my feet. "We got to get you to the hospital quickly here."

I did as I was told and he wheeled me towards the open door and out to the ambulance. He strapped me into the back and put a mask over my face.

"Take deep breaths," he commanded. *Again? What's with all the breathing?* With the mask over my mouth, I couldn't ask any questions.

"I just hope you can hold off on this baby until we get to the hospital. I hate getting blood on my hands if I don't have to," he added.

He didn't make me feel very secure.

I gazed out the back window as we drove off and saw the group of girls and staff standing there like a picture, their indifferent faces staring at me while they became smaller and smaller.

I can't remember the rest until I woke up under a starched white sheet in a bed with railings. I stared up at a stark light in the ceiling. I felt no pain. I ran my hands down to my belly and it was gone. *They've stolen my second heart,* I thought. I was all alone now. I screamed and screamed until a nurse appeared at the door.

I screamed, "Where's my baby?"

"Calm down young lady. Your baby is fine. The doctor is just checking him over and the social worker is on her way to talk to you.

Did she say he? It's a boy?

"I want to see my baby!" I cried.

"It's best that you don't, deary," she said, in her condescending tone.

What does she mean by that? Aren't babies supposed to be with their mothers when they're born?

"You're stealing my baby, aren't you?" I screamed, trying to get out of bed. It was no use, I was too weak. Just then the woman from the social welfare office hustled in.

"We need to talk about the baby," she said, and sat down beside me.

BILLY *1957*

Hope Fades

I was delivered to a different prison some distance away from my hometown. There had been a shortage of solitary cells and they didn't dare try to reintegrate me after word had gotten out that I'd raped a young girl. Although living amongst criminals was not my choice of company, being alone with my thoughts all the time was torturous. This was the beginning of my isolation from everybody I had ever known. Edna had come to check on me from time to time, kept me updated on Molly, but after my relocation I'd lost complete touch with the outside world. I wondered if anyone even bothered to learn where I had disappeared to. I would run my hands over my body sometimes to convince myself that I did exist. My sense of invisibility deepened.

At first I had held onto that illusive hope that somehow, miraculously, I would be cleared ... that someone would come forward and undo this terrible wrong. I pleaded with Mr. Cullen to do whatever it took to get an appeal. I sold my farm so that I could pay his fees. I needed to keep fighting, to do whatever it took to clear my name and return to my little girl.

"I managed to talk to Natalie," he claimed on a subsequent visit. "She is fully denying that this ever happened. She has written an affidavit to that effect. She is no longer living with her family and is speaking out. I will present this to the judge."

It was my only hope. They had to listen to the complainant herself. In the meantime, I tried to learn about prison survival in my new location. I learned the lingo and how to appear tough and fearless even when I was crumbling inside. I learned to keep my nose clean and to stay out of trouble. I was smarter than most of them and I used those smarts in my favor. I watched the dynamics between prisoners carefully before I picked sides. I knew which side would most likely have my back. I learned how to entice others to trust me, to feel they had something to gain through their connection with me. I may not have had the brute strength many of them had, but I had a charisma that put them at ease. They knew I was no threat and so I was often considered inconsequential and overlooked, which was the way I wanted to be. I stayed on the sidelines and observed. I never antagonized the guards, and after a while, they looked out for me. I made these no-mind apes feel important, even though I despised them. In other words, I learned to play the game of survival in a jungle of men who were wild with anger.

Mr. Cullen returned some time later to deliver news. "I'm sorry, but no luck. The judge questions the validity of Natalie's statement ... said that her motive to retract the accusation could not be established without another trial. She could be trying to get even with her parents. There were rumors of a falling out in the family. Nevertheless, the chances of getting another trial are slim."

I was crushed.

"What we could try," he continued "is to collect evidence that the brother was not a reliable witness and perjured himself. We could try to discredit him. He has a history of being an unsavory sort."

I knew he was grasping at straws, but I wasn't going to let any chance of clearing this up slip by. I watched the last of my funds disappear into his big black suitcase and waited patiently for his return.

I had been given laundry duty as my job in the prison. I looked forward to it. I needed to keep busy and productive. After some time of showing them I was a model worker, I convinced the warden to allow me to utilize the farming skills that I had. I craved the outdoors, even in the dead of winter. At first it involved digging ditches, which was back-breaking labor. However, I didn't mind. I felt the anger drain out of every pore when I had physically exhausted myself. I felt calmer inside. My nightmares subsided. They must have been impressed with my work ethic, because I progressed onto garden chores that took more skill and less hard labor. I built walls; I landscaped pathways and planted trees. In the winters, I shoveled snow and identified and insulated the more delicate shrubbery. I was put in charge of others who also preferred outdoor work. They called me the farmer and that got some respect, even from the more hardened criminals. Who could hate someone who dedicated himself to something as benign as digging in the earth?

After a long absence, Mr. Cullen returned for one last visit.

"Sorry," he started, shaking his head.

My heart sank.

"I've tried, but I'm running into dead ends. Mr. Dickson is dead. The missus won't talk. Even Natalie has disappeared. My only lead was the brother, who is now in a minimum-security prison for some petty crime. I tried to reason with him, told him he has nothing to lose if he comes clean. He refused."

"But what about proving he's someone who lies through his teeth? That he is not to be believed?" I asked in desperation.

"I tried going to the judge with evidence of his character, of his criminal record. The judge said that unless he revokes his statement, the record stands. Just because he's in prison now, doesn't prove deception, or what kind of character he *was*. He could have become hardened after the fact. It doesn't prove his character at the time of his appearance at the trial. Sure I have witnesses that say he couldn't keep a job and drank too much, was dumb in school. But whether he lied? That would be difficult to prove. I'm hitting a brick wall here."

Mr. Cullen sheepishly buckled his suitcase to leave. He knew I had no more funds to pay him.

I wasn't surprised by the news. I knew we were desperately trying to find something. My hope of exoneration was evaporating. I had only one final strategy left. That was to be on my best behavior as a prisoner so that I was out on parole by the ten-year mark. There were eight long ones still to go, but what other choice did I have? The only thing that would keep me going was knowing that, at least then, I would see my Molly again.

DORA *1958*

The Uneaten Cake

I spent the morning baking a chocolate cake and decorating it with Smarties. I wrote "Welcome Home Molly" with them. I had asked the cleaner to work extra hours to make sure the house was spotless. She even polished all my silverware. Collin wasn't on call this weekend, so I was relieved that there would not be any interruptions. I set a table in the garden with pink napkins and colored tumblers as Collin prepared the BBQ. The skies were cloudless, the breeze gentle, and the gardens were perfectly manicured. I rechecked the pool temperature to make sure it was nice and warm in case Molly wanted to go for a swim. I don't know why I felt so nervous. This was my daughter coming over for heaven's sake, not some stranger. I cut a few pink and white daisies from the garden and placed them as a center piece on the table. I stood back to gaze at it all. From what I remembered, pink was Molly's favorite color. *Perfect,* I thought.

Collin came up from behind and wrapped his arms around me.

"You are such a good hostess." He kissed the side of my neck. "And such a pretty one too."

"Do you think she'll like it here?" I asked, needing his reassurance that it was as perfect as I thought.

"Don't worry about a thing. Molly will absolutely love it here."

I knew he had to be right. What child wouldn't love this garden? Collin had even had the gardener hang a swing from the large oak tree in the back corner of the lawn. I had bought stuffed bears, a monkey, and giraffe and placed them together on her new bed. I had a princess canopy hung from the ceiling. Every detail had been attended to. I was so excited to finally have my daughter back with me. It would make this house more of a home, and create a family once again. All this space was feeling lonely for me, especially with the long hours that Collin was away at work.

The doorbell rang. I quickly, removed my apron and threw it on the kitchen counter. I then scooped it back up and stuffed it under the sink. I glanced in the mirror in the hallway and patted down my hair and checked that my lipstick hadn't smudged. The doorbell rang again and Collin joined me at the door. I tried to contain my excitement.

"Well hello there, Edna. Good to see you Jake," I said in greeting. "I'd like you to meet Collin, my husband."

They stepped inside and shook hands. I realized how awkward it might have been for them to hear those words. The divorce between Billy and I had gone through without difficulty, given that he was going to remain incarcerated for a long time. Even though I was sure they had feelings about it, I was grateful that they were making an effort at reuniting me with Molly. There was obviously some discomfort as they stood there in silence. Edna looked away.

The contrast between us was stark. Edna had on her frumpy brown dress and her large bonnet, dotted with flowers. Jake wore a jacket with sleeves too short and patches on the elbows. He wore a red bow tie and suspenders that pulled his pants almost to his chest. Meanwhile Collin was dressed handsomely in his crisp white shirt, with sleeves rolled up to his elbows, and his neatly pressed suit pants. His watch glistened on his wrist as they shook hands.

"C'mon in, make yourself at home." I gestured towards the living room.

In between them stood Molly. She also wore a bonnet that was neatly tied under her chin. Her dress looked like something that Edna had sown for her, perhaps from some old discarded curtains. She had on white knee socks with white, patent leather shoes that she was obviously proud of, judging by the way she placed her feet forward, leaning back against Edna. In her hand was a delicate bouquet of buttercups, which she handed to me.

"Why thank you Molly, these are lovely," I raised them to my nose. "And they smell so fresh. Let's get them into some water right away." I noticed they were becoming wilt.

I put my hand behind her shoulder and led her into the kitchen, while Collin took Jake's coat and hung it in the closet. Molly looked around the kitchen. Her eyes grew wide as she spun herself around and caught sight of the pool through the glass doors.

"Would you like to go for a little swim before we have our dinner?" I asked. She nodded excitedly.

"Well I've bought you the cutest little bathing suit to wear. I expected you might need it. Let's go upstairs and I'll show you your room."

Molly followed me up the winding staircase. I realized that she had still not spoken a word to me.

"Have you ever been in a big house like this before?" I asked.

She shook her head.

"Well it's a lot fancier than that old farmhouse that we used to all live in before."

Suddenly she stopped, halfway up the stairs. Her expression turned from wonder to something else. She looked down. I was kicking myself for having mentioned anything from our past. It was a bad memory for all of us, I was sure. I tried to quickly change the subject.

"Wait until you see who is waiting for you in your room. I opened the door. She hesitated.

"Come, come," I coaxed. "These are your roommates." I held up one of the bears on the bed. "And look in here," I opened the door to her closet. "Look at all these pretty new dresses and this shelf is full of games and puzzles and—"

Molly turned suddenly and ran down the stairs.

"Molly stop!" I called, but she wouldn't turn around.

I felt devastated. What had gone wrong? I followed after her, calling for her, and found her squeezed up against Edna on the living room sofa with her face buried in Edna's arm. She wouldn't look at me. Collin rolled his eyes.

"What's this all about now," Edna cooed, as she stroked Molly's hair. She dug her face farther into Edna. I knew that it was time for me to back away.

We made it awkwardly through the meal. Collin tried a couple times to engage Molly in conversation with his questions about school and sports. But she never let go of Edna and refused to answer. Edna said that she was just a bit shy. She hardly ate her food, even the chocolate cake. She never did go for her swim.

We'll try again another time," Edna tried to reassure me on their way out. I bent down to say goodbye to Molly. She looked at me from the corner of her eye as if I were not to be trusted.

"Molly, I hope you come back again real soon. That pretty new bathing suit will be waiting for you."

I stroked her arm as she coiled away from me. I shut the door quickly before I burst into tears.

NELL *1956*

Something Perfect

Why I suddenly wanted my baby so badly at that point, I'll never know. Up until then, all I could think of was getting it out of me and away from me so that I could return to normal. Did I even know what normal was anymore? Had my life ever been normal? What would I return to? I didn't want any connection to my brother and wasn't this baby his as well? Yet when I woke up, and it no longer was a part of me, it felt like my heart had been ripped out of me. Every cell in my body craved having him next to me. My breasts ached as they swelled up with milk, and my womb reminded me of the loss as it painfully constricted. I cried inconsolably as the social worker tried to calmly talk to me.

"You are only sixteen years old. Think of what's best for this child. You have no family, no way of looking after it. I think it best that you not see the baby and that we have it adopted immediately by one of many qualified couples who have eagerly been waiting a child of their own."

Her detached manner made me even more fearful. She had no idea how I felt.

"You have no right; he's mine!" I cried. "I want him back! I want to see him!"

"Now be reasonable. What good could come of you seeing him? It will only make it much more difficult—"

"He's my baby! I want to see him!"

When she realized she wasn't getting anywhere, she got up and straightened the white gloves that seemed to protect her hands from the people she worked with.

"Very well, if you insist. I'm only thinking of your own good, but if you won't listen to reason, I guess I have no choice." With that, she left the room.

While I waited for my baby, my breasts started to dribble out a white sticky substance. My body ached more with every minute I had to wait.

Finally she arrived with a light blue bundle and placed it in my arms. I looked at the tiny wonder that had lain next to my heart these past months. I had been warned that a baby created through incest may not come out normal. But he was absolutely perfect in every way. His tiny fingers grabbed tightly to my baby finger as if its life depended on it. I caressed his soft forehead and he made a cooing sound.

"I'll protect you little one," I whispered. "I promise."

I exposed my breast to him and his tiny mouth found the nurturance that my body offered. I'd never felt so at peace as I did in that moment. His tiny heart beat next to mine again. Here was something I had done right. I'd produced this lovely little boy and it was now my job to look after him. I would do whatever it took to make his life better than mine. I knew that no one else could love him more than me.

The social welfare lady looked on with resignation.

"We'll see what we can do to find you proper housing. You are going to need somewhere to live with a baby. It's not going to be easy you realize."

I looked up at her as the baby suckled.

"Easy has never been part of my life," I said.

I had found my reason to carry on. My purpose. I'd call him Nathan—a male version of Natalie, my name at birth. It felt like I was claiming back a piece of my original identity and letting go of my battered one. I gazed lovingly at what I had created. Nathan had saved me.

BILLY *1958*

The Unwelcome Visitor

Life in prison had become a mindless routine. I went through the motions. There was no other choice. The sadness hit me at night, when I curled up in my cell and thought about Molly. I took the one picture I'd managed to keep with me all these years out of my pocket and kissed it goodnight.

"Sleep tight my darling," I whispered.

I wondered what she looked like now. She would be eight years old and the last time I saw her she was five. I wondered if that thin hair of hers had thickened with age. Was it still the color of sunshine? I wondered if she'd lost her baby fat … whether she had her new front teeth. How tall she might be now? I wondered if she was still with Edna. Since they moved me from my hometown prison, there were no more visits. There were a couple of letters. Molly would send me a picture, usually of something happy like a flower or bird. There used to be pictures of us as a family, but she'd stopped drawing those. When she was able to write, at the end of Edna's letters Molly would add a heart and say that she loved me in big bold letters. I cried like a baby as I looked at them over and over.

Then the letters stopped completely and I didn't know why. It was as if she had vanished. I hoped with all my heart that she hadn't given up hope. Hope was all that kept me going, and without that I knew I would be dead inside. In the last few letters I'd exchanged with Molly, I asked her how Mommy was. She would say "fine" or "okay" and nothing more. Was that what Edna instructed her to do? I wondered why no one was telling me what had happened to her. Then I got the letter from her lawyer, demanding a divorce. She had deserted me. As painful as it was, how could I deny her?

Then came a glimmer of hope: I had a visitor. Finally! Could it be Molly? I braced myself as I walked into the waiting room. There stood a young lady. I didn't recognize her at first. She stood there fidgeting, running her hands up and down her arms as if she were cold, and shifting her weight from foot to foot. She was tall. Her hair was pulled back into a ponytail. She offered me a faint smile, even though her eyes looked sad. I looked around the room to see if there was anyone else but there wasn't.

She extended her hand to greet me.

"Hello Billy."

I recognized the voice. It took me a moment to place it. My past came rushing back to me. It was the voice of someone I had once cared for but had buried. Someone whom I felt nothing but cold hatred towards now. How dare she be here after what she had done to me? To my family?

"Guard!" I yelled, as I froze on the spot.

The guard turned towards me quizzically.

"Take me back to my cell, now!"

He looked at her as if he was wondering what he should do.

Now!" I repeated and started for the door. I banged on it as if that would make it open.

"Hold on, hold on!" he shouted. "I'll open it."

"Wait!" I heard Nell call. "Please Billy! I need to talk to you!"

I put my hands over my ears. I didn't want to hear her voice or anything she had to say to me. I kept my ears blocked until I heard the door slam shut behind me.

DORA *1958*

My Worst Fear

"That was utter nonsense," Collin said later that evening. "Look at all you did for her and there wasn't an ounce of gratitude."

As sad as I felt that Molly had rejected me, I felt I needed to defend her.

"She's a sensitive child, always has been. I guess like her mother," I said, looking up at him demurely. "We've got to give her time to adjust. She's not used to us and this house. She's used to Edna's family, which is so different."

"Well Edna's family isn't an option for her. We've imposed on them long enough. This is now her home and that's that. What child wouldn't be grateful for all of this? We will pick her up from Edna's next weekend with all her things and that will be the end of it."

I knew when Collin had made up his mind there was no point arguing with him. I was also aware that he didn't have the patience that I had nor the compassion I felt. Fatherhood for him was a duty he would perform and a child's respect was what he would expect in return. I had a bad feeling in my stomach but tried to ignore it.

"You know what Molly needs?" he asked in a gentler, more compromising tone. "And what *we* need?"

I was hesitant to ask. I looked up at him inquisitively.

"She needs a little brother or sister. It's not too late for that. We need a real family."

I suddenly froze. I could feel my palms perspire and my heart beat faster in my chest. Was he crazy? Did he know what he was saying?

Having Molly was what had made me so ill. I had just finally recovered. How could he suggest such a thing?

He must have read my mind.

"I know what you're thinking. It won't be that way again, Dora. Trust me. I'm your husband, but I am also a doctor. I will watch you carefully and know what to do as soon as there is any sign."

I still sat there unable to speak. My tongue was so dry it stuck to the roof of my mouth. Collin got up from across the room and came to sit beside me.

"It would be the best for all of us. A child that's ours and a sibling for Molly." He reached over to kiss me. My mouth couldn't respond.

"I think we should get started tonight." He ran his hand from my cheek down my neck to the top button of my blouse. How could I deny him? He was my husband now. He deserved to have his own child. Would he stay with me if I were to deny him? I couldn't take that risk. Perhaps it was naive of me to think that Molly would have been enough for him. A second-hand child. I closed my eyes trying to block out the flood of thoughts and fears and let him carry me off to the bedroom.

NELL *1958*

Never Giving Up

I did whatever it took to keep Nathan. Whenever I faltered, they threatened to remove him and I fought to keep holding onto him. I worked at any job I could find. I cleaned toilets during the days and worked as a waitress at the Five and Dime at night. I hated having babysitters and public daycares watch Nathan while I was gone. At the end of the day, my life's purpose was to return home to him. I thrived on watching him grow, from his curious exploration of the world around him to forming his first words. I was there every step of the way. Perhaps he provided a focus for me so I could avoid dealing with the rest of my life. I didn't have friends and I didn't have any interest in dating. I couldn't risk being vulnerable to anyone. I had only one purpose and everything else was superfluous.

The one thing that tore away at my insides was what I had done to Billy. My conscience was ridden with guilt as I thought of how kind he had been to me and how that kindness had caused such an injustice to him. I knew I had to set things right. I did what I could to locate the lawyer who had defended Billy during his trial. I wrote to him.

"Mr. Mulgrave is innocent," I declared. "A huge injustice has been committed and I want to set the record straight."

The lawyer took his time but eventually responded. "I've taken your declarations to the courts for review."

Again I waited and waited. Finally a letter arrived.

"Sorry to inform you that a retrial has not been granted." No further explanation was offered. I wanted to scream. How could they not listen to my plea? I felt like that helpless child I'd once been, years ago, never having a voice. All through the trial people had spoken for me. I was forced not to contradict my parents under fear and duress. Well, all that was different now. I had my own voice, but it was too late. The damage was done.

"Could you please inform me where Mr. Mulgrave is incarcerated," I inquired in my next correspondence. "I would like to visit him."

"I would strongly advise against that, for your own sake," he advised. "Nothing good could be accomplished by contacting Mr. Mulgrave. I am sure you can understand that there is much justifiable bitterness."

I insisted. "I need to know where he is. I can handle anything I have coming to me and I deserve every bit of it. I just need to see him to apologize, and more than that, to explain. I beg you to at least allow me that. Please."

I couldn't live with myself if I didn't try to set things right. If I couldn't get him out of prison, I could at least try to make it up to him in any way that I could.

"Very well, Miss Dickson. You can't say I didn't warn you, but if you insist."

I called my work and asked for a couple days off without pay. I took what money I had saved and bought a train ticket.

He refused to speak with me the first visit, and the next. I refused to give up. How could I give up on someone whose life I had destroyed? I often thought of his precious daughter Molly and wondered what had happened to her. Her mother wasn't the most stable person for her to rely on. I couldn't imagine how Billy must be feeling, being away from his daughter. I couldn't imagine being apart from Nathan. My heart ached for them. I would have traded places with him if I could. Anything to correct the injustice. With every attempt I made, I was stone-walled. The message I got over and over again was that it was too late. He wanted me out of his life. Maybe it was too late to change what had happened, but it was never too late to reach out to him and try to do what I could to help him endure the wrong. I knew that his anger towards me was justified, but I wasn't going to give up. I would keep persisting until I could break through. I wasn't even sure what I could offer him, but I knew that if I just gave up, I couldn't live with myself.

BILLY *1959*

Sorry Is Not Enough

I thought I had made it perfectly clear that I didn't want anything further to do with Nell, but she remained relentless in her efforts to see me. She sent me letters almost daily. I ripped them up without opening them. When they wouldn't stop coming, I started returning them with a note scribbled on the front stating 'do not send!' She ignored my command and continued to send more, with a plea to open them. Finally my curiosity or my boredom got the better of me. What could she possibly have to say to me at this point? Did she not know how much damage she'd caused? I read how sorry she was. Did she honestly think that saying sorry could undo the damage? The lies? I crumpled up the letter and threw it against the wall. I stared at it on the floor for days before I uncrumpled it to read more. She explained that she had refused to accuse me of that terrible crime but her parents had forced her. Their only goal was to protect her brother, as they had always done. They threatened to throw her in the streets if she didn't keep her mouth shut. Eventually she couldn't stand it anymore and had left them behind, even though she was penniless and pregnant. The hatred she felt for what they had done had made it impossible for her to stay. She said that she was determined to somehow make things right. "Too late for that Nell!" I said out loud, laughing bitterly.

The letters kept coming, and now that I'd started, I continued opening them. She explained how she'd had the baby, and despite the urging of social workers, she was determined to keep it. Despite the fact that it was a child of someone she despised, she felt for its innocence. It was not to blame for being born. It deserved to be loved. She explained that, against all odds, she had managed to keep him and how glad she was for that decision. He was the sunshine of her life. Again I cursed her and shredded the letter into a million pieces. I didn't care if she was happy. She didn't deserve to be happy with a child while I sat here rotting away, having lost Molly. She could burn in hell for all I cared. I started sending the letters back again. Then packages started arriving. She sent me home-baked cookies. She sent me magazines, newspapers, books... I took them willingly as it was my only tie to the outside world. I had missed that connection for so long and it made me aware once again of the world beyond these prison walls. Suddenly I was in touch with what was going on again. I read voraciously to kill the monotony of my existence. On the cover of every package was written, "Please forgive me." I never would.

Then came a note.

"I will help you find Molly."

That got my attention. Everything else I didn't care about, but if there was any hope that what she was saying was true, I couldn't ignore it. For the first time, I wrote her back. One word: "How?"

She pleaded to see me, so she could explain. I didn't see the point of seeing her in person, but I relented. There was something about Nell's persistence that rang true. It was the Nell I used to know, full of tenacity and determination. When she put her mind to something, she wouldn't give up. For now it was to see me again, for some reason. She had found the means to do so.

I wrote back, "Okay."

She was in the visitors' room the next day. I wondered what I had done? How could I have agreed to meet with the devil herself? How could I ever put any faith in a person who had let this happen to me? I also realized that I had nothing to lose at this point. She sat at the table, her hair pulled back, her eyes fixed on me as I walked in. She didn't look like the same person. The Nell I had known was shy, demure, and hidden from the world. This woman looked strong. Determined. She made no sudden moves towards me, for which I was grateful as I probably would have turned around if she had. For what seemed like forever, we sat in silence, although I was conscious of her searching eyes. She was waiting for me to allow her to speak.

"What do you want Nell?" I asked dismissively.

"I know that forgiveness is too much to ask," she said. "I have ruined your life and even though I felt helpless to do anything at the time, I am stronger now. I want to somehow make it up to you."

I looked at her incredulously.

"I don't think you should waste your time." I got up to leave.

"Please listen to me," she pleaded. "There is not a day that goes by that I don't think of you and wish I could somehow undo everything that has happened. I can only imagine what you have been through, but I have also been tormented by this. If I could, I would trade places with you in a second." She paused and wiped the tears that were welling up in her eyes.

"I have tried. I have put aside every spare penny that I've made so that I could hire a lawyer to help me make this right. I have pleaded with the courts to listen. I have written endless letters and I will not stop until I see you walk out of this place."

I was not going to give her any recognition or sympathy here. She did not deserve it.

"Don't waste your time or your money. It won't work. I have spent every penny I had and it got me nowhere. I've lost everything. *Everything!* My home. My family." I was emphatic, my anger brewing. "It's all in the past now. I've accepted that it's not going to change. I have no other choice. I'm doing my time and counting the days until I'm free again."

"Let me help. Tell me anything you need and I will do whatever I can to get it for you," she pleaded. "I will do anything to try to make this time easier for you."

I felt sickened at the thought of giving her the satisfaction of helping me. She didn't deserve anything from me to ease her guilt. The only reason I had agreed to see her was because of her comment about Molly.

"You said you can help me find Molly. That's all I care about. Or was that just another lie?"

"No. I will do whatever I possibly can to find Molly for you. I am following every lead. I already know a few things."

She finally had my attention.

"Such as?"

A noise erupted in the hall, and she paused and leaned back in her chair. It was a scuffle between a guard and some other prisoner. We tried to ignore it. It was always hard for them to say goodbye after a visit and (at times) they needed to be dragged away. When the screaming subsided, she continued.

"I was able to track down the family she was living with. I know that she is no longer with them. They told me that she is back with her mother. That's all that they would tell me."

She wasn't telling me much about my sister and her family. I knew that part anyway. I had been wondering why they stopped bringing her in. I figured they just lived too far away now that I had been moved. I didn't realize she was back with Dora. I shook my head in disbelief.

"You mean Dora has Molly and she hasn't made contact with me? She knows how much Molly means to me. She may despise me, but why would she deny me contact with my own daughter?"

"I don't know Billy. I'm trying to find that out. I want to help you find her, because I do understand what she meant to you. I was there, remember? I saw everything. I also have a child now, and I can't imagine what it would be like if I lost him."

I had to have some hope ... something to hold onto in here. I knew I'd be a fool to send her away without letting her try to locate my daughter.

DORA *1959*

Stuck in the Middle

Molly did come to live with Collin and I, albeit reluctantly. All the pretty new dresses, trips to the soda shop, and stuffed toys couldn't pull her out of her morose mood. She spent more time talking to her damn dog than she did to me. I don't know why she was punishing me when I was trying so hard to make up for lost time, but she seemed intent on doing so. With Collin it was even worse. She merely tolerated his existence. His patience with her was waning.

"Give her time to adjust," I requested after another evening of silence at the dinner table.

"Oh for heaven's sake. Children adapt easily to new situations. She's just being spiteful and it doesn't help making excuses for her. She is obviously lacking in manners. A please or thank you would not be too much to expect over dinner."

As difficult as it was for me with Molly, I didn't want to also deal with Collin's resentment.

"She's just not comfortable with you yet," I said. "I think that's why she's so quiet. Maybe it would help if you spent some time getting to know her a little. You know, try to play with her after dinner or take her to a baseball game or something."

"Dora please," Collin said, rolling his eyes. "I come home late most nights after an exhausting day seeing patients. I barely have time to eat, read the paper, check my mail, and get ready for bed. If she were around on the weekends, then that might be different."

"You know that Molly had a hard time leaving the Stone family, and Edna offering to have her back for visits on the weekends is what's gotten her through."

The only time I saw any excitement in Molly was when she was packing up for those weekend visits. I was envious to see her run into her aunt's arms the moment she arrived at the door.

"Well it's time for those visits to come to an end. We are her family whether she likes it or not. I know they meant well to take her while you were ill, but they are simple people, Dora. She is not learning refinement in that household and it's time to teach her some etiquette. Besides, soon the baby will arrive. Once she has her own little brother or sister, she probably won't want to leave."

I wrapped my arms around my belly protectively. Yes. The baby. It was due in only a month. Was I ready for this again? Collin seemed convinced that everything was going to be fine. He explained to me that I had a post-partum depression with Molly and how it was caused by my hormones changing after the birth. He explained how that had developed into what he called a depressive psychosis. As I understood it, I had become out of touch with reality and saw things in distorted ways. He said that now that I had been properly treated, the chances of that reoccurring would be unlikely. Besides he was by my side to make sure that I would be taken care of properly. Even though I remained apprehensive about how I would cope with a new baby, I trusted Collin. I knew I would be safe with him.

Maybe he was right about needing to curtail Molly's visits with her cousins. I was still holding on to hopes of creating more of a family with Molly and this new baby. How could the baby not create more of a bond for all of us? I was tired of being torn between keeping both Molly and Collin happy. This time I had to side with Collin. It was time for Molly to stop the weekend visits and get used to this as her home. She may not like it, but she would get used to it.

"I think you're right dear. I'll have a talk with her," I said, to his nod of approval.

NELL *1960*

The Audition

I had been drowning in my guilt, and in my exhaustion as a single mother, and I was discouraged with what looked like a road to nowhere. It was a fluke really when things suddenly turned around for me. I was reading the classifieds, looking for yet another job to help subsidize my salary. I wanted something better for Nathan than our hand-to-mouth existence. He was now ready to start school and he seemed so much further ahead of the other children his age. Maybe it was the time he spent alone while I was away. He couldn't seem to get enough of reading books. He also enjoyed building things. My only concern was that he took life far too seriously. Maybe that was something he had learned from me. There never seemed to be enough time to play and have fun. He was already starting to read and write, and drawing vivid, imaginative stories. I wanted to give him the opportunities to develop his abilities, but with my salary there was little I could provide for him other than a roof over his head and food in his stomach—and barely that.

What caught my eye was an ad for an audition:

"Talent scout in town looking for bright new talent. If you think you have what it takes, come down to Ambrose Stadium on Saturday for an audition."

Was I kidding myself? What did I know about acting? I flipped the page to ads for waitresses and started circling jobs. I started making calls. I stopped myself on the first number and put the phone down. I picked up the paper and flipped it back a page to the audition. I tore it out and tucked it into my purse.

I was discouraged when I arrived on Saturday to find that just about everyone in town had shown up to audition. I took my place in the long line up. I was sure that many of these people were real actors. I didn't belong here. But something in my gut coaxed me to stay. To at least try. I'm not sure if it was pure fantasy or a belief that I could actually do this. Not knowing what I'd be required to do and what I was up against was daunting.

After several hours of waiting and wondering and missing Nathan, I got inside the door. I was given a piece of paper to read and asked to be seated. There were several other hopefuls surrounding me, with sheets that they were avidly reading. They took down my name and said they'd call when it was my turn.

I read over the script as I waited. Obviously I was going to have to read it to them with whatever acting skills I could muster. I knew I didn't have any. But as I read it, there was something in there that I could identify with. It was a about a character who was struggling in a situation that she had no control over. It seemed very real to me.

"Natalie Dickson," someone called, "come in please."

I had decided that Natalie was a much more dignified and professional name than Nell.

I quickly collected the pages as I watched a disheartened contender leave the room before me. I walked in feeling shy. Before me sat two men and a lady behind a long table. They were busy scribbling notes and finally looked up wearily at me. I could imagine how many times they had gone through this today and I felt sorry for them. Now here I was wasting their time.

"Thank you for coming in, Natalie," the older man with the scraggly beard finally acknowledged. The younger man never looked up. The woman sat at the end, swiveling in her chair while twirling her hair. She looked familiar and I wondered if she was an actress. She didn't say anything.

"Let's see how you do," the older man said, without introducing himself or the others.

"Anytime you're ready, you can start." He took a long gulp from his coffee mug.

I closed my eyes to block them out. I somehow knew that was what I needed to do to get through this. I took several deep breaths and felt myself going inward. I was no longer aware of their presence. I remembered my first line and I started. I paused. Then like a blur I continued. At one point, I started to cry. I felt like I was the person in the narrative and I felt her pain. I spoke it. I cried it. I screamed it and I surrendered to it. When it was over, I felt a sense of exhaustion and peace. I had to orientate myself back to the room and the audience of judges before me. The older man was sitting upright staring at me. The younger man had finally looked up at me. The woman had stopped swiveling in her chair. There was what seemed like a long silence in the room.

"Wallace," the woman leaned forward to address the older man. "What did you think?"

Wallace didn't take his eyes off me. "I think I'm dumbfounded."

The younger man exchanged glances with the other two and nodded.

"Well, that's the best we've seen all day," he said. "Are you currently working as an actress?"

"No sir," I said. "It's just something I always wanted to try."

"Well, you were amazing," the woman said. "Just absolutely amazing. You almost had me in tears."

They all got up and came out from behind the desk to shake my hand and introduce themselves for the first time. I couldn't believe this was happening to me. I had actually done something right.

"We are definitely going to be giving you a call," Wallace said, after taking down my phone number.

"Thank you so much," I said, my shyness creeping in again.

"You were just great. We will have a contract ready for you to sign. How quickly would you be able to start with us," he asked.

I had to pinch myself. Was this happening for real or was this a dream?

"Anytime at all," I said, barely containing my excitement. "Thank you! Thank you so much."

"No, thank you for coming down," Wallace replied. "You've made my day."

As I left the audition, I was walking on air. I had no recollection of my performance itself. It was as if I had gone into a trance and was now waking up. I just knew that, whatever I did or wherever I had gone while I was performing, it was a place I wanted to be.

BILLY *1961*

Forgiveness

It took me a long time to warm up to Nell and trust her again. She never faltered once with her weekly visits. One time she left me a newspaper review of a show she performed in. It described her as someone to keep an eye out for. I studied the photographs of her on stage. She looked like she had truly found her calling. The drive and tenacity to make something of herself was evident. I'd known she had it in her even back in those summer days so long ago, when she was able to keep going despite the horrors she dealt with at home. I knew she was proud and that she was seeking my acknowledgment.

Sitting there looking at the review, I had a flashback of Nell. She had been just a child when I knew her. She needed protection back then and yet refused to ask for help. I'd tried my best to help her and failed. Maybe she was not the devil I had made her out to be. She was a victim herself. This happened to her as much as it happened to me. I saw that pleading expression on her face that day when she had run up my driveway looking for work. I didn't realize that behind it was her desperation to get away from her abusive family. The same pleading expression was on her face now, as she came by to drop off what she could in her attempt to make peace with me. She may not have been imprisoned by these four walls I was in, but she had been imprisoned by her family. She managed to break away from that and had worked hard to create a life for herself. She was now reaching out, trying to help me stay connected to something outside of here. I had needed to hate her, but realized that I no longer could.

"Congratulations," I said, holding the article in my hand the next time she came to visit. "You've done well for yourself."

Nell initially beamed at my approval, but then I could tell that she was recoiling back into her feelings of guilt. She was out there living her life while I was in here on hold.

"You don't need to say anything," I reassured her. "I know I've been bitter, and now I see that the bitterness has been eating me up inside. I have to let it go. Everyone let me down and I've been rolling around in self-pity. I'd given up on my faith in humanity and kindness and all that I once believed. I thought I hated you, but what I really hated was all the bad things that happened to you and what it did to us both. I realize that you're not to blame."

Tears started rolling down Nell's cheeks. "I'm so sorry—"

"Shush," I said, placing my finger against my lips. "No more apologies." I cracked a smile while holding up the article. "You've made something of yourself, Nell. Well done!"

She wiped away her tears and managed a smile in return. "Hey, there had to be a silver lining somewhere in all of this. My acting is my way of dealing with my pain. I can play some pretty desperate, deranged characters pretty well. My agent always sends me out for parts that require someone who can cry a lot."

We both chuckled. Something I couldn't remember doing for so long.

I leaned back in my seat, studying her. She was now a professional woman, a mother, and a caring friend to me, and yet she still had that vulnerability about her. Emotionally, she was still that lost waif I'd once known, seeking reassurance.

"I'm proud of you, Nell."

Her eyes glowed as if I'd just given her a precious gift.

She then dipped into her pocket and pulled out a photograph.

"Do you want to see what makes me proud?" she asked.

I nodded and shrugged simultaneously. She handed me the photo. It was a picture of her and a young boy. He was blowing out candles on a birthday cake. Nell stood behind him, her hands resting on his shoulders and a happy grin on her face. It took me back to the tender moments I had once shared with Molly. I felt a moment of sadness but pulled myself out of it. I handed the photo back to Nell.

"He's a handsome boy. He's very lucky to have you as his mother."

She looked as if a weight had been lifted. She let out a heavy sigh.

"He means the world to me. I'd like you to keep it," she said, looking unsure of how I would respond. "That is if you'd like to."

"I'd be honored," I said, and slipped it into my pocket.

We looked at one another for another minute in silence. There was so much to say and yet nothing at all.

"Now tell me your preference for the next book I bring you. Fiction, mystery ... Playboy?"

We both laughed and it felt so good. We remained smiling in silence until the guard came up behind me and motioned for me to go.

I thrived on Nell's visits. Through her, I felt I had a life outside these mundane walls. She kept me informed of all the mind-boggling developments that were happening so quickly in the world. Now the information was at my fingertips and I read what she brought me veraciously. She sometimes made me laugh, which was something I had forgotten how to do. I was feeling a full range of emotions again, instead of just anger. Those feelings made me feel human again. She brought me fresh-baked bread and fruit and vitamins to supplement the prison gruel. She brought me books to read and paper to write on. I wrote letters to the people I had once known but never mailed them. I sometimes wrote short stories, and even poems. It was amazing how creativity that I never knew I had would come out in my moments of solitude. There was a part of me coming alive that never would have emerged in my past life on the farm. She knitted me warm vests and socks to wear to bed at night. I started to trust again, to believe in kindness once more. She may not have found Molly for me, but I knew she did what she could, and somehow being connected to her was a connection to the world I knew Molly lived in.

DORA *1962*

Eavesdropping

Rex lay on the bedroom floor parallel to Molly. He was an addition to our family that I couldn't deny Molly, despite Collin's protestations.

"This house is no place for an old farm mutt. Just think of all that fur and smell."

I picked my fights with Collin carefully. This time I was not going to give in.

"Rex is the only consistency Molly has had in her life. She would be heartbroken without him. He used to be my dog as well at one time you know."

"Well then he stays in the yard only. A house is no place for a large dog."

When Molly took to sleeping in the dog house with him and crying inconsolably when we ordered her inside, Collin relented.

"Okay, okay. I don't want to deal with the theatrics night after night. Rex can sleep in Molly's room at night, but then back outside during the day."

We found that took Molly outside as well for most of the day, as she couldn't stand to hear him whining. When the weather changed and fall winds began to blow, he was allowed into the back mud room. Molly set up her toys in there and insisted on doing her homework on the dirty floor beside him in the evenings. Finally he was allowed into her room for the evenings.

Timmy was now three years old, and rambunctious as any little boy. He adored his older sister. He lay on the opposite side of Rex on Molly's bedroom floor, playing with his set of farm animals. He took to his older sister instantly, following her around like her shadow. I was relieved, as it gave me a break away from watching him in the evenings. Even though I was so much better, I still found that if I didn't get my rest, my mood would deteriorate. I'd often snap at the kids or dog and then feel bad after. I didn't want to go back into feeling guilty for something I had no control over.

The door to the bedroom was ajar so that I could hear their conversation while I folded towels in the bathroom next door. Timmy rhymed off his animals.

"This is a cow. This is a horse. This is a pig. This is a goat."

"What sounds do these animals make?" Molly asked.

Timmy made the sounds for her.

"Where do these animals live?" she asked.

"They live on a farm," he said.

"That's right."

"Molly, what is a farm?" he asked.

"Well," Molly hesitated and my ears perked up, "it's a place far away from a city. It has lots and lots of space to play in and for the animals to roam around in."

"Have you ever been to a farm?" he asked.

"Yes, I used to live on a farm once," she said.

"With Mommy and Daddy before I was born?"

"Not exactly," she said quietly.

"Did you like it on the farm?"

"Yes, Timmy. I loved it on the farm. There were so many fun places to play. I'd play hide and seek behind the haystacks. There were cats with kittens in the barn. Rex was there with me too, along with pigs, and chickens that lay warm eggs every morning. We would eat the eggs right away and they tasted much better than the eggs we eat now. I learned to milk a cow. It was so funny watching milk squirt from those udders into a bucket, sort of like shooting your water pistol. Oh and our apple tree! Those apples were so delicious that when I bit into them the juice would drip down my chin. Mommy would make us apple pies. Sometimes Daddy," she hesitated, "not your daddy but my real daddy, would take me down to the river for a swim. I would come home with a bucket full of tadpoles and try to take care of them, hoping they'd turn into frogs. It never happened though, so before all my tadpoles died, Daddy would make me take the bucket back to the river to set them free."

"I didn't know you had another daddy," Timmy said inquisitively.

My heart felt like it wanted to stop.

"Yes, I had the best daddy in the world. But he died."

"Why did he die?"

There was a pause.

"I don't know. He just did. Now what sound does a rooster make?"

Timmy imitated the sound with a loud crowing sound.

"Molly, who did you play with on the farm?"

"I played with Rex. I also had a friend named Nell, who was *so* much fun. She took care of me."

"Didn't Mommy take care of you?" Timmy asked.

Another long pause. I leaned in even though I wasn't sure I wanted to hear anymore.

"Not very much. She stayed in bed most of the time."

"Why?"

"You ask too many questions, Timmy. Now let's put all these farm animals away, shall we? Rex looks like he needs to go for a walk. We'll play again later, okay?"

"Molly, I want to go see a farm. It sounds like fun."

"Yeah, I want to go back someday too."

I shut the bathroom door so she wouldn't see me standing there. I stared into the mirror for a long time. Was I really so absent all those years that I didn't see any of the beauty that Molly recalled? What did I remember? A place that was far removed from people. Something that I preferred after a while. A man who was kind to me but I pushed away. A small child who used to tuck me in at night. A girl offering a helping hand that I resented. Was that really me? I turned the shower on and stripped off my clothes. I tried to wash the memory away.

NELL *1964*

Fulfilling a Dream

I had been acting for a while. Nothing really big but enough to pay the bills. I was starting to feel a void, like something in my life was missing. As much as I treasured the opportunity of working as an actress, it wasn't enough. There was a churning in my gut and I didn't know what it was. Until one day I woke up and realized.

The next time I went to the prison for a visit, I felt uplifted. Billy was a year away from his parole hearing. His freedom was finally within reach. He was looking more tired than ever. It was showing in his posture, the way he hung his head when he walked, and the way he slouched forward when he sat. His hair was starting to show gray at his temples. Time was moving along and he had wasted so much of it in here. What did remain was the gentleness in his eyes. Even after what he had been through, I could see his soul was pure. He sauntered in and sat in his regular spot across the table from me. The room echoed with voices, and guards milled around in the corners, waiting and watching. I passed him an article I had cut out of the paper. He picked it up and pulled his reading glasses out of his shirt pocket, unfolding them with one hand and slipping them on. I noticed that he squinted more now. He had a puzzled look on his face as he read.

"You're thinking of moving?" he asked.

"No, no," I exclaimed. "I wouldn't uproot Nathan. It's just a space I want to rent." I couldn't control my enthusiasm. "I've been giving this a lot of thought, Billy. I've developed a few skills along the way with my acting. I love acting, but what I really want to do is inspire others to do what I so much enjoy doing. I want to open an acting studio. I want to teach others."

Billy ran his hand across the top of his head several times. His hair grew ruffled with each stroke. He stopped and looked at me over his reading glasses.

"You realize there are costs involved to get this started. There's advertising, buying equipment, and decorating costs, just to name a few."

I knew Billy was being cautious. I didn't blame him for wondering if I was being impulsive or careless. But I was more determined about this than I'd ever felt about anything.

"I've given all of that thought. I've managed to save some money. I've set up ads at the local schools. I've already received some calls. I have an excellent acting resume. I have colleagues in the business who believe in me and that can help—"

"Why is this suddenly so important to you?" Billy interrupted.

I paused to think before I answered. I knew it seemed rather sudden and it must have seemed out of the blue to Billy, and yet I also realized that this had been brewing for some time. Just as I took enormous gratification in trying to make things better in Billy's life, by giving to him everything that was within my capacity to give, I knew that giving of myself—of what I believed in—was going to give me the greatest satisfaction in return.

"You know, when I was really young, long before you knew me, I dreamed of being a teacher. I had no idea what I was going to teach, but whenever anyone asked me what I wanted to be when I grew up, there was no hesitation with my answer. Now that flew out the window when all I could do was keep my head above water, first at home and then with Nathan, but now? Now that I can dream again, it's all coming back to me."

Billy observed me closely. I knew he was listening, taking it in, and mulling it over in his analytical way.

"What about your acting career? What will you tell your agent? She's invested a lot in your career."

As much as I didn't like having to think of the practical stuff when I was feeling so excited about this, I could understand Billy's concern.

"I know. I've thought about that. I'm not totally unrealistic about this. I know I have to continue acting, keeping to my contract. Over time, I hope to start winding down, and put most of my energy into developing the studio.

I know it's going to take some time before I can rely on it fully. At least I have a plan. This is the place I'm going to do it," I pointed to the picture in the ad. "I'm going to get started and I'm going to help other young girls try to live their dream. I will make them work for that dream the way that I did. I've gone down that path and I have something to give back now. I want to instill that inspiration in others. I know that I can."

Billy took off his glasses and put them carefully away. He leaned back in his chair, studying me.

"You are a very determined young lady. That I know for sure. If you put your mind to something, I have no doubt that you will make it happen. I wish you all the best with this. I mean that sincerely," he added.

I beamed. There was nothing that I wanted more than his blessing. I was sure that I was going to be able to help some young girl like myself someday. Even if I was only successful with one person, it would be worth my effort.

Fall 1965

MOLLY

Twigs

I gave Ringo a big kiss—the life-size poster of him on my bedroom wall that is.

"Why do you like him the best?" Vicki asked.

Why did I? He was not nearly as cute as Paul. His big nose and crooked smile made him look goofy. I guess I was just more attracted to the underdog. The one who others wouldn't pick.

"He can't even sing as well as Paul and John," Vicki said.

"I don't know. He seems like he's nice," I said.

"Nice. You like nice? That explains why you always hang out with Dwayne the Dweeb at school. He's probably nice too, right Twigs?"

I flopped down on my bed. Vicki looked at me with that too familiar smirk. She felt that she needed to somehow fix me or educate me to the hip way of life. I twirled the ends of my hair with my fingers.

My friends at school would say, "Twigs, you are so lucky. You're so skinny and gorgeous." I didn't try to be skinny and didn't particularly like it, but no matter what, I couldn't put on weight. Twiggy was 'in' and everyone wanted to look like her. Clothes always seemed to look good on me and that's how my nickname started. It didn't bother me being called Twigs, and after a while it grew on me. I guess I was lucky to be considered pretty, but with that came an expectation to be a certain way. I had to hang out with the popular girls at school, even though I much preferred the friendships I had with the ones who didn't quite fit in. They were more interesting and had more to talk about than just boys, clothes, and makeup. As for boys, I could feel their eyes watching me as I walked down the school corridors. I found it embarrassing and looked away, unlike the other girls who hung out with me because they enjoyed the attention.

"Dwayne's my friend," I said. "I've known him since the fourth grade. He's not my boyfriend or anything."

"I would hope not," Vicki said, bouncing onto the end of my bed. "You know you can get any boy in school, and what do you do? You hang out with Dwayne. How uncool is that?" She looked up at Ringo's picture. "About as uncool as having Ringo staring at you on your wall."

When Vicki left, she took several of my newly bought skirts and tops with her. I didn't mind sharing my clothes with my friends. I had more than I needed. Mother always insisted on buying me the latest fashions, even though I could care less. Vicki was a couple of sizes bigger than me, but didn't seem to realize that there was any size difference between us. She'd try to pull herself into my clothes, bulging over the waist line and sleeves. Often the seams would be ripped when she returned them, if she returned them at all. It didn't bother me. I liked keeping others happy. It was important to fit in with the girls who were most popular at school. I saw how badly they treated those who they thought were below them. I wanted to stay on the good side of them, but I also felt like I needed to support those who they picked on and humiliated. I'd do what I could when these preppy girls weren't looking. I'd smile at them in the hall or tell them they looked nice or something. I'd invite them over secretly and then I'd have to pretend I didn't know them when I was back at school. I didn't understand these barriers that were not to be crossed. All I could do was try to play both sides and survive these social rules of high school. I was good at surviving most situations.

I sat at the desk in front of my bedroom window. I liked gazing at our maple tree. It was starting to shed its brilliant leaves. I liked watching them drift to the ground in the breeze. Beyond the tree was the street, with houses that all looked very much the same. The only difference was the color of the roofs and front doors. Our large tree reminded me of the countryside. It brought back memories of the trees I used to climb when I was little and the endless fields I could play in. When the leaves dropped from the trees in the winter, there was nothing but these look-a-like homes and gray concrete.

"Time for dinner," a voice called from down the hall.

I snapped out of my daydream, the quiet place I often retreated to. I closed the text book that I should have been reading. It was my job to set the table and Mother would get angry if I dawdled. I glided down the wide spiral staircase. The giant chandelier that hung above was bright and glaring. I preferred dim lights that cast shadows and made everything look softer. Mother liked having all the lights on bright. She said it cheered her up, especially in the fall and winter.

I set four place settings on our over-sized dining-room table, one that could easily seat ten people. Mother always kept fresh flowers in the middle. She had started taking classes in flower arrangement. She said it made her feel cheerful to have bright colors to look at. In the winter, when flowers were hard to come by, Collin made sure to bring home a fresh bouquet every week. He said that it was the least he could do for her with all the times he was late getting home from work.

I didn't particularly like Collin, but I tolerated him. What choice did I have? He was all that I had now as a father. He was just so different from my real dad, whom I remembered as being fun to be around. Collin didn't have a funny bone in his body. All he did was work all the time, have a few drinks after dinner, and go to bed. I only saw him at the dinner table if he got home in time. I secretly hoped he wouldn't make it. If I had my preference, I didn't care to see him at all. In his eyes, I could never do anything right. I was worried that I would start believing that about myself. He did seem to give my mother what she needed: a nice house that she enjoyed decorating and showing off to her friends, a name in town as the doctor's wife, and medical care if she started feeling ill. I was thankful for that, as I needed his help in keeping my mother well. When Collin was around, Mother was at her happiest. He noticed when she wore a new dress and told her she looked pretty. Her favorite time was after dinner, when they would sit together with a drink and talk about their day. On the days that he didn't make it home until late, I tried to avoid being with her. She'd become sad and mopey. My mother's world centered around being a good wife. She said that she wouldn't be here if it wasn't for Collin and owed him everything.

It was a big change for me, moving out from a family of seven with Aunt Edna and Uncle Jake and all my cousins. I remembered when it was just the three of us at one time, when my real parents were together, and how much I enjoyed that. This was different. It was like the two of them and then me by myself. All I'd ever wanted was to have my mother and father back, so I didn't dare complain. At least I had my mother back. She no longer stayed in bed all day long as I once remembered. I still felt that I needed to be careful not to upset her. She would still have bad moods. I had learned not to expect much from her before and I still felt that way. I missed Aunt Edna, Uncle Jake, and the rest of the family terribly after I left them. We now lived several hours apart, so visits became less and less frequent. After a while, I never saw them again.

A year after I moved back with my mother, my little brother Timmy was born. That was the beginning of my babysitting duties. I did a good job looking after him for my mother. Collin was away at the hospital so much and Mother would often feel tired, so I was expected to take over. Soon all the neighbors wanted me to also babysit for them. I liked kids and enjoyed my own pocket money, but felt I didn't have enough time to myself. I liked to just lie on my bed and daydream. I'd remember happier times in my life. Times when I felt secure, loved, and that I belonged. I'd remember those golden streaks of sunlight over the meadows and the sound of chirping birds and crickets at night. I remembered running through those fields until I'd collapse under the apple tree in our garden with Rex by my side. I remembered my father. Oh how I still missed him so much. I never understood why those days ended.

"Honey, we only need three settings." Mother came into the dining room carrying a casserole. "Collin just called from the hospital. He won't be home until late."

Not going to be a good night for her, I thought.

Timmy was sitting at the table with his feet swinging, playing drums on the table with his knife and fork. I gave his head a playful rub and took the seat across from him. He was six years old, with sandy curls and sky blue eyes. He had trouble sitting still and Mother found this exhausting.

"We won't have that at the dinner table," she scolded.

Timmy's playfulness drained out of him. He dropped his utensils and pouted. I tickled him with my foot under the table and he giggled.

Mother sat at the end of the table and started passing around the casserole. I held my breath as Timmy dripped his food on the tablecloth.

"Now look what you've done. I just washed that this morning."

Timmy dipped his finger in the mess, trying to scoop it up, but only smeared it around more.

"Just leave it!" she shouted.

I could tell he was on the verge of tears, so I quickly jumped in. "Very tasty Mom," as I took my first bite. "Sorry that I'm not very hungry." I actually wasn't sure what it was. Fish? Maybe chicken with a lot of cream sauce and mashed vegetables.

She took a bite. "No, it's much too salty. Good thing Collin isn't here to taste it. I will have to work on my recipe."

We sat in silence for some time as I moved my food around the plate. Mother asked me a few questions about school that I didn't feel like talking about. It felt like she was just trying to make conversation. Then she glanced over at her flower arrangement.

"Oh dear, those flowers are starting to look sad, aren't they? I do hope Collin remembers to pick up new ones on his way home."

I knew that was unlikely, with stores being closed by now.

"I can pick some up for you on my way home from school tomorrow," I offered.

That didn't seem to help cheer her up. It was not only the flowers themselves; it was the gift from Collin that mattered. It was his peace offering after missing an evening at home.

"I wish you would eat more, Molly. You're looking thinner all the time."

I chewed each bite for a long time but struggled to get it down. I just wanted to leave the table and get back to my room. Mother looked like she was drifting away. I knew when she needed to be left alone.

"Do you want to come and hang out in my room, Timmy?" I asked. "We could get your coloring books and I'll get my homework and we can lay on the floor together."

"Can we have popcorn?" Timmy asked.

"I don't see why not," I said.

I picked up our dishes from the table and placed them in the sink. Timmy looked at my mother in much the same way as I had when I was close to his age. It was a search for something to grasp onto that remained unreachable.

He followed me up the stairs.

Trying to be Normal

Vicki was back in my bedroom the next day after school. Mother had taken Timmy to a dental appointment so we had the house to ourselves.

"Let's raid the fridge," Vicki suggested. "I'm famished."

She pulled out a bottle of Coke, some leftover macaroni salad, ice cream, and a bag of chips and laid everything on the counter. I was conscious of the mess this was going to create. I picked up an orange that sat in the fruit bowl and started to peel it. Vicki gave me that familiar grimace of hers.

"No wonder you're so skinny," she said, "eating just that."

I felt like telling her that maybe she'd fit into my clothes better if she also ate like this.

"I like oranges," I said.

"Better than ice cream? You are not well, Twigs," she said, reaching to feel my head.

She proceeded to eat everything at once, dropping chips on the floor. Fortunately Rex was nearby to lick up the crumbs. I gently patted his head. He was starting to show his age, struggling to get up on his feet. I didn't want to think about the fact that my time with my lifelong friend might soon be coming to a close.

Mother was fussy about neatness and cleanliness. I didn't want to deal with her mood when she got home to see things out of place. I didn't dare tell Vicki that Mother would be upset. I just wanted my home life to look normal to everyone else, even though I felt it was not like everyone else's. At Vicki's, her house was never *not* messy.

"I like your house," Vicki said, looking around at the expensive furniture my mother had recently purchased for the living room. Whenever we sat on it, we'd get scolded, so I didn't see the point in having it. She made us wash our hands before we touched anything in that room. She said it was for her and Collin and guest use only. That, of course, did not include my friends.

Vicki picked up a family photo sitting on our dining-room cabinet.

"I've never seen your father before," she said. "You don't look anything like him."

"That's because he's my stepfather."

"Oh!" Vicki looked up at me quizzically. "I didn't know your parents were divorced."

This was the conversation I wanted to avoid.

"My father's dead," I said.

"Aw, what happened to him?"

How was I going to explain what happened to him when I didn't know myself. All I knew was that he had been put into prison for reasons no one would explain to me, and after one visit, I never saw him again. My mother told me he died in prison. There was no mourning, no funeral, he just disappeared. I felt like a part of me died with him, but it was not something I could share with anyone. I had held onto his promise to return to me. I wanted to contact Aunt Edna to find out what had happened to him. Mother told me that they had moved away—a job transfer for Uncle Jake. She claimed she had no contact number for them. That whole side of my family vanished from my life, as if they'd never existed.

"He just died," I said.

I was not willing to talk about it any further. Vicki was left holding the photo with a stunned look on her face.

"I should clean up before my mother gets home," I said.

I felt like I was ruining Vicki's fun, and was sure that she'd talk about how weird I was to the other girls at school tomorrow. No matter how hard I tried to mask my life, to pretend that I was the girl who had it all together, I felt that it was a facade. What I really felt like inside was the frightened little girl who was abandoned by her parents ten years ago.

The Relief of Not Being Me

One thing that I absolutely loved was theater. I loved acting and being someone I wasn't. I had been successful in scoring the title role of Cleopatra in the school presentation last spring. I was beaming when I stood up there at the end of the performance, watching the sea of faces, the sound of clapping and cheering ringing in my ears. Mom and Collin were in the front row, and it was one of the few times I felt that I had made my mother proud. She loved the praise that was showered on her from the other parents after the show. For me, acting was an escape from my life. I felt the character I was playing surge through me like I was really that person for those brief moments on stage. My teacher convinced my mother to put me into acting lessons on the weekends. She told her that I had real talent that needed to be nurtured.

"As long as you don't let your school work suffer," Collin warned me. "The lessons are conditional upon that, understand?"

I would have agreed to anything to be able to study what I thrived on doing. I started attending a small theater group on the weekends. I couldn't get enough of these lessons. I tried my best to get my school work completed nightly so that this would never be taken away from me.

I was in awe of my new theater instructor, Natalie. There was something so real about her. I could tell that she put everything into her teaching and expected the same in return. I tried to memorize and copy her fine, subtle techniques. I practiced them for hours in front of a mirror at home to perfect them. I wanted to please her more than anyone. I think that I did. She pulled me aside after class one day.

"Twigs, I've noticed how hard you've been working. I'm impressed with how quickly you've been picking things up. Keep it up and you'll be going somewhere someday."

I beamed with her praise.

"I just want to be as good as you," I said. I didn't want to pry, but I wanted to know more about her.

"Do you ever actually act on stage or on TV?" I asked. "That is, when you're not teaching?"

Natalie sat down and wiped her brow with the towel she carried around with her.

"It's a tough business," she said. "I've done bit parts, commercials, a few theater productions locally. Mostly I teach. I love seeing students like yourself learn and develop and do what I also love to do so much."

She motioned for me to sit across from her, which I gratefully did. I felt it was an honor to be speaking so personally with my teacher. I had taken in every detail about her as I'd watched her so intently, week after week. She was not what most people would consider classically beautiful, but she had a unique look about her. Her nose was not perfectly straight and her ears stuck out a bit too far, but there was something about her that made her statuesque. Maybe it was the way she carried herself, with her head held high, and with graceful movements that made her the most beautiful woman in the world to me. She wore her hair swept up into a bun, and I started wearing my hair in a similar way, even purchasing the same berets that she used. I checked several department stores before I found the exact ones. She had radiant skin and her eyes sparkled like sunlight on water when she laughed. Her body was long and slender but never awkward. She seemed so elegantly in control of every aspect of her looks and her movements, unlike my clumsiness. I wanted to be like her.

"How long have you been acting for?" I asked.

"For just over five years now. Getting recognized as an actor is not an easy feat. I came from a background that didn't encourage anything artistic or cultural, to say the least."

She looked down as if she were remembering something she'd rather not speak of, then sighed and brought her gaze up to meet me again.

"Sometimes the difficulties one faces in life are the motivating force behind creative expression. I think that was the case for me. I found what I loved to do and then it became critical that I be the best that I could be at it. I've still got a long way to go, but I'll never stop doing what I love. I hope you don't either, since I see the same passion in you."

There was something familiar about Natalie, but I couldn't put my finger on it. Maybe it was our mutual love of acting, but there was something else. Perhaps we'd both been through some difficult times. Little did she know of my background. She probably thought I'd been part of this wealthy family all my life and never had to struggle for a thing. She didn't know how I would reach deep down to those painful memories inside myself—the losses I felt and the disappearance of my father—when I performed.

"I'm practicing really hard at home so that I can be as good as you someday. My stepfather gets mad at me though when my marks are not all A's. He thinks acting is a waste of time and that it takes time away from my studies."

Natalie looked at me intently.

"Education is important. I never had a chance to finish school. I would have liked to. If I hadn't started my acting career, who knows where I'd be right now." She looked back at me. "Don't give up on school, but also don't give up on acting. You're lucky that you can do both. So do both really well. I know it's in you."

Collin had given me the same lecture before, at least about school. Listening to Natalie was different. She looked like someone who had gone through some tough times and had somehow survived with new-found strength that was contagious. I felt a kindred spirit with her. I had never felt this with anyone else before.

Going Deep Within

I stayed for talks quite regularly with Natalie after my Saturday classes. I could tell the other girls were envious of the extra time she gave me. They'd deliberately bump into me and would tell me I was in their way or turn their backs on me when I tried to join their conversations. They'd glare over their shoulders and giggle amongst themselves. I was the outcast of the group, but that didn't matter to me. I was already trying hard enough at school to fit in. I wasn't going to waste my energy trying to be a part of this group as well. I was not here to be popular or to socialize. I was here for one thing only and that was to be an actress. I knew the other girls hated me when Natalie would stop the class and have me demonstrate something that they weren't getting. All I cared about was that Natalie thought I was great.

"I got the lead role in this year's theater production," I said, when I saw Natalie.

I could see her excitement as well and ran up to hug her, but she held back.

"I'm proud of you, Twigs!"

"I just used everything you taught me when I auditioned. The school judges applauded me. Can you imagine?" I was beaming with excitement. "Collin says my life is becoming nothing but theater. I started crying when he said I had to make a choice between accepting the lead and coming to your classes. I told him that if I had to make a choice, I'd rather continue with you. That's when my mother finally put her foot down. She said that she was so proud of me in last year's play, that she would not miss seeing me in this year's production over her dead body. Collin gave in. So I can continue with both. I'm so excited!"

Natalie hugged me after all. It felt good to get her reassurance.

"I'm so proud of you." She stepped back and put her hands on my shoulders to make eye contact.

"Now what you need to do is prove to Collin that you can do this and not let your schoolwork slip. Right?"

"I know, but how do I find the time to do it all? I also have to take care of my little brother a lot."

"Listen, I know you can do it. You're smart and you're determined. If you want something bad enough, you'll do it." She hesitated and added. "You don't know this, but I'm a mother. I have a boy that's almost ten years old. No one helped me raise him. I did it all on my own. There were times when I didn't think I could do it all, but I did it for the love of my son and for the love of acting."

I was taken aback by this bit of personal information. I had always viewed Natalie as a free spirit. She didn't seem like someone who would be cooking meals and taking her son to school and doctor's appointments.

"You seem too young to be a mother," I managed to say when I was able to get over the initial shock.

"I started young, not out of choice. Remember what I told you before. These challenges are what builds strength."

Now that she'd shared this personal bit of information with me, I wanted to confide in her. I wanted her to know me better.

"I think I know what you're talking about. Sometimes when I'm acting, I mean really acting, I go back in time to a place when my life was not like it is today. When I think of people that I've loved and lost… " I paused to contain myself, "I can feel the sadness and express it through the character I'm playing. It may not look like it to you, but I have had some pretty tough times myself."

Instead of reacting with surprise as I'd expected, she just nodded and stroked my hair.

"I could have guessed," she said. "I know what's real and what isn't. No one could put the kind of energy into their acting that you do without having felt something very deep themselves. That's what sets you apart from the other students."

I felt so close to Natalie in that moment. I could tell her anything or everything—something that I couldn't trust doing with anyone else—and she'd understand. I had forgotten what being close to someone was like, and now I was finally starting to feel it again.

The Report Card

I proudly put down my report card on the dinner table. Mother and Collin were seated and Timmy was chatting away, even though no one was listening. Collin slowly took the envelope and opened it. I studied his expression as he read it.

"Okay, you did well in English, Art, Theater, Geography, and History. But why only a B+ in Math and Science?"

He looked up at me over his reading glasses. I was stunned. I had worked really hard for these marks.

"Look at the grade point average," I proclaimed. "The average is only C+ for Science and Math. I got one of the highest marks in the class!"

He took off his glasses, methodically folded them, and placed them in his shirt pocket.

"I don't care what everyone else got. I care what you got. If you want to get anywhere in life, you have to do extra well in those subjects. This is not good enough. Math and the sciences, those are the important ones. B's won't do. I know you can get A's if you work harder."

"But I got A's in the Languages and Arts," I pointed out, feeling exasperated.

"And where is that going to get you in life? If you spent half the time that you do on those acting classes on your math instead, your marks would be where they should be. The classes need to stop."

Collin put the report card down on the table and continued his meal.

"No. Please," I said. "I don't want to be a doctor like you. I know that's what you expect of me, but it's not what I want. I've got the lead in the school play again this year and my acting instructor called me gifted. Please don't take that away!"

"You are too young to know what you want. Dora, I think it's time that she cut back on those acting lessons. That time can go to better use." With that he returned to his meal. "Great sauce on the potatoes dear. New recipe?"

I couldn't contain my outrage any longer. "You can't do that! I worked hard at school like you asked. I can't believe you're upset with two B pluses.

You just don't want me to do what makes me happy! You think being a doctor is the only answer in life. Well I don't *want* to be a doctor like you! All you do is work all the time. Does that really make you happy?"

Mother looked at me with her mouth agape and glanced nervously over at Collin.

Collin pounded his fist on the table. "That's *enough* young lady! I pay the bills in this house and what I say goes. You may not appreciate it now, but you'll thank me someday."

I looked at my mother pleadingly. "You *can't* agree with him?"

She looked away. I should have known that she didn't have it in her to come to my rescue when I needed her the most. I stood up so quickly that my chair toppled over and I threw my napkin on the plate.

"I'm not hungry," I said, and ran towards the stairs to my room.

"Come back here young lady, now! I won't have such impetuous behavior in my house!"

"Let her go, dear," I heard my mother say.

"Why is Molly sad?" I could hear Timmy ask.

"Molly is acting spoiled," Collin responded. "When Molly doesn't get her way, she cries, hoping that we'll change our minds. But it won't work. Just like you cry when I take your toys away after I've asked you to clean them up and you don't. You then learn that I mean business, whether you cry or not. You then learn to put your toys away."

"But Molly doesn't have any toys," Timmy said.

"Never mind. You're too young to understand."

"No I'm not!" Timmy yelled and started to wail.

"Enough!"

The wailing got louder as I slammed my door.

I threw myself on the bed and pounded my pillow with my fists.

"You can't do this to me!" I cried and cried until there were no tears left. I lay there staring at the ceiling. If this had been my real father, would he have been so mean? All I remembered of him was that he wanted me to be happy. He spent his time teaching me nursery rhymes and fun songs. If I had a sour face, he would tickle me until I laughed. He carried me high up on his shoulders so that I could tower over the world below. I know I was only five years old then, but would Collin have done any of these things? Judging by the way he never did anything but lecture Timothy, I knew it wasn't in him. I suddenly missed my father terribly.

Natalie was the only person left in this world who understood me. How could they take her away from me? I wouldn't let it happen!

Meet My Mother

I begged and pleaded with my mother to take me to one more acting class the following Saturday.

"Collin would be furious with me if he found out," she said.

"He'll never know, Mom. It'll be our secret. Please? I've *got* to say goodbye to Natalie."

My mother had been quite concerned about me this past week, when I refused to come out of my room and sit at the dinner table with Collin.

"You've got to eat something," she said. "You can't afford to lose any more weight."

Collin told her to let me be and that, when I was hungry enough, I'd come back down and be part of the family. My mother knew how stubborn I could be. She'd sneak food inside my door after Collin had gone to bed. But I wouldn't touch it. I was on a hunger strike.

"Okay," she finally relented. "I'll take you there Saturday, *if* you promise to eat something."

I agreed and ravenously gulped down the meal she brought me.

At the following class, I anticipated that Natalie and I would have our few minutes together as had become the routine. I dreaded having to tell her that my classes were over.

"I'm sorry, but I can't talk today, Twigs. I need to pick up my son."

I felt hurt by her abruptness. She didn't know it yet, but this might be the last time I ever saw her.

"I need to talk to you." I fought back tears.

She stopped what she was doing and took notice.

"What's wrong?"

"Collin won't let me come back again. I begged and pleaded, but when he makes up his mind, it's final."

"Oh no! Why?"

"He didn't like my report card. It was a good report card but not good enough for him. He wants me to be a doctor like him. He says I'm wasting my time with 'this acting business'."

Natalie came over and embraced me like never before. My tears flowed freely now.

"Twigs, you are very talented. Don't give up the dream, no matter what."

"I can't do this without you," I cried. "I need you."

When I said it, I realized that I needed *her,* far more than just an acting coach.

Just then I heard my mother's voice calling. I wasn't ready to leave. I hadn't had a proper chance to say goodbye.

"Molly? Molly, where are you?"

"I'll be just a few more minutes, Mother!" I cried.

She walked into the auditorium.

"You know that I have to pick up your brother and get dinner ready. We have to get going."

She was now face to face with Natalie. Mom looked at Natalie, with a forced smile on her lips, and stretched out her hand.

"Pleased to meet you. I'm Molly's mother, Dora. Molly's talked so much about you. I was hoping to meet you sooner but things have been hectic. I'm sorry that this didn't work out."

As my mother chattered, Natalie stood there like she'd seen a ghost. Her face lost its color, and for a moment, I was worried she might faint. Her lips moved a couple of times to form words, but no sound came out. She tried again as she reached out her hand in return.

"Nice to meet you, Dora," she said.

A Ghost from the Past

It was hard to concentrate on being in character for the school play. My heart wasn't in it like it was when I had Natalie to coach me through. I hadn't even had a chance to say a real goodbye to her at our last class. I wondered if I could ever say goodbye to her. Then one day, when I spotted Natalie watching my school performance from the sidelines, my heart skipped a beat. I bubbled up with excitement that she was there watching my rehearsal. I wondered why she had come. Was it because she couldn't say goodbye either? I couldn't wait to finish the act and run off the stage to be with her.

"Oh Natalie, I'm so glad to see you!" I cried as I ran to embrace her.

"Is your mother here?" she asked.

"No," I replied. I wondered why she was asking. "She's coming later to pick me up."

"Good. I need to talk to you. I need to ask you some questions."

I was taken aback by the tension in her tone. It was not the Natalie I was used to. Whatever it was that she wanted to know sounded serious.

"What kind of questions?" I asked.

"Can we go somewhere else to talk? Somewhere a little more private?"

This time of day, the students had left the building. Any one of the classrooms would be empty. I peeked down the hall and found a room with the door still open. No teacher was in sight.

"Let's go over there," I pointed. "Is something wrong?" I asked.

She didn't answer.

"I'm so glad to see you, Natalie," I said, grinning at her. No smile was returned.

When we stepped into the room, Natalie shut the door behind us. She motioned for me to sit down at one of the desks and pulled a chair up beside me.

"Twigs..." She paused. "I've always called you Twigs, thinking it was just short for something. What's your real name?"

I had gotten so used to being called Twigs that I never used my real name anymore.

"My family calls me Molly, but all my friends call me Twigs. Why do you ask?"

"Molly, I need to know where you grew up."

I was confused about why she was asking. What difference did that make?

"I grew up here."

"All your life?"

"Well, no ... I lived for a while with some relatives and—"

"I mean when you were little. When you were five years old. Do you remember the name of the town?"

"I lived on a farm when I was little. We sometimes drove to a town called Fenton. Why do you want to know?" My voice was breaking from the strain of not knowing what was going on.

Natalie leaned back on her chair and paused. She looked like she had trouble speaking.

"What's the matter?" I asked. "What's this got to do with my acting or anything else?"

She reached out her hand and touched mine. Then she closed her eyes.

I was feeling very uneasy, as if something bad was about to happen. I had no idea what.

I waited.

"I think I knew you when you were a little girl," Natalie finally said.

Natalie left me with that. She said it wasn't the time or place to elaborate, and that she would come see me again after another school play rehearsal. She said she needed to talk with me and that she had to let me know some things, but that was all she'd said. Then she left.

I didn't know when I was going to see her again, but in the meantime, I went through the motions of going to school, attending rehearsals for the play, doing my homework, and talking to my friends like everything was the same. I waited anxiously to speak to Natalie again, wondering what she was going to tell me. How had she known me? Why did she turn pale when she met my mother? All these questions swirled around in my mind without answers.

Days passed that felt like weeks with no word from her. I wondered if she would keep her promise. Then I saw her, clear as day. She sat in the auditorium watching my rehearsal the following Friday afternoon. I stopped what I was doing and stared at her. She nodded with that familiar look of approval, the one that said 'carry on; you're doing well'. Knowing she was there made me try so much harder. I was performing because of her. I wanted to make her proud. She stood up and clapped when I finished and the other students looked at her, wondering who she was. I ignored them and ran to her.

"That was brilliant," she said. "Remember to raise your chin when you speak. The voice takes on a clearer tone. Otherwise, fantastic!"

"I've been waiting all week to see you!" I exclaimed.

"Me too," she said reassuringly. "Is your mother picking you up?"

"No, I take the bus home after rehearsal. I have to be home at six for dinner."

She glanced at her watch. "So that's in an hour." She took a moment to think as I waited in anticipation.

"How about I drive you home, but we stop at a café along the way. I'll drop you off around the corner from your home so no one knows."

It was a café I'd never been to before. She wanted to make sure we wouldn't run into anyone that would know me. She explained that she didn't want any trouble. We sat across from each other and sipped on Cokes.

"I really miss my classes with you Natalie." I sat gazing at her across the booth.

"Don't worry, you're going to do just fine without me. You're way beyond anything that I could teach you at this stage. I just want to be acknowledged when you accept an Academy Award someday. Okay?"

I smiled. She suddenly looked serious.

"There is something I need to let you know. I wasn't sure how to tell you and thought about it all week. That's why I took this long to contact you again. I just decided it was best if I say it straight out."

I took a long sip of my Coke, even though all that was left was the melted ice on the bottom. A slurping sound came out. I never took my eyes off her. I felt a knot growing in my stomach.

"This is going back a long ways for you—a different life I imagine. Do you remember a girl who used to work on your farm that last summer you lived there?"

I thought back to that summer. It was like a dream to me. I remembered every detail of that farm. The veranda with the swinging door, the barn with the hens and stray cats, and the pond where I'd catch tadpoles. I remembered my daddy, with his curly sun-drenched hair and the piece of straw that he'd chew out of the corner of his mouth, and yes, I remembered a girl who came to take care of the animals and sometimes me. I remembered that my mother didn't like her very much.

"Yes, her name was Nell. She lived next door."

Natalie reached across the table, grasped both of my hands in hers, and looked deep into my eyes. I watched hers grow moist.

"I'm Nell," she said.

I pulled my hands back. I stared at her in disbelief.

"What are you saying? I thought your name was Natalie. How could you be Nell?"

"I know this is a huge shock to you. It was to me too. I knew who you were when I met Dora, your mother. She looks a little older of course, but I recognized her right away. Fortunately she didn't recognize me."

Suddenly I felt excited. Here was someone from my past. Someone who was there with me and knew that life existed for me. Not like my mother, who never made any mention of it.

"Nell ... you've grown up."

I realized how stupid that sounded after I said it. I had grown up too.

"But why have you changed your name?" I asked.

"Natalie *is* my name. Nell was a nickname that my family used. After I left home, I used Natalie. With wanting to become an actress, it was more sophisticated. Besides, I didn't like who I was as Nell and wanted to leave her behind."

I felt like I had found a long-lost friend. I felt there was so much to catch up on all of a sudden, but Nell stopped me before my questions started.

"I have a lot more to tell you, but we'll have to meet again. There's not enough time. I'll come and meet you again next Friday, okay?"

I felt disappointed but realized I was already going to be late getting home.

"Can't we meet sooner?" I asked.

"No it's best this way," she said. "I don't want to raise any suspicions with your mother. I don't think she'd want me to be talking to you. Please don't tell her about our meeting."

I remembered that Mother didn't care for Nell back then, even though I could never understand why. But Nell was a different person now, grown up with a child of her own.

"I won't, but I don't understand why," I said.

"We'll talk more next time. For now, it'll have to be our secret."

Remembering

What did I remember about Nell? And about that summer? I ran through it in my mind over and over again throughout the following week.

Natalie didn't look anything like the Nell that I remembered. Odd to think that she was my age when I knew her. I remembered that she rarely smiled or laughed. She worked really hard for my father, even when it was so hot that even Rex wouldn't leave the shade. She would sometimes have dinner with us, but whenever she did, my parents would argue afterwards. She never ate much, sort of like me. I could tell my mother didn't like her, because she'd get into one of her bad moods whenever she came around. I wondered why, since she was helpful around the house, folding laundry and doing dishes. She did all the things my mother was too tired to do. Nell hardly ever really spoke to any of us. I remembered that she had long hair that hung in her face making it hard to see her expressions. I could tell if she was having a sad day by whether she had her hair pulled back or had it falling forward. On her sad days, she didn't want anyone to see her face.

I adored her when I had her to myself. Those times were rare, but I remember them well. Sometimes we'd play tag in the yard or hide and seek. Other days, when it was too hot, we'd play cards or board games in the shade. I had fun because she always let me win. We would play word games that she'd invent. She'd start a sentence and I'd finish it. Then we'd think of all kinds of different endings we could use instead. I remember one particular book she read to me; it was about a family of ducks. The mother duck scolded her baby when he wasn't nice to his little sister. The brother kept being mean to his sister whenever the mother wasn't around, and it took a long time before the mother came to the baby girl duck's rescue. It was a really sad story, but I was especially sad when I saw Nell cry after reading it. She rarely showed any emotion, so this was unusual. She always greeted Rex playfully and he got excited when she arrived. She said that she was happy to have Rex and me as friends. I wondered why Nell didn't have any other friends. She seemed like such a nice girl. I was glad though, because it meant she would spend more time with me. I felt like she was my big sister and my best friend.

Unlike that Nell I remembered, Natalie, my acting instructor, always wore her hair pulled back in a ponytail or bun, her eye contact was direct and expressive. She wasn't afraid to touch and hug, unlike the Nell who pulled away uncomfortably whenever I reached for her. Natalie spoke clearly and distinctly while Nell kept her head down and mumbled. How weird that she was now teaching me to project my voice. How had she changed so much? I guess people do when things happen to them that force them to change. I was thinking of my own life. Natalie had mentioned having a ten-year-old son, so she must have had him shortly after that summer. I never saw her with a boyfriend at that time so it seemed odd. I couldn't imagine having a child at my age. Why would Nell have wanted that? Maybe it was an accident. Either way, it was very out of character for the Nell that I had known.

Nell disappeared from my life when that summer was over. The end of that summer was the end of the life I then knew. It was the end for me in so many ways.

The Lies I Was Told

Natalie picked me up after my theater practice the next Friday. It was unusually mild for a late fall day. We drove to a park a few miles away from my school and got out of the car. The afternoon sun was casting shadows through the trees. The last of the fall color hung to the branches and the crisp foliage crunched under our feet as we walked.

Natalie made small talk along the way but I could tell she was preoccupied. I was full of questions that I was afraid to ask. There was something ominous about our reconnection. She gestured for us to sit on the park bench and we both climbed up on the table. Natalie looked ahead silently as if she were meditating. I clasped my hands as if in prayer.

"I have something to tell you," she started.

I studied her profile. Once again, the word "statuesque" came to mind. Her eyes glistened at the corners. She let her head drop down and she wrung her hands.

"Your father," she began and then hesitated. "This is so hard for me." She stopped and composed herself before continuing. "Your father is still alive."

I felt faint. What was she saying? My father died a long time ago. How could this be? I gathered myself enough to speak.

"My mother told me—"

"Your mother lied," she said, interrupting me. "Your father may have been dead in her eyes, but he did not die in that prison."

My whole world felt like it was collapsing. Everything I knew was thrown into question.

"How would you know?" I managed to ask.

She finally looked at me. Her eyes were welling with tears.

"Because I know where he is," she said. Her voice cracked with emotion.

Suddenly I felt like that five-year-old girl again who had lost her daddy but held onto the hope that he would return. Since then that hope had been buried, and a new life had emerged. Now that glimmer of hope returned. Just a glimmer though. How could this be true? I was so overcome by mixed emotions, questions upon questions, that no words came out as I moved my lips. I thought about how I had lost my voice once before. A rush of fear ran through me at this possible recurrence. I let out a moan, so I knew my voice was still there. I didn't know what to ask. There were just too many questions—so much I wanted to know all at once. I needed to know the whole story. What? When? How could this be? Mostly I was overcome with wanting my daddy back again.

"Where is he?" I asked. "Does he know where I am?"

Natalie took a deep breath, as if she were trying to get her emotions under control enough to speak, and wiped away the tears that spilled down her cheeks.

"Molly, he has been in prison a long time. He is just getting out, but he is a broken man. He needs to build his life all over again. Your mother deserted him a long time ago and he lost contact with his whole family. I believe his sister Edna visited him a few times and then she stopped coming as well. He just gave up on everything, except you. He has always been determined to find you again."

I had held onto the image of my father as that strong man I loved. The one on the farm where we were a family. I couldn't imagine him as a broken man who had given up all hope. I didn't want to think of him that way. I felt angry at Natalie for saying that. She obviously didn't know my daddy like I did.

"How do you know all of this?" I demanded.

Another heavy sigh. Natalie hung her head as if she were in confessional.

"Because I stayed in contact with him. I was the only one who did. It wasn't easy at first but I kept trying and finally he let me. I had no idea you were his daughter. If I had..." she hesitated, to collect herself, but couldn't hold back her sobs.

I felt numb inside. I shifted away from her. I was unsure of myself and how I would react as all this information came pouring over me like hot coals, burning my heart, my soul, my senses.

"What are you saying? How? Why did you visit him? Why you?"

I stared at her, desperately needing the answers.

"Because it was my fault that he went to prison. I'm so sorry Molly," she said, trying to reach for me. I moved farther back.

A stream of whys flew through my mind—the questions that no one would answer for me for the last ten years. What had my father done to end up in prison? Why would such a kind and gentle man, who took in strays and put baby birds back in their nests, be locked up? None of it had ever made any sense to me. Here was Natalie finally offering some answers. But it still made no sense. What had he done?

"Why did my father go to jail? Why? Why?" I screamed.

"That summer that I worked for your father, things were rough for me at home. My brother used to—" She stopped herself for a moment and rested her head on her hands. "He used to do things to me that brothers shouldn't do. He's the father of my son."

When she gathered herself again, she continued.

"My parents knew that he was kind of sick in the head, so they were very protective of him. When your father found out what he was doing to me, he tried to report it to the police, so my parents blamed it on him instead. They accused him of raping me."

I sat there trying to absorb this, afraid to say a word. My father hurting anyone was absurd. How could anyone have believed that?

"I'm so sorry Molly. If only you knew. I was a scared fifteen year old, pregnant with nowhere to go. They threatened me. I'm not making any excuses for what happened. I'm just trying to explain. Now that I can look back, it's different. But at that time I was a frightened child."

I tried to gather the words.

"My father went to jail for something he never did?"

"Your father was a good man. He was trying to help me. I tried to keep him from getting involved, but being who he was, he couldn't walk away from what he saw."

I felt a rage growing inside me.

"Did you lie to the police? Did you accuse my father of raping you?"

Natalie looked desperate. She shook her head emphatically.

"No, no! I denied it all! I never, *never* said what my parents wanted me to say. The lawyer made it look like I was too scared to admit it. They said that with the circumstantial evidence and my brother as a witness there was enough to convict. Even your mother thought he was guilty. They had some merchant in town who testified at the trial that he seemed to show an unusual interest in me, even though he was only trying to protect me. All the cards got stacked against him."

I thought about my mother and how she had lied to me. How could she have done that? How could she have turned against my father—her husband—like that? How would I face her now?

As if Natalie were reading my mind, she said. "Don't blame your mother. I believe she tried to do what was best for you. He wasn't coming out of prison for a long time. She tried to move on with her life, and she wanted you to move on too. She didn't want you to know why he was in jail. She thought it best that he be dead, for your sake. I'm sure of it."

I got up and walked to a pile of leaves on the ground and knelt down on them. The crumpled organic matter felt like the death of a life—a pretend life built on untruths. My life. Natalie followed me and stood there looking at me.

"Not that it matters to you, but I got out of that family of mine as soon as I could. I went on welfare for a while with the baby. Then I started working as a waitress at night, but during the days I went to acting auditions and it was what kept me going. I put my pain into something that I loved to do. My father died of alcohol poisoning, and the last I heard, my brother has been in and out of prison for different misdemeanors. I've lost contact with my mother. I've buried that family. I have gone to see your father in prison for many years. He replaced my family before he ever went to jail and remained my family while he was there. I have never forgiven myself. That's how I know he's alive, Molly."

He's alive. I couldn't believe what I was hearing.

"When I met you," Natalie continued, "I had no idea you were the same girl that I knew ten years ago. Not until I saw your mother. And then I knew. I've been looking for you for years Molly, for him! I haven't mentioned anything to your father yet. I had to tell you first. All this searching and you were right under my nose. All I can say is thank God I've finally found you!"

"Take me to my father!" I demanded.

BILLY

The Parole Hearing

At my ten-year parole hearing, I sat before the prison board. A row of men in suit jackets sat across from me. I clasped my handcuffed hands in my lap and folded my hands in prayer. I didn't know where to look—whether to make eye contact or avoid it. So I looked down until I was spoken to.

The plump fellow with rosy cheeks, sitting at the end, pushed back the few wisps of hair that remained on his head and spoke first.

"Mr. Mulgrave, we have reviewed your records carefully. It appears that you have had an exemplary record ever since you entered prison. No incidents noted," he continued, glancing at his notes. "You have worked cooperatively with other prisoners and been compliant with the guards. I have to commend you on that."

I nodded, offering a recognition of his words and gratitude in receiving them. I recognized the warden at the other end of the table, a stout man with a thick neck and fingers that looked like they were swollen. I could only glance at him before I started feeling intimidated and looked down. There was far too much power in front of me to feel safe. My life was in their hands.

"Mr. Mulgrave," the warden said. "Your crime was a serious one. However, according to my records, the victim has been visiting you quite regularly and has forgiven you. That is quite remarkable. Have you anything to say about your rehabilitation?"

I felt like screaming at them that there was no crime committed. That the only crime that occurred was my being wrongly convicted and imprisoned for ten years. I also knew that every prisoner in here proclaimed their innocence and denial was frowned upon.

At this point, I managed to raise my head and look them in the eye.

"Whatever happened in the past is in the past. I am a new man and will work hard on the outside to keep up the behavior you have commended me on and be a worthy citizen."

I meant those words, but it killed something inside of me to not be able to say that I had never in my life deviated from being a man with probably far superior morals than any one of them.

"What are your plans should we grant you your release? Do you have family to help you?" another man asked, who looked like he was getting quite bored and fidgety and would have rather been somewhere else.

The word 'family' hit a cord. The one thing that had meant everything to me no longer existed.

"I no longer have contact with my family. I lost that when—" I stopped myself, careful not to lay blame on anyone else. "I lost that when I was imprisoned for my crime. I have a rooming house that I can stay in and work for my accommodation. It will be a humble start toward building my life once more."

Nell had made the arrangements for me.

They all nodded in agreement and I knew that I had given them what they wanted to hear.

"You have been a model prisoner, Mr. Mulgrave. You will be released immediately and will report weekly to the probationary board for one year. If after that time, you have met the conditions of your parole, you will be unconditionally released. Do you have any questions?"

"No, I don't. Thank you," I said, feeling a heavy weight being lifted. *A model prisoner*, I thought. Not quite the same as the model citizen I had been before they took that away from me. I released my damp, clasped hands when they undid my handcuffs.

A free man at last. All I could think about was that now I could finally go and find my little girl.

DORA

Elusive Memories

We sat in the living room after dinner. I had my gin and tonic and Collin had a scotch on the rocks. He read the paper, ignoring my presence. I felt so disconnected from him. From everyone. "How was work today, dear," I asked.

"The usual," he replied gruffly, as he flipped the pages.

Why is it so difficult to get conversations going?

"Did you have any interesting new patients today?" I asked, trying to engage his attention.

Collin didn't look up from his paper. "You know I'm not going to discuss confidential matters with you, dear."

I gulped down my gin and tonic and got up for another. I grabbed his glass for a refill, but he put his hand over it.

"That's not necessary." I knew he didn't approve of me having another, but I didn't care. As I stood at the counter pouring myself a drink, I tried again.

"Did Nurse Campbell have her baby yet? Last time I saw her she looked like she was ready to explode she was so big. Brave lady for working as long as she has."

Collin looked as if he were trying to remember who I was talking about. "Oh yes, she had an eight-pound baby boy. She brought him in the other day to show him off. Sturdy one. Looks like he's ready for the football field already."

Not like our Timmy, I thought to myself, *who prefers to draw rather than throw a ball.* I was sure he was a disappointment to Collin, even though he never admitted so. It was the comments that he made. Like wanting me to get him into team sports, even at a preschool age, so that he would get used to tough and tumble play. The time I tried to put him into the mini-mouse baseball team, he squished his eyes shut and ran out of the way of the ball every time he was at bat. The other boys laughed at him and he wouldn't go back.

I always thought he was hard on Molly, but after having Timmy, I realized it was in his nature to be critical. I was hoping that Timmy would be what mended the gap in our family, but despite his easy-going nature and physical resemblance to Collin, he couldn't meet Collin's expectations. He was too fidgety, too whiny, and not tough enough, according to Collin. Even though I was grateful that the pregnancy had gone well and I did not experience the nightmarish lows that I had gone through with Molly, I had somehow fallen short of producing a child that met his expectations. I felt that whatever shortages he thought Timmy possessed were due to something I was or wasn't doing. I realized that, in Collin's mind, he thought he was doing the best for us. I also knew that when his mind was made up about things, questioning him would only cause him to dig his heels in more.

"I'm doing the best for Molly," he claimed after one of our disagreements. "God knows she didn't have the guidance she needed as a child and she's not to blame for that. I'm trying to give her the direction she needs to be successful in this world, so she doesn't go down a wrong path."

Like her father, I thought he wanted to add. It was almost as if he were looking for the flaw in her that would lead her to failure. He was that much harder on her because he thought he had to get that devil out of her. What he didn't realize was that his criticisms were not only driving her further away from him but from me as well.

I took a few more sips of my gin and went to bed early.

I still thought of Billy now and again. He entered my dreams when I least expected it. My life was so different now than it once had been with him. I now lived in this beautiful manicured home in the city. I'd always been a city girl and thought this was what I wanted. We had security gates at the front and high hedges giving us privacy all around. We had a pool in the yard. We had a gardener who came and trimmed the perennials and cut the lawns every Thursday. I had a cleaning lady who scrubbed the house from top to bottom every Monday. I had my own car to drive the children and do errands. I had more dresses, coats, and shoes in my closet than I really needed. I went to the beauty parlor every second Friday to have my hair and nails done. Collin had given me everything that I could possibly want. So I didn't understand why Billy still haunted me. Collin said that it was best to bury him, as if he had never existed. He said that it's for Molly's good if she thought he were dead—said that she could then move on with her life and accept him as her father. This was my chance to create the family life that I'd always dreamed of, which never happened with Billy. That dream was cut short with his criminal choices and my decline into the abyss. If it wasn't for Collin, I might not be alive today. He brought me out of that never-ending fog and offered me hope of something better. He sat by my bedside during those long hospital days, bringing me back from that dark hole I had fallen into. I had taken enough pills that awful day to put me in the grave. It took a long time for me to accept that I was still here when I didn't want to be. Collin was my doctor, but he was more than that. He seemed to be the only person on this earth who truly cared about me. He became my reason to live and through him I mended.

I was now indebted to Collin for all of that. Yet I still had these dreams of Billy. The dreams were of the Billy I once remembered. The man who had made me laugh, who brought out my deepest passions, and whom I had once trusted with my soul. Why did he have to destroy what we had? I might not have been the wife he needed at that time, but to be so foolish as to succumb to his temptations with a teenager? He committed a crime that he was now paying for and that destroyed everything we had. I should have despised him, but I didn't. I still got this nagging feeling that maybe my perceptions weren't as accurate as I thought. After all, even Collin said that I was out of touch with reality during that time. However, why would the police have arrested him and the courts sentence him if it wasn't true? I just wondered how I could have been so wrong about him. He was the kindest, most gentle, most moral man I'd known. I believed in him. How I wished that Molly could let him go—forget about him and accept Collin as her father. He was a good provider and a person she should be proud to call her father. His reputation in the community spoke volumes. He'd left the hospital I was once in and started a practice here in town. Everyone knew him and I got treated special for being Mrs. Collin Holston. Yet none of this seemed to matter to Molly. She held onto those elusive memories of a man who once was and no longer is. I guess in some ways that's the dream that reoccurs for me as well. Collin has been a wonderful husband in many ways, but he fails to have the warmth that Billy had. In moments of weakness, I realize that I'll never love Collin like I once loved Billy. My dreams remain the closest I'll ever come to him again.

NATALIE

Redemption

I've grown to believe that there is a higher purpose for why things happen the way they do. I didn't always feel that way. As a child I felt that I was running from the devil. Everything seemed to evolve so unfairly. Life just happened to me and I had no control over any of it. I didn't understand why a kind person like Billy was punished while an evil person like my brother got away with an easy ride, why he was protected by my parents and I wasn't, and why the man who tried to protect me was being punished. I've never been religious. Never went to church. Perhaps that was my sin. I questioned how I had survived with the hardships and challenges I had faced. If I'd continued along the path that seemed destined for me, I would have ended up in some back alley, maybe no longer alive. My baby would have ended up in some other home and I would never have known him. With no education, no money, and no family, I should have led a life of depravity. But something changed and I realize that change was within myself. I defied the direction my life was heading. I was determined to do whatever was in my power to change its course. Mixed into that determination came a bit of luck and opportunity.

As I felt some sense of accomplishment, the haunting skeletons of my past started to fall behind. I was moving forward and kindness was finally making its appearance. The cycle of it reinforced itself. I grew stronger every step of the way, and the more I gave of myself, the more I received in return. I started to believe in a cosmic order. I believed in karma. I believed you reap what you sow. How could I not? I brought joy to the children I taught and felt an immense personal satisfaction in return. I was giving something of myself that I was good at. More than the skill or talent that I may have possessed, I developed the heart of giving. Nathan, whom I once viewed as the product of the devil, became the blessing in my life. He was my initial reason to turn my life around and now not a day goes by that I don't feel myself eternally blessed by his presence. He was my gift in disguise. I punished myself endlessly with guilt over the fate of Billy. I wondered how I could have let this happen to him when I'd had no control over what happened to me. I tried my best to make it right but failed to realize that no compensation could make up for his enormous loss. All I could do was try to achieve his one request, which was to find out what happened to Molly. Just as I had lost hope of ever resolving that, Molly appeared miraculously before me. I finally had my chance at redemption. I finally felt deserving of the good that had come my way. All the suffering finally had some purpose.

MOLLY

The Performance

When I walked into my home that night, it felt like I was walking onto a stage. We were all actors. Dora was pretending to be my mother, and Collin was doing a poor job pretending to be my father. It was the biggest acting performance of my life. I had to act like there was nothing wrong. I wouldn't dare jeopardize a reunion with my father. I had to pretend that we were a family going through a normal evening dinner.

"You're late for dinner," Mother said, as I came in the door. "What took you so long?"

Lie number one.

"My bus was late. Then I ran into someone from my school and we got talking and I lost track of time."

"Well your dinner is cold," she said, "but help yourself."

I felt too nauseous to eat.

"I'm not hungry. Do you mind if I just skip dinner tonight?"

Collin put on his stern expression.

"You are part of this family and whether you eat or not is up to you, but you will sit at the table."

The script in my mind had me pretending to be a normal teenager at the dinner table with her family. I sat down.

"How was your day?" Mother asked.

Lie number two.

"It was like any other day," I said.

Mother wanted to know about my play. Collin wanted to know how I did on the science test. Timmy wanted to know if I'd play Snakes and Ladders with him after dinner. I passed the performance. I had to be a really good actor to get through this one.

It wasn't until I was in my room alone that night that I pulled out my old photo album and let myself remember. The flood of emotion overtook me and I sobbed for all that I had lost, for all the lies that I had been living with for all these years: the loss of innocence, the loss of trust, and the loss of the family I was meant to have. There we were, the three of us in the photograph, with Rex happily panting by our side. I took the photo out of the album and I ripped off the part where my mother stood, leaving only my father, myself, and Rex together. I took the part with my mother and stared at it for a long time. *Who was she? How could she have lied to me about my father like this?* Then I ripped it into a hundred pieces and threw it into the trash.

BILLY

Finding Molly

Jazzy curled her slinky body around my ankles, purring with contentment. I reached down to stroke her back, which arched at my touch. He belonged to the owners of the rooming house I was renting and had taken to meowing at my door in the mornings. I welcomed the companionship.

I swept the last of the dust into the bin. The owners of the rooming house had hired me to maintain the old building. My room was free in exchange and I even got a few dollars to buy some groceries. It was now time to start the painful rebuilding of my life, one step at a time. I was ten years older and had lost everything I ever worked for. The cold and damp from my prison cell had made my bones ache. My fingers wouldn't bend without pain and my one knee was weak. I couldn't put much weight on it, which caused me to limp. My hair had strands of gray, my skin was pasty, and I had lost my muscle tone. Hard labor like I'd once done on the farm was not something I could consider doing again. Scrubbing the floors and walls of this building and fixing broken toilets and sinks was about as far as I could extend myself physically. Even though it wasn't much of a life compared to what I once had, I took great moments of pleasure in the simple things I'd missed for so long. I appreciated the smile that Mrs. Atkinson would offer when she passed me in the hall. I wasn't sure if it was from a genuine friendliness or pity, but I didn't care. I couldn't remember anyone smiling at me all those years in prison. I looked forward to my morning walk to the grocery store to pick up my bread and coffee. I appreciated the simple exchange of niceties with Jed, the store owner I'd gotten to know on a first-name basis. I appreciated the sun when it broke through the clouds and even the rain on my skin. My world was now in bright colors instead of shades of gray. I enjoyed being able to work again, to be useful. I also valued planning my days as I chose, having some control over my life once more.

I took it upon myself to take a trip out to the farm after my release. I wish I hadn't. I cherished the memory of how it once had been, and perhaps out of some naivety, I thought it might still exist the way I remembered it. I had lost the farm long ago to lawyer fees, and with that loss, I should have just let it go. It sat there on the hillside looking sadly neglected. I had taken such pains to create a home there. Now the paint was peeling, the porch sagged, and the roof needed repair. I resisted the impulse to go to work and fix it. It was no longer mine. There was no sign of livestock in the fields and the barn was boarded up. The fields were no longer cultivated and weeds had taken over. The fence was broken in many places. I thought about knocking on the door, but what was the point. Perhaps a drunk like Nell's father lived there now. It reminded me of how they had let their farm go after the grandparents passed away. I had held onto the memory of this home for ten years, and even though I knew I had lost it, the memory of how it once was kept my sanity. Now I had to put this behind me or I would remain bitter.

The anger that I'd felt in prison over the unfair hand of fate had diminished to sadness. The sadness was now replaced by resignation. What hurt the most was my loneliness. I didn't know where to begin to find Molly. I searched intensely through all the nearby city directories for Dora or Molly Mulgrave but nothing showed up. I didn't know what her new married name might be. Edna no longer lived at her old address and the new owners did not know where they had moved to. I had totally lost touch with even my own sister. I couldn't let go of trying to find Molly. She was all that really mattered to me. My tormented thoughts haunted me as I lay in bed at night, and I'd thrash through my nightmares. I ached with the loss of my daughter. She was my heart and my heart was out there somewhere.

Then one day I found a note under my door. Nell had been by while I was out. The note said that she needed to talk to me. She said it was important and she'd come by this evening. I went out to buy a pound cake for her visit. I even bought some tea and milk for her, as I knew she preferred that to coffee. She was the glue that had held me together in prison, through those dark days, and I was grateful to her for that. I washed the floor and made my bed and set two plates on the card table the neighbor had given me. I pulled up an extra stool and waited for her arrival.

Nell wanted me to call her Natalie now. She said I was the only one who still knew her as Nell, but she preferred that Nell no longer exist. While she wanted to leave her past behind, I wanted to hold onto it.

As I sat by the window watching a squirrel scold a dog at the bottom of the tree, my attention shifted to footsteps outside my door and a gentle knock. I ran my hand through my hair, straightened the freshly washed shirt I'd put on, and headed for the door.

Nell stood there with that mournful grin I had grown accustomed to seeing over the years. It was a forced smile full of remorse. How I had wished I could have hugged it away behind those bars. Now I could. She stepped through the door and into my embrace.

"How are you, Billy?"

I stepped back to look at her, still holding onto her shoulders. I admired how she had grown into such a lovely young lady. Her presence was full of confidence, her eye contact solid, and her chin strong and determined as she held it high. I remembered when I once had that strength and determination and how feeble I now felt in comparison.

"I'm better now that you're here," I said. "Hey come on in; make yourself at home in my make-do home." I signaled her in.

She looked around. "I like what you've done with the place. It feels homey."

She went over to admire a print I had hung on the wall. Her eyes dropped to the bureau below. She picked up the framed photo of Molly. It was the only one I had left of her. I'd kept it with me throughout those years in prison and would look at it daily. Nell didn't say a word, just gently put it back down.

"I've got some tea for you. Let me boil some water. I bought some lemon pound cake."

Nell seemed unusually quiet and apprehensive today, not her normal bubbly self, full of stories to tell about her boy or her latest acting auditions or students. She put up her hand and shook her head.

"It's okay Billy. This is not just a social visit. I have something important I have to talk to you about. I want you to sit down before I speak."

I suddenly felt a sense of trepidation. Something wasn't right.

"Are you okay, Nell?" I asked, thinking she might be ill.

"I'm fine Billy; don't worry about me."

She took my arm and made me sit across from her at the table.

"I have some very good news for you. Something that I know you've longed to hear. Something that I've promised you for a long time but failed to deliver."

She hesitated, looking fidgety … uncertain. I held my breath. If it was good news, why did she look so anxious?

"I've found Molly," she said.

I sat there dazed. I couldn't utter a word. I could feel my heart start rapidly beating in my chest. Why did Nell not seem excited telling me this? My first thought was that something bad had happened to Molly.

"Tell me she's okay," I said, holding my breath.

"Yes, yes, she's fine. More than fine."

I breathed again. This was the day I had been dreaming of. I couldn't contain myself.

"Where is she? Does she know about me? When can I see her?"

The questions poured out of me in a torrent as my eyes tried to hold back the tears of joy. It was what I had wanted to hear for ten years. I couldn't believe it was for real.

"Slow down a bit, Billy. Let me explain."

Nell looked out the window as if she were gathering her thoughts. I sat motionless in my seat, frozen with anticipation.

"Remember that girl I told you about who I was teaching in acting class? The one I mentioned was extra talented?"

I had to think for a minute and nodded as I remembered something, vaguely. Why was she bringing that up now?

"Well, I had no idea that I was telling you about your daughter. I didn't know it at the time, but then I met her mother and recognized her as Dora."

It took a moment to grasp this. Molly was her student? She had been talking to me about my very own daughter. How could this have been?

She stopped speaking and gently placed her hand on mine. I shook my head in disbelief.

"Molly was there all along and you didn't know it?"

"Billy, the last time I saw Molly she was five years old. She's now fifteen. I never made the connection. She even used a different name: Twigs, a nickname she had adopted."

I suddenly realized that if I were to see her today, I probably wouldn't recognize her either. I had spent ten long years away from her while she was changing from a child to a young lady.

"How stupid of me. Of course you wouldn't have known." I hated myself for putting her on the defensive. "Does she know who you are now? Does she know anything about me?"

"Yes, I told her."

I raised my head and closed my eyes letting out a heavy sigh. "FINALLY! You have no idea how much this means to me, Nell!" I opened my eyes and looked at her.

"Wait there's more," she said reluctantly, and paused for a moment. "I don't know how to say this, but Molly thought you were dead all these years. That's what Dora had told her. It has all been a great shock to her."

I couldn't believe what I was hearing. I stood up so hard that the chair toppled over behind me. I slammed my fist on the table.

"Damn that Dora! It wasn't enough that she never once came to see me! Wiped me out of her life like I'd never existed. Then to lie to our daughter!?"

I looked around the room for something to punch—something to throw. My rage was at a boiling point. Nell grabbed my wrists and pulled me back down.

"Listen to me Billy," she said. "She was very sick for a long time. She's created a new life for herself and for Molly. You weren't a part of that. I'm not defending what she did, but I *do* think that in her mind she was doing what she believed was best for Molly."

"I'm her father, goddamn it! I'll always be her father, no matter what. She had no right to take that away from me!"

I sat there and rested my head in my hands. I felt the rush of rage that had overcome me slowly dissipate. It had been a long time since I'd felt such anger. Mostly I'd felt impotent. Over the years, feelings were inconsequential. For the most part, I had become numb. Now I was boiling over with emotions and didn't know how to handle them. I felt like laughing and crying and shouting all at the same time. Nell looked uncomfortable, not sure how I might react next. She kept being reassuring in her calm, even voice.

"I need you to know that Molly has missed you every bit as much as you've missed her. She may have thought you were dead, but she never stopped thinking about you and loving you. The new family has not been the replacement for her that Dora had hoped for. Her heart is still with you."

"I need to see her, Nell," I said, wiping the moisture from my eyes. "I need to see my baby girl."

"You will, Billy. She wants to see you too. But remember that Dora knows nothing of this. Her new husband has been parenting Molly and we don't want anything to go wrong here so that they try to stop you from seeing her. We need to do this carefully."

I was struggling to let all this sink in. A new father? No wonder Dora wanted that divorce. I had felt invisible all these years and now I felt like I'd been buried too.

"I won't let them take her from me again. They've caused me enough pain. I will see my Molly again and there is nothing that anyone can do to stop me."

Nell stayed for a while longer. The pound cake remained untouched. She was worried about me, about how I might react. She was right to be concerned. I was torn between my impulses and my reason. After I calmed down and reassured her that I was not going do anything rash, she left. I needed to be alone. I lay in bed staring at the ceiling. I knew her new last name now, and the town where she lived, merely one hour's drive away. I had to hold myself back from catching the next bus that was going that way to appear standing on her doorstep. I could see her in a matter of hours. But I knew Nell was right. I had to tread carefully. I had waited far too long for this to let it slip away. Nell said that she'd help set up a meeting for us and I trusted her. The wait was going to be excruciating.

I had lost my faith in a higher being many years ago when I'd been abandoned, left to the tormented hell hole of the devil. Now my faith was beginning to be restored. I clasped my hands tightly together and whispered a thank you.

DORA

The Truth

Lately something had changed in Molly. Her reactions had an edge to them. She'd become sharp, impatient, and angry with everyone, even with Timmy. At first I thought it was just a moody teenage thing. Then I started to worry whether she was getting depressed like me. Collin said that these things are passed along in families. That's when I decided to look around her room one afternoon when she was out. I wanted to see if I could find out any clues as to what was going on with her. Maybe there was a boyfriend who I didn't know about. Maybe she was hiding drugs of some sort. Nothing turned up, but I was tempted to peek at the diary I found in the bottom of her drawer. It was securely locked. I just needed a clue about what was going on with her. I looked for the key in her other drawers, her jewelry box, and under the mattress, but no luck. I started sorting through the papers on her desk, and buried at the bottom, I found an old photograph. There she was in Billy's arms when she was young, with Rex at their feet. Part of the photo was ripped. The part where I had been standing beside them. My first thought was how foolish it was of her to hold onto these reminders of her father, whom she hadn't seen for ten years. I had protected her by not telling her of the terrible things he had done. Meanwhile she had created some fantasy of him in her head. Then I wondered why I was ripped out of the photograph. I looked in her waste bin, and there I was in shreds. I had been discarded with bitter animosity. Why this obvious rejection of me after all I had tried to do for her, and the privileged life that Collin and I had created for her? I was overwhelmed with both hurt and anger.

Just then I heard the door open. I froze. I had been so absorbed in what I had discovered that I had not paid attention to the time of day. She would have been arriving home. I looked up and there she stood at the bedroom door, looking at me with disdain.

"What are you doing in my room?"

I was not going to make any excuses. I felt outraged. I threw the pieces of the photograph in the air and watched them land around me.

"Why?" I screamed, as if I'd been unleashed for the first time in years. "Why do you hate me so much?"

"You tell me why I *shouldn't* hate you!" she shouted back. "Tell me one good reason!"

My anger turned to tears.

"You ungrateful child! After the home I've given you? With nothing lacking? Any child would give *anything* to have the life you have, yet you discard me as your mother! You heartlessly rip me up like I don't exist!"

Molly stood there staring at me, challenging me.

"It's all been a lie. My whole *life* has been a lie!" she screamed back. "This family is all pretend! None of it is real!"

Molly saw the picture lying openly on her desk and grabbed it.

"This was the only real thing in my life." She held up the photo. "And you took that away from me!"

I felt like I'd been slapped so hard that I saw stars. I had to sit down before I fell down.

"What are you saying?" I managed to ask.

"Don't play dumb, Mother. You know *exactly* what I'm talking about."

I was stunned. Could she know?

We stared at each other in a standoff, each daring the other to say something. She broke the silence first.

"I know. I know everything! How could you have lied to me? How could you have taken my father away like that?"

Oh my Lord. How on earth did she find out? My heart melted as I watched her break down in sobs. I tried to reach out to her, but she pushed me away.

"Molly, I did it for your own good. Your father was as good as dead in that prison for the rest of his life—" She cut me off as I tried to explain.

"Well it's *not* the rest of his life! He's out now."

I was stunned by her words. I stood there grimacing. How could that be? As far as I had heard he had a twenty-year sentence.

"How do you know this, Molly? Tell me."

"Nell told me." I gasped. "Nell?"

"Nell! Now called Natalie. My theater instructor? Small world isn't it, Mother!" she screamed mockingly through her tears. "She also told me that he was innocent. He never laid a hand on her! He was wrongfully convicted and went to jail for a crime he didn't commit."

What she was saying was coming at me at a staggering rate and I sat there with my mouth agape. No words came out. She continued.

"It was her *brother* who raped her! It was *his* baby she had. That she has now! Daddy was only trying to help her and he got accused by the family, and then by the cops who wanted an easy arrest. He was innocent Mother, and you buried him like he didn't exist anymore! How could you have done that to him? To me?"

Molly grabbed her pillow and I watched helplessly as she sobbed. I knew there was nothing I could do to comfort her. I was the enemy in her eyes. But how could this be? How could any of this be true? I saw him watching Nell, spending endless hours with her on the farm, driving her places. What about the time in the barn when I found him holding her? Was that all my warped imagination? I had questioned myself, hoping it wasn't true, but then came the police to take him away, confirming everything I'd suspected. The truth of that moment had nearly killed me. And now, after years of recovery, all of what I had believed was thrown into question. Billy was wrongfully convicted? It didn't make sense. Suddenly my life felt like an illusion. Nothing seemed real.

"Molly, are you sure of what you are saying?" I asked in a voice so calm, it surprised me.

She rolled over to face me, her face streaked in tears.

"Yes," she said nodding. "Natalie is taking me to see him." She paused. "And there is nothing that you can do to stop me."

I looked at the determination in her eyes and I knew it was true. Billy was a free man. An innocent man.

That night I didn't sleep. I cried instead. In the morning, Collin noticed my swollen eyes.

"Has Molly upset you again?" he asked. "I tell you that girl has the devil in her. Look at what she's doing to you."

I didn't say anything. I was afraid to open my mouth, because I wasn't sure what might come out. I knew he cared about me, but he just wouldn't understand any of this. I didn't understand it either. I felt so confused and conflicted that I needed to just stay inside my silent self for a while. He put a prescription note on the table as he left for work.

"You need to get some sleep. Get this filled first thing today and it will help."

He kissed me on the cheek before heading out the door, as I sat there motionless.

Later that morning, Molly put on her favorite pants and sweater and fussed with her hair and makeup in front of the mirror. She ran down the stairs when she heard the beep of a horn outside. I managed to stand up and walk towards her. We stood there looking at one another for a few seconds and I knew where she was going. I knew it wasn't in my power to stop her, nor did I want to at this point. I went to the door and tried to take her into my embrace. She pushed me away but then resigned limply. I held onto her and buried my face into her freshly washed hair. I could feel her pulling away.

"Stop for a second!" I said. "I know I have no right to ask this, but could you please say hello to your father from me. Can you tell him that I'm so very, *very* sorry?" I could feel my tears starting up again.

She hesitated and I thought she'd turn away. Instead she reached for me and really held me for the first time. "I will Mom," she said. "I will."

The horn tooted again outside.

"I have to go," she said and let go of me.

I stood in the doorway and watched her run outside. She looked beautiful, more confident, at peace. She hesitated and waved before she got into Natalie's car. I waved back and blew her a kiss.

I kept standing in the doorway as the car pulled out of the driveway. I watched the taillights grow dim in the distance. I watched the paperboy ride by on his bike and toss the newspaper towards our doorstep. He looked at me quizzically and waved. I waved back. I noticed that the roses were in second bloom despite the fall that was upon us. I thought that I should go and cut a few and put them in a vase. I loved the smell of roses. A gray squirrel ran across the porch and hesitated as he saw me. His cheeks were stuffed full of treasures that he was off to bury. He looked comical and I smiled. He scurried away, his tail twitching. The air smelled of the rich earth and of decay. I took a deep breath. The cycle of life was turning into its dormant phase before new life could reemerge once more. The clouds were beginning to break apart, allowing for small glimpses of sunshine to break through. I went back inside and looked at the prescription on the table. I tore it up. I changed into my jeans and plaid shirt. I was going to go outside and rake the leaves into big colorful piles in the yard.

NATALIE

The Queen in the Fortress

It was late when I arrived home after teaching my evening class. Our place was small but cozy for Nathan and me. Nathan had his own bedroom and I slept on the sofa bed. I didn't mind as I was always in bed after him and up before he rose. Some nights I was so tired that I just collapsed in his bed while I read him a story. He was nine years old and starting to outgrow having his mother cuddle with him. It was hard for me to let go. He was my world.

"Nathan," I called, as I stepped in the door. He poked his head out of his bedroom and signaled me over. He seemed excited.

"Come see what I've made," he proclaimed. Nathan was a creative boy, probably from having so much time to himself and living in his imaginary world without me around much of the time. I threw my coat on the chair and entered his room. He sat at his desk and beamed at me.

"Look!" He pointed to the elaborate fortress he had glued together. I pulled a chair up beside him and he showed me all the chambers and courtyards he'd built.

"This is the knight." He held up a figure he'd created. "He has power over this whole kingdom. He fights for the good of the peasants."

"It's beautiful," I said, giving him a squeeze.

"This is the queen that lives there." He held up another figure. I named her after you Mom. I wanted you to have this special place to make you happy."

His words took me back.

"Why thank you," I said. "But what makes you think that I'm not happy?"

Nathan busied himself with his creation avoiding my question, so I pushed a little harder.

"Sometimes in life it's not what you have but who you have in your life that makes you rich with happiness. I have you in my life and that makes me very happy. I don't need a kingdom."

Nathan hesitated. "Then why do you sometimes cry at night?"

I was surprised that he would have noticed, assuming he was always fast asleep at night when I allowed myself to grieve.

"What makes you think that I've been crying?" I asked.

"Remember, I always keep my door open so that I can see you. I sleep better if I know you're there. Sometimes I see you crying and wonder what I've done to make you sad."

"Oh honey, nothing," I gushed, as I grabbed him for a hug. "You are everything that makes me happy. It's other things that make me sad. You know how you feel when Johnny picks on you at school? We get sad because of other things that happen and then come home and cry later."

"What other things make you sad?" he asked.

How was I going to answer him? How could I explain something that had happened so many years ago? Then I came up with an idea.

"How about you put on your pajamas and crawl into bed and I'll tell you a story. Maybe I can answer your question that way."

He gave me that look and said, "Mom I'm too old for bedtime stories."

"Honey, it's not a fairy tale but a true story that I want to tell you," I assured him, hoping that would make him want to listen.

He got ready and climbed into bed. Once he was under the covers, I snuggled up next to him and began.

"Once there was this little girl. She had a mean old father and brother. They used to make her do all the cooking and cleaning until she was exhausted. They never said please or thank you, and she could never do enough for them. No matter what, they continued to be mean."

"Where was her mother?" he interrupted.

"Well her mother was away at work and didn't really know much about what was going on."

I wondered if Nathan was thinking about how much I worked away from home as well, so I added,

"Most mothers who work make sure that their children are taken care of, but this mother didn't."

He seemed satisfied with that.

"Anyway, one day this little girl met a man who was very kind to her. He helped her by making her feel special, something that her family didn't do, and she was very grateful to him. This man cared so much about her that he became concerned when he saw how tired she was every day. The little girl didn't want to tell him how mean her family was, so she kept it a secret. This man was wise and one day he sat outside her house and he watched. That's when he saw her brother hurt her. He tried to rescue her, but by trying to help her, bad things happened to him. The family lied and said that *he* was the one who hurt her. Even though the little girl said it wasn't true, no one believed her and the man was taken away and locked up in a bad place."

"You mean a jail?" he asked.

"Yes. For many years."

"I feel sad for that kind man," Nathan said in a mournful voice.

I kissed him on the forehead. "Well I feel sad for him too and that's why I sometimes cry at night. You see, I was that little girl many years ago. I'm now grown up and my life has changed, but I still feel sad for that nice man who was locked away because he tried to help me. If he hadn't sacrificed himself for me, my life may never have gotten better. Because of him, it did. I now have you and I have no one being mean to me anymore."

Nathan snuggled up closer to me. I closed my eyes and held onto him.

"Mom what happened to your mean father and brother? Will they ever come back and be mean to you again?"

"No, they are gone forever. My father died from the bad things he did to himself. My brother," I hesitated, as I cringed with the thought that he was also Nathan's father, "well he is locked away for doing many bad things. He deserves to be locked away, unlike that kind man."

I added with a positive tone. "You know what though? That kind man is now free and I know that some good things are going to happen for him."

"Like what?" he asked.

"Well he had a little girl that he had to leave behind when he was locked away. He searched and searched for her but could not find her. Then through a miracle, Mommy found her. He is soon going to be together with her again and that is like a dream come true for him."

Nathan smiled. "That's good. I bet she is happy too. I would have been very sad if you were taken away from me for a long time."

"I can't even imagine it, sweetie." I tried to smother him with kisses.

He pulled away. "Aw Mom, don't slobber on me," he said. I realized that he was growing up much too fast and kisses from his mother were not welcome anymore.

"Okay sport, no more slobber. Just know that I love you very much."

I tucked him in and turned to leave the room.

"Mom?" he called. "I'd like to meet this kind man someday."

Nathan's words stayed with me long after he had fallen asleep. The thought of having him meet Billy had never occurred to me. Nathan had never had a man in his life of any sort, good or bad. I guess I had always tried to protect him against all men. The ones who had taken an interest in me and wanted more by meeting Nathan were quickly shut out of my life. I never wanted to take the risk of hurting him. But he was a boy, and as much as I tried to be his everything, I couldn't make up for the father he never had. Just like Dora, I had to lie and tell him his father was dead to protect him. However, unlike Billy, *his* father was evil. If there was any man in this world I *did* trust Nathan meeting, it was Billy. The thought of that gave me comfort. I slept more soundly than I had for a long time.

MOLLY

Let's Go Fishing

The house appeared ominous, with shabby gray siding. Maybe it was just the way I was feeling. There was a sense of trepidation and elation all mixed in one. The front steps creaked as Natalie and I slowly climbed them. I hesitated at the front door. Through that threshold was my past. I felt like that five-year-old child once more. I was stepping back in time to another life. I was excited but terrified. My hands trembled as I turned the knob. Inside was a gleaming wood banister leading to an upper floor. The hallway had a kaleidoscope of light cascading from the stained-glass window. It made the wooden floors and railing shine. *My father cleans these floors,* I thought. As usual, he doesn't stop short of perfection.

"He's one story up," Natalie said.

We slowly started our ascent. It felt like the longest staircase I'd ever climbed. I felt faint. Natalie took my arm to steady me and offered a reassuring smile.

"Here we are." We arrived in front of a row of doors down a narrow hallway. A part of me wanted to burst through his door and another part wanted to run. I was confused and frightened. I remembered my father so clearly, but that was such a long time ago. What was he going to be like now? I never thought I'd see him again … and here I was mere feet away from him. I was no longer five years old and he was no longer the same man I had loved on that farm we lived on together. I knew that living in this house with dark hallways was not in character with the father I knew.

Yet I realized that this was probably so much better than what he'd been living in for the last ten years. I quivered at the thought.

I stood there motionless, so Natalie went ahead and knocked. I held my breath. The door opened slowly, revealing a man who was older and more tired-looking than the father I remembered. His face had creases that had not been there before. His tanned and rosy cheeks were now pasty and his eyes had crinkles in the corners. His hair was thinner. The thick windswept curls I used to love to run my fingers through were gone. He looked smaller than I remembered, or was I just was so much bigger now? I stood there awkwardly gazing at him. A familiar, gentle smile came to his lips, crinkling the corners of his eyes and he reached out his arms to me. I rushed to him and wrapped myself in his embrace. I clung to him as if he would vanish if I were to let go. I could feel his heart beating rapidly against mine. He gently stroked my hair. He no longer smelled of hay and cornfields, but of something unfamiliar. Our arms circled around each other as if we were one. Even with all that had come between us, he felt so familiar.

I finally released myself from his embrace. He touched my cheek gently and we gazed at one another.

"You've turned out so lovely," he said softly.

"And you are ... so much older than I remembered."

We both broke out in laughter. It felt so good to laugh that I kept laughing until I felt tears running from my eyes. He wiped them away like he used to.

"We have a lot of catching up to do," he said.

"There's lots of time for that now," I answered.

"Come!" He motioned me inside. "Come in."

Natalie had slipped away without a word.

"It's not much, but it's home for now."

I gazed around the room, at the cramped quarters, and drab, minimal furnishings. I couldn't help but think of the contrast to the house I now lived in ... of what my mother had gained and my father had lost.

My eye caught a framed photo. I went and picked it up. It was a photograph of me when I was a young child. I was sitting on a rock by the river that he and I would frequently visit. He would throw in his fishing line while I would wade around the stream in my knee-high boots, Rex in tow, searching for hidden treasures. Rex would try to catch anything that moved in the water. In the picture, I was squinting into the sun, straw hat on my head, and I was laughing. I remembered the funny face my father had made on the other end before snapping the photo. A rush of memories swarmed through me. I was so innocent. So full of wonder and adoration for my father. It was written all over my face in this photograph. I choked back the sob in my throat as I placed the picture down. I felt a reassuring hand on my shoulder.

"That picture stayed in my pocket all those years, Molly, and not a day went by without me kissing you goodnight."

I spun around and hugged him again. I clenched my fists around his collar and buried myself in his shoulder.

"I missed you so much, Daddy!"

We remained rocking in each other's arms until we heard a light knock at the door.

Natalie cracked open the door slightly. "Sorry to interrupt, but I have someone here who also wants to say hi." She pushed the door open wide.

There stood Rex on his wobbly feet. He was old and weak now and Natalie would have had to carry him up the stairs. He stood there briefly, and then headed eagerly for my father with a whimper and rapid beating of his tail. Father knelt down and gently stroked him.

"How are you doing old boy?" Rex licked his face.

I guess dogs never forget.

"Rex and I have been best buddies through everything. He's been there with me every step of the way." *How would I have coped without him?* I gazed at them lovingly. He had been my silent partner throughout all of this. He stood there gazing into my father's eyes with a big grin on his face and rapidly wagging his tail, expressing the pure joy that we both felt.

My father knelt down and rubbed Rex's head. "If only dogs could speak, the truths they would tell."

How very true, I thought. He'd witnessed it all and was still smiling.

"There are so many years I've missed in your life and so much I want to catch up on," my father said, gazing up at me. "I don't know where to start."

I looked over at the photograph again.

"How about we go fishing?" I suggested. "You, me, and Rex. Like old times."
The crinkles at the corners of his eyes deepened with his familiar, radiant smile.
"I'd like that."

Epilogue

One year later

We did go fishing the following weekend and the weekend after that. We sat in the canoe, listening to the distant cry of a loon and the gentle ripples on the water. The earth around us stood still as we talked and laughed and cried and talked some more. The shattered puzzle pieces between us were slowly being reassembled. We had each other back in our lives and that's all that seemed to matter. We had both limped along without one another and now we were becoming whole again.

A short while after my reunion with my father, he took me to visit Aunt Edna and Uncle Jake. He had finally managed to track them down. They were like ghosts from my past. Aunt Edna still had that soft, plump flesh I used to cherish melting into when I was young and frightened.

"Look at you child," she said. "We got to get some meat on those bones. You're probably just as stubborn about what you eat as you were then."

She went to get me some homemade cookies. She still wore her feather hat and gray shawl with the lace-up ankle boots. Uncle Jake seemed smaller and more frail than I'd remembered. They had sold their city house and the two of them had retired to a small hobby farm. Aunt Edna tended to her vegetable garden, pickling everything for the winter. She kept a small collection of chickens and a goat. Uncle Jake whittled wood into furnishings that he sold to friends and neighbors. He had developed a new hobby of going to the race track to watch the ponies run. He claimed he made a small profit at it. I guessed it was to get a break from listening to Aunt Edna's chatter.

I was eager to find out what had become of my cousins. Aunt Edna pulled out a family photo taken the previous Christmas. In the photo, Aunt Edna and Uncle Jake sat in the middle, surrounded by a group of adults. I had no idea who anyone was.

"This is Sally," she said, pointing to the one standing closest to her. She was shorter than everyone else and also wider. Her confidence was illuminated in her broad grin.

"She's studying to me a grade-school teacher," Aunt Edna said.

I remembered her as my childhood tormentor, and felt pity on the poor students who would be under her hard-handed style.

She then pointed to a beautiful and majestic woman with long flowing hair and lots of makeup. She was thin, except for a rounded tummy.

"This is Elizabeth. She was a dance instructor for a while at the local community center, but is now almost ready to have her first child. This is her husband," she pointed to a handsome older gentleman standing behind her with his arm around her. "He's done well with some business dealings and they've already bought themselves a big city house. I suspect more children are in their plans." I remembered her as a beautiful diva prancing around the house. It didn't surprise me that she'd done well for herself. She wouldn't have accepted less than perfection in her life.

Standing behind them in the photo were two men. They reminded me of the characters in the Laurel and Hardy show, one being rotund while the other was small and diminutive.

"Ricky trained and tried out for a pro-football team but didn't quite make it. He enjoys coaching junior football in his spare time," she said fondly. "He drives a delivery truck for a living. It's a good living. Drinks far too much beer for his own good though. Look at this stomach," she said, pointing at his girth and shaking her head.

Her finger moved to the smaller man and a proud grin appeared. "Leonard is an English scholar. Already has his first novel published and was quoted in The Tribunal as the new and upcoming writer to watch for. I just hope he doesn't write about his crazy family," she said with a chuckle that made her jiggle.

I gave my Aunt Edna a lingering hug at the door.

"Thank you," I said. "I don't know how I would have survived without you all those years ago."

"Aw honey, you were family," she said. "I missed you when you were gone and so did everyone else." She choked back a sob and wiped her eyes with the back of her hand. "I'm just so glad you are finally with your father. That was all I ever wanted to see. Take good care of her now, Billy!" she shouted at him over my shoulder as she turned and walked away.

I smiled as I stood there watching them toddle down the pathway arm in arm.

Natalie continued to coach my acting career and became my personal agent. She encouraged me to join a small theater group that performed seasonally in local shows. I auditioned for commercials and small TV productions and was proud of the portfolio that I was slowly putting together. Natalie was my biggest fan, and I wouldn't have had the courage to keep going without her encouragement. She continued to teach theater students and her enrollment grew so large that she had to start a waiting list. She hired another instructor to help her so that she could spend more time with Nathan. Together they moved into a larger two-bedroom flat with a yard.

Natalie introduced Nathan to my father and they took a real liking to one another. Dad showed him how to fish and swim, and how to catch tadpoles and make grass sing and all the outdoor fun stuff we'd shared when I was a child. Watching them was like watching what would have continued between him and me if our lives hadn't been so dramatically altered so long ago. For him it was like starting over again from where he'd left off. Nathan clung to him, absorbing every moment of the time they spent together like a sponge. There were times that I even brought along my little brother Timmy for our visits. Nathan treated him like his younger brother, passing on what he had learned from my father. There was a whole new family forming among us. My world was becoming expansive, forgiving, and kind.

I continued to live with Mother and Collin. As long as they did not interfere with the time I spent with my father, I was able to continue my life in the home that I was familiar with. I didn't have the heart to desert little Timmy. Collin and Mother knew that I was of age to choose where I lived and eased up on their expectations of me. Without saying it, they were communicating that they did not want me to leave.

I observed a certain peacefulness about Mother that had not been there before. Although we never spoke of what had happened, I sensed that she had rid herself of the internal demons that had haunted her. She took up gardening and painting, and started to volunteer at the hospital. She joined the P.T.A. at Timmy's school and let him join a model-making class. She would help him paint the little wooden airplanes that he'd assemble. When Collin complained that he needed to be more involved in team sports with other boys, rather than these pansy, girly activities, Mother would put her foot down and speak her mind.

Collin backed off on interfering with my acting career. He no longer mentioned anything when I brought home the occasional B. In turn, I gave up the grudge that I'd held against him. I still didn't care much for him, but we had a mutual tolerance for one another. I knew that Mother and Timmy needed him in their lives. He realized that I had my father back and that there was nothing he could do to change that.

It took me a while to forgive my mother. It was my father who was able to convince me to do so, for my own good.

"The anger will eat you alive," he said. "Trust me, I know."

"She kept us apart all those years with her lies," I argued. "How could I forgive that? How could you?"

"I was consumed with anger and hatred for both Dora and Natalie. I blamed Dora for deserting me and causing our separation. But my anger was only hurting me. I was able to forgive Natalie when I realized that she was as much of a prisoner in her family as I was in jail. It was such a relief to finally let those feelings go. I once loved Dora and I expected her to support me as my wife. I never really accepted just how ill she was. It was not her fault. She did what she thought was best for you. She did the best that she knew how."

He was right. I knew the anger I felt would just eat away at me and I needed to forgive. Although Mother and I still had some healing to do, we were on that road.

My father moved out of the rooming house and found a small one-room house situated in the back fields of a farmhouse. In exchange for rent, he helped work the farm. He had come full circle back to what he enjoyed doing most. When I went to visit, I'd often find him sitting on a log in the field staring into the meadow or by the brook that gurgled beside the woodshed. I knew his sadness lingered. How could it not after all he'd been through? I could also see him slowly healing through his love of nature. He'd look up at me in wonder whenever I appeared, as if he were seeing me for the first time. We never ceased to be grateful for having found one another again. My father had promised me he would come back, and despite the years of lost hope, he had kept his promise.

Rex passed away the following summer. He was content those last days, laying under a shady oak tree in our yard. I sat there with him, rehearsing the scripts Natalie had given me, and he seemed to listen to my every word. I brought him water, which he accepted gratefully with a flapping of his tail. Food he refused, despite my coaxing. I stroked his head and protruding ribs and told him I loved him. Then came the morning I went to check on him and his eyes didn't open. He appeared to have gone peacefully in his sleep. I sat next to my lifelong friend and reflected back over the years. He had been my only true companion through it all. I thought about the new chapter that was unfolding before me. One that I was looking forward to. As much as I had relied on Rex through the years, I was able to let him go now. I was feeling the strength in myself growing. I was feeling fully visible and not afraid of it now. Just like those fields my father once cultivated, I was now cultivating my own. "Thank you buddy," I mouthed, as I gently stroked Rex's head and laid a lingering kiss on his temple, one last time.

About the Author

Maret Johanson has been working in Mental Health, Academia and as a Family Therapist for over 35 years. She has promoted journaling/writing as a tool towards recovery with the people she has counselled. She has written numerous articles for newspapers and magazines. She has now turned her hand to fiction. This is her first novel.

Maret grew up in Toronto but has spent the second half of her life working and raising a family on the west coast. She lives with her husband in a quiet seaside cove in West Vancouver. Her desk top writing companion is her big orange cat.

Printed in Canada